TO LURE A LORD

Just a Touch of Scandal Book II

CARO KINKEAD

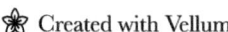 Created with Vellum

For everyone who's struggled to write in 2020.

CHAPTER 1

Augusta Eastleigh smiled politely as her partner made his final bow to her and, with a brief nod to her mother, departed. "He asked if I would consider a second dance after supper," she said, her voice pitched to ensure the words did not carry beyond Lady Eastleigh's ears.

"Only if no better opportunities arise," Lady Eastleigh replied. "Pleasant enough, but he's a younger son and his older brother is married with two boys. Precious little hope he'll inherit the estate. His family has been friends with your grandfather forever, otherwise I wouldn't always give him a first dance, much less a second." A sideways glance. "You aren't encouraging him, are you?"

"Not beyond politeness. I find him tolerable company, but…" She shrugged, letting the gesture speak for her.

"Tolerable is better than some," her mother muttered, casting her gaze backward. Augusta didn't need to turn to know Charles Wilverton hovered, as he often did during such events. "I'll be forced to give that man a public cut soon."

The fluttering of her fan revealed Lady Eastleigh's agitation as she surveyed the guests. "I wish Lord Chalton would appear. Perhaps I should allow Mr. Stanton that second dance. His attention might prove useful at some point."

How Augusta wished they were done. She wearied of smiling at gentlemen who did not meet her mother's specifications, but whom they dared not turn away. Or those who did, but with whom she found no affinity.

Most of all, she wanted to escape the gossips eager to repeat the rumors her mother maneuvered her father into an elopement when with child by someone else.

All this would be easier if her grandfather, the Earl of Forebridge, wasn't one of those who believed the rumors.

Lady Eastleigh looked as if she had more to say, but Lady Knowle's approach caught her attention. "My dear, I have the most fascinating news to tell you."

Speaking of gossips. She turned away to hide a grimace, only to find the movement brought her face to face with Wilverton. "We should dance the next set together," he said, "as no other gentlemen have asked. You did promise."

How kind of him to point out her suitors were a bit thin on the ground that evening, and in such a delightfully condescending tone. "You are mistaken, sir," she began, careful to keep her voice neutral. "I did not promise—"

"The supper dance as well, I think," he said, cutting off her words. "That will give me the chance to speak with your father as Lord and Lady Eastleigh will most certainly insist you and your partner eat with them."

No. To this point, Baron Eastleigh had managed to avoid all but the briefest conversations, sidestepping the question the man clearly wanted to ask. He met neither her mother nor her grandfather's requirements, but if Wilverton proved the only man to make an offer, Forebridge might give his blessing anyway. "I do not believe my mother will agree, sir, as she has plans."

He leaned in, close enough for Augusta to take a step back. "So do I, Miss Eastleigh. So do I."

His expression was smug and certain, making the urge to tell him to go to the devil difficult to resist. A deep breath steady herself, before beginning. "Sir, I must insist—"

"Lord Chalton! We had begun to wonder if we would see you this evening."

Happily, she turned her back on Wilverton to find Simon Mercer, the Earl of Chalton bowing over her mother's hand. "Augusta especially missed your presence," Lady Eastleigh continued as he acknowledged Lady Knowle, gesturing for her to step forward.

"My mother exaggerates somewhat, but it is good to see you, my lord," Augusta said as she dropped a curtsey.

Chalton offered her a lopsided grin in return. The one bright spot in this ordeal, an unexpected friendship she hoped might prove the basis for something more. For the moment, an invitation to dance would suffice to extract her from Wilverton's presence. Once on the floor, she might be able to enlist his aid in ensuring her supper dance was spoken for, just as she had aided him in the past few weeks.

He did not ask. "You are familiar with Lord Blair, but I do not believe he and Miss Eastleigh have been introduced."

He indicated the gentleman at his side, and she found herself caught by piercing blue eyes focused entirely on her. She'd spied him many times at one gathering or another, but never in such close proximity and never with his attention on her. The effect was…unsettling.

"Of course I remember Lord Blair," Lady Eastleigh said. The slight edge to her voice broke the spell Augusta found herself caught in. "We've not seen you of late, sir."

Slowly, his gaze moved from daughter to mother. "Recently returned from the Peninsula. Business took me there."

A muscle twitched in his cheek, hinting more to the tale. Some romantic whim suggested a dashing spy in the efforts against Napoleon, but Augusta wagered the truth more prosaic. He did, however, glance inquisitively from Lady Eastleigh to Augusta, and back again. "May I present my daughter, Miss Augusta Eastleigh," she said, taking the hint. "Augusta, Lord Blair MacDonald. His father is the Marquess of Rutherglen, a friend of Lord Forebridge."

The last signaled a warning, but Augusta concentrated on making the most graceful curtsy possible, He bowed in response, his eyes still on her. She couldn't read his expression, only that he studied her deeply for some unknown reason. She did not find the attention unwanted.

Then, he smiled graciously and held out his hand. "Miss Eastleigh, would you favor me with this next dance?"

Would she? Augusta almost laid her hand in his without hesitation, then remembered her mother had yet to give her permission. Lady Eastleigh would choose the earl over a third son, even if his father was a marquess. Then Wilverton stepped forward, his chest puffed out. "Miss Eastleigh promised me this dance."

Wilverton's words threatened to throw everything into chaos. Etiquette gave her two choices: acquiesce to his demand to avoid a scene or publicly call him a liar. Lady Knowle, still standing nearby, would hang on every moment.

She didn't want a scene. She didn't want to dance with Wilverton.

Choosing a third path, she laid her hand in Blair's. "I believe I shall, sir."

Surprise flashed across his face, but he did not hesitate to lead her away as her mother began to object, her words drowned in the noise of Wilverton's indignation at this very public rejection. Some would say she behaved just as Lady Eastleigh did during her season. At this moment, Augusta did not care.

"Did I just usurp another gentleman's place?" Blair asked as they found a spot in the line of dancers now forming.

"The gentleman presumed," she replied, her words a bit clipped. "No promise was made or implied. His intent is to frighten away any potential rivals, no matter my feelings on the subject."

Blair lifted an eyebrow. "I do not frighten easily."

She found it difficult to suppress a slight shiver underneath his gaze. *Stop that. Enjoy the dance, but don't think you mother will let things go further than that.* "I'm certain you don't."

He chuckled as the orchestra played a chord and they paid their courtesies to one another. The music began, and Augusta stopped thinking of what her mother would say when she returned.

Augusta did not often find dancing pleasure in London. One worried about the correct steps while keeping up an appropriate and scintillating conversation with her partner. As she and Blair moved through the opening figure, she relaxed, enjoying the ebb and flow of the pattern, something she experienced only with Chalton.

Unfortunately, where Chalton and she engaged in lively conversation, Blair remained silent as they completed the first repetition, moving down the line to face a new couple. The second repetition also passed in silence. *If I simply wanted to look at a handsome figure, I could sit in front of a portrait.*

Halfway into the third repletion, she decided to break the silence. "Were you on the Peninsula for the government?"

The danced required him to circle around the other lady in the figure, then return and take her hands. "No."

She blinked as they made their own circle. He'd asked her to dance. Why was he now taciturn? In other circumstances, she might amuse herself by gazing at his stylishly tousled light brown locks, blue eyes, and strong chin.

With a slight shake of her head, she pulled herself out of a daydream. "Is something wrong?" he asked, a frown causing a crease between his brows.

"No, Lord Blair." Augusta offered her most dazzling smile. "A passing thought."

A nod, and she feared they would lapse into silence again. Another turn and as they took hands to proceed down the line, he said, "When did you and Lord Chalton meet? I don't recall him dancing with you before I left London."

Her turn to frown. "Near on a month. Lord Abernathy made the introduction at a dinner."

"Abernathy, newly married, believes everyone should be mated."

Something in his tone sounded a warning. "You do not agree?"

"Lords must ensure their line continues, but gentlemen who find happiness seem determined to foist the same on all their fellows instead of allowing them to find it in their own time."

Another circle away, which gave her a moment to consider her words. "The purpose of the London season is for gentlemen to meet young ladies with the intention of matrimony."

"So you have fixed your eye on Chalton."

It was a challenge, and she knew his purpose now. He objected to the idea of his friend paying court to her for some reason. Her imagination supplied several. "I find him kind, intelligent and enjoy spending time with him when we meet."

"Yet you chose to dance with me rather than wait for him."

"You offered and allowed me to escape a most disagreeable gentlemen who assumes prerogatives he is not entitled to. Why did you ask if you believed I should wait for Lord Chalton?"

"Am I wrong in wishing to become acquainted with the lady my friend spent time with in my absence?"

No, but Augusta nursed a growing suspicion his reason might be to determine if he must rescue said friend from someone he deemed inappropriate. "I'm glad for the opportunity. Lord Chalton speaks highly of you."

The words were the most polite answer, though far from what she wanted to say at this moment. The game had rules, ignored at the peril of gossip and a ruined reputation. They passed the next few steps in silence, each moving gracefully about the other. Any pleasure in the dance, though, vanished as she tried to anticipate his next move.

"I did not realize Chalton looked to court a young lady. In the past, he experienced…ill luck in his attachments."

Not the direction she expected him to take. "They say there was a match his family objected to."

Her mother had said much, much more. No need to mention that. Not as Blair's eyes narrowed, his jaw tensing. "Now you are willing to step into the breach."

"I enjoy his company, and am flattered he enjoys mine. Should he wish things to develop further, I am not opposed."

"There is talk, Miss Eastleigh, your mother is eager to see you married off quickly to as well-placed a gentleman as she can manage, or the matter will be taken out of her hands."

A chill moved down Augusta's spine. "A gentleman would not listen to such gossip about lady." She avoided spitting the words at him, but it was a near thing, her voice tight. "Or, if he did, he would not repeat the tales to her."

Blair appeared surprised at her response. How did he think she would react? Quake in fear? Run from the floor in tears? "You met me only this evening, yet you pass judgement on who I am and why I enjoy Lord Chalton's company. You accuse me of mercenary intent in the plainest of terms. You do this after giving every indication you wished to partner me because you might find me pleasing company."

She circled away, then back to him. "You do this all cloaked in 'concern' for actions Lord Chalton took during your absence. You say my motives are suspect, sir. I submit yours are no better."

The last words brought a snicker from the other gentleman in their foursome. *Lovely. Another bit of gossip to rage about the town.*

Blair glared at the man but did not speak again until they moved down the line once more to face a new couple. "I see you inherited your mother's tongue."

Augusta smiled sweetly, more than a little pleased when he lapsed into silence once more. If he did not speak another word before the music ended, she would be more than pleased. Confident of the steps, she let her attention begin to wander, small scenes catching her attention. The Duke of Stockwood simpering at the latest in a long line of young ladies he fell in and out of love with. Sir Roger and Lady Phipps partnering one another in the second line of dancers.

"Oh, she didn't."

Blair's head swiveled in the direction Augusta looked, a frown crossing his face at the sight of Chalton and Lady Eastleigh among the dancers. "At least it keeps him away from Mrs. Hibbert," he muttered.

She could only imagine what he might be thinking. She wished otherwise.

Once the dance ended, he offered her his hand, and steered them directly toward Chalton and her mother, the two couples meeting on the floor. "That was naughty of you, Augusta," Lady Eastleigh said. "You know better than to slip away with a gentleman without my approval."

Impossible to miss the steel beneath the teasing tone. "Lord Blair's father is a close friend of Grandfather's. I did not think you would object."

7

Lady Eastleigh frowned, but the messaged had been received. "Naturally, he would wish Lord Rutherglen's son be given consideration. Still, it was wrong to let yourself to be whisked away."

"Her actions allowed me the chance to dance with you," Chalton said, offering a slight bow to Lady Eastleigh. "With Miss Eastleigh as my partner, I am certain I will enjoy the next set as much as this one."

"But—" The word exploded from Blair's lips, earning him a glare from both Chalton and Lady Eastleigh. Ignoring both, he gestured toward the doors, trying to communicate something he didn't want to put into words.

Chalton stepped closer and lowered his voice to a near whisper. "Meet me in the entrance hall when this is done, and we'll leave. Don't argue," he added as Blair opened his mouth once more. "Don't make things worse."

Blair shut his mouth, stepped back and bowed stiffly, leaving the way clear for Chalton to offer Augusta his arm. "Shall we, Miss Eastleigh?"

Augusta laid her hand atop Chalton's arm and allowed him to lead her away. She swore she felt Blair's steely glare focused firmly on her back. Not that she would give him the satisfaction of a backward glance.

CHAPTER 2

That was a disaster.

He had not expected her to accept. He had not expected to ask. He suspected this might be his lone chance to take some measure of Augusta Eastleigh before he gave his father his answer. Blair didn't like to make a decision without at least some of the facts, considering his decision would last a lifetime.

He also hadn't counted on Simon courting the girl. When he left London, his friend had still been resistant to the idea of dipping his toe into matrimonial waters. He must one day, but the hurt from Eleanor Shelby had not yet receded enough. Yet, the responsibility for carrying on the family line still hung over him. Just as it now seemed to hover over Blair.

He shouldn't have come tonight. But he'd been eager to be out of the house, away from his father's somewhat patient anticipation of a response to his suggestion.

Home was the last place Blair needed to be at the moment. So was an assembly, watching Simon partner a young lady who stalked him as a potential mate. The woman Blair's father wanted him to marry.

Worry about his elder children must have driven the Marquess of

Rutherglen mad while Blair journeyed to Spain to fetch Hamish home. Otherwise, why consider such a waspish woman as his son's bride? Worse, a woman around whom gossip and innuendo flew.

Through no fault of hers, Rutherglen had said. *She'll make you a fine match.*

Attractive enough, yes. A bit tall for a woman, but given his own height, that might be seen as an advantage. Part of him wished she'd been more congenial in her conversation, even if he might provoke her.

Conscious of Lady Eastleigh watching him, he offered a bow. "Please excuse me."

He turned away, but she spoke. "A moment, if you please."

No secret from whom Augusta had inherited the chill in her tone. "I forgive you for snatching my daughter away to the dance floor without seeking my permission," Lady Eastleigh said. "This time. I confess some disappointment at such behavior. Your father is the most courteous of gentlemen."

Hardly the first such warning received from a mother who took exception to his attentions. Politely as he could, Blair inclined his upper body. "I understand."

"I must wonder," she said, "why you are not pursuing an heiress. Let us be frank. Unless the plague sweeps through your family, there is little chance you will inherit the title. Which means you have no fortune of your own save whatever allowance you get from your father." She tilted her head to one side, considering him. "Do you possess some secret source of income? You're not Mrs. Porter, writing dreadful novels filled with blood and terror to delight young ladies?"

Blair's spine stiffened, not from the insinuation he might be a writer of cheap fiction. She couldn't possibly understand how close the arrow hit home. "No, I am not," he replied, finding civility difficult.

"Then you should understand my concern. I'll see her well settled, with a man possessed of proper social standing and a fortune to keep her secure. Do I make myself clear?"

Clear Forebridge had not bothered to share his plans with his daughter-in-law. "Perfectly, madam. I'll not waste any more of your time."

He bowed curtly and made his way around the edge of the floor, ready for the moment when the current dance would be done and he and Simon could get away, as far as possible from the clutches of Lady Eastleigh.

"I should apologize for her dragging you out onto the floor," Augusta said as she curtsied to Chalton, ready to start the dance.

He chuckled, taking her hand for the first steps of the dance. "I asked her. Mrs. Hibbert was lurking, and I thought the dance floor would be safer than avoiding her attempts to catch my eye."

They circled away from one another, and around the other couple in the figure. When they drew close to one another again, he said, "I'm the one who should be apologizing. I'm not certain what Blair was thinking."

She hesitated before answering. "I understand he is your friend…"

Chalton rolled his eyes. "Said something foolish, didn't he?"

"More like insulting and annoying. Does he make a habit of being rude to ladies he's just met?"

Her words caused a wince as Chalton moved to circle with the other lady in the set. "Don't tell me," he said when the dance brought them together again. "He tried to warn you off."

"I do not mean to distress you, my lord, but how can you be friends with such a disagreeable man? I'll not repeat what he said or implied, but rudeness does not begin to describe the words."

Now Chalton hesitated. "Two things you should understand," he said at last, his voice softer. "Blair stood by me when my father prevented my marriage to Miss Shelby, saw the pain the loss caused. He knows the hurt has not healed and I fear that causes him to believe I am vulnerable to the machinations of over-zealous matchmaking mamas. He's been very helpful in avoiding Mrs. Hibbert." Chalton flashed a smile at her. "As have you, these past weeks."

Augusta's conscience pricked at the words as they moved apart from one another, wondering if Blair was something she must accept.

"He went to the Peninsula to fetch his brother home. The wound's quite severe, I understand," he continued as the figure ended and they proceeded down the line.

Any other complaints died on Augusta's lips. "I'm sorry to hear that. Doesn't the army usually handle such things?"

"Special pass and dispensation from the Regent. Made him swear up and down to be back for this grand fete planned for June." Chalton paused. "Unless Hamish doesn't recover. I get the impression he's worse than they originally thought."

"That's why Lord Blair was eager to leave."

Chalton smiled ruefully. "I don't believe he's in a party mood. Might I beg some indulgence?"

With an effort, Augusta smiled. "I will endeavor to be kinder when next we meet."

A slight squeeze of her hand, and they parted to circle the other dancers. The squeeze was encouraging, an intimate gesture. Mayhap things were progressing as she hoped.

They danced several more figures before she happened to notice a figure hovering at the edge of the crowd. "We are being watched," she said.

"Damn. The Hibbert doesn't give up, does she?"

"Is the fact you're not the only one she's pursuing any comfort?"

Chalton snorted. "The Duke of Stockwood flees at the sight of her. Gives the impression of a wounded sea bird."

He smiled at her laughter. "Better. I enjoy seeing you laugh."

"She'll be waiting to pounce the moment you escort me back to Mother. You won't make it to the door.."

Augusta glanced down the line. "You said Lord Blair needs to talk?"

"He's more upset than he lets on. I fear Hamish may still be in danger."

In that instant, Augusta felt a genuine pang of sympathy. Her only brother was far too young to even think of joining the army, but she knew how she would feel if he were mortally wounded. "We are but two away from the bottom of the set," she said. "When we step out, I shall tell you I need to go to the retiring room. Thank goodness etiquette insists on vagueness for such things."

"But…"

"You'll escort me there, naturally, and send word to my mother where I am."

They stepped apart, then together once more. "You can then make your escape. We'll catch Mrs. Hibbert off guard, and she'll be slow-footed in pursuit since she is on the opposite side of the floor from the entrance."

Chalton blinked twice, then a slow grin spread across his face. "Have I told you, Miss Eastleigh, how glad I am to have made your acquaintance?"

"Tell Lord Blair he is in my debt for ensuring you are not delayed." She cocked her head to one side. "I like that idea."

He chuckled as they reached the final figure. They danced their way through, then stepped out to let the couple waiting step in. "I fear I must retire, Lord Chalton." Augusta made no effort to moderate her voice. "I am afraid the room has become too close for me."

Chalton did not hesitate, escorting her toward the room's entrance, Augusta doing her best to look slightly ill. Halfway to the door, Blair joined them, his expression more annoyed than concerned. "What's wrong?"

"I'm escorting Miss Eastleigh to the retiring room. She is unwell."

"Mrs. Hibbert—"

"Is probably already following us," Augusta replied tartly. "I suggest you not delay things by arguing."

The look of shock across Blair's face was satisfying. He didn't argue further, and they continued to move, reaching the retiring room in short order. Chalton bowed over her hand. "I am once again in your debt, Miss Eastleigh."

"Hurry, or she'll catch you," Augusta warned, one eye still trained on the ballroom door. "Do send for my mother, please."

He squeezed her hand, then released it, and she turned to enter, confident he would do as she asked. Inside, the maid was understanding. She was not the first miss in need of some cool refreshment and a few minutes of quiet. Not that she enjoyed the quiet for long, as Lady

Eastleigh arrived quicker than she expected. "My poor darling," her mother said, taking a chair next to the chaise where Augusta half-reclined. "I worried this might happen."

"I'll be fine, Mother. I just needed some time away from the crowd."

Augusta did her best to sound a bit wan, but the narrowing of Lady Eastleigh's eyes warned her excuse rang false. Reaching out, Lady Eastleigh smoothed a fold of Augusta's skirt. "You should take care. The evenings will only get warmer as we move into summer, and if you take ill too often, it will be a cause for concern."

Where that concern might lie was unspoken, but Augusta caught the meaning. "Besides," Lady Eastleigh continued, "other gentlemen desire a dance with you. True, you've partnered the best already, but we should hope one of them might ask you for another turn after supper. Perhaps Lord Chalton—"

"He had an appointment elsewhere," Augusta said. "He and Lord Blair planned to depart once he sent for you."

Lady Eastleigh's eyes narrowed again. "You must tell me more of this, my child. Later."

Augusta did not respond but nursed the refreshing drink as long as she dared. All too soon, though, she rose to her feet. A moment longer while her mother fussed at her dress and tucked a stray curl back into place, then they moved toward the door.

They were not more than a step or two outside the retiring room when Charles Wilverton planted himself firmly in their path. "I wondered where you were, Miss Eastleigh. It was wrong of you to accept a dance from others when you had promised one to me. I would like my dance now."

Augusta opened her mouth, but Lady Eastleigh was quicker. "Augusta would be most happy to oblige you," she said, sliding a protective arm around her daughter. "Unfortunately, she is overcome by the warmth of the evening and I think we best take her home to rest."

She gestured to a nearby footman. "We will need our wraps, and our carriage. Please find Lord Eastleigh and tell him we are ready to depart. I believe he may be in the card room."

The footman bowed and moved to do as she asked, and Lady Eastleigh turned toward Wilverton once more. "I'm certain you understand Augusta's health must be my primary concern. Perhaps another evening?"

Wilverton frowned, but etiquette demanded he acquiesce. "I will hold you to that, Lady Eastleigh. Miss Eastleigh."

With a short, sharp bow, he disappeared back into the main room. "Odious toad," Lady Eastleigh muttered.

"I thought you wanted me to dance more," Augusta said.

"Not with Charles Wilverton. Be warned, though; if you're not careful, you'll find yourself matched with someone like him. Here's hoping Lord Chalton comes up to snuff soon."

They were being helped into their wraps when Lord Eastleigh appeared. "What is wrong, Goose?"

Augusta started to speak, but Lady Eastleigh quieted her. "You're feeling ill, remember?" When Eastleigh looked questioningly at her, she added, "All will be explained in the carriage."

With their wraps in place, the party stepped through the front door to find their carriage waiting. "At least we were spared the expense of hiring one this year," Lady Eastleigh said as she climbed in.

"Does mean he gets a report as to everywhere we go," Eastleigh said. "Now, what is this about?"

Both of her parents looked at Augusta expectantly. "Lord Chalton attempting to avoid Mrs. Hibbert."

"Understandable," Lady Eastleigh said. "I saw her hover nearby as he spoke with us."

"He and Lord Blair planned to depart as soon as his dance with me was done. I suggested, as we were near the bottom of the set, I could announce my need to retire. This would force Mrs. Hibbert to take a more circuitous route in her pursuit, giving him more time. Lord Chalton was most grateful for the suggestion. You know the rest."

Finished, she steeled herself for the scolding her actions had earned, beginning with her agreement to dance with Blair.

The silence stretched on. Eastleigh looked at his wife, Lady Eastleigh looked at her husband. "The idea's not a bad one," he said. "Got him away from someone he didn't want to associate with."

"Hmm. A bit too dramatic, perhaps."

Eastleigh chuckled. "I remember you enjoying the dramatic."

The two of them leaned their heads toward one another, and Augusta turned her head away from the intimate moment. It was uplifting to see love and affection enduring after twenty years. At times, though, she wondered if her parents wouldn't be happier without a family to worry about.

At last they turned back to her. "It's best you don't mention this to your grandfather," Lady Eastleigh said. "If he asks why we came home earlier than usual, stick to your story."

"Why did we leave early?" Eastleigh asked. "Surely Goose didn't feign that much illness."

"No, but Mr. Wilverton accosted us just outside the retiring room, reprimanding Augusta for accepting dances before him. Then he demanded she partner him immediately."

"He still lives?"

"Sadly, yes," Augusta said, trying to determine if she was in trouble or not. "I believe he also wants to speak with you, Papa. At least, he hinted broadly at it during the evening."

She gained some satisfaction in seeing both her parents grimace. "Another thing not to tell your grandfather," Eastleigh said. "We don't want to give him any ideas. I just hope you're right about Chalton's interest."

"He is in her debt," Lady Eastleigh said, "and he does seek out Augusta's company. I think we should hope." She sighed. "He just needs to show some tangible sign before your father runs out of patience."

Or Lord Blair convinces him a match is a bad idea. That, however, was not a worry to share with her parents.

CHAPTER 3

They were barely in Simon's carriage and away from the curb before Blair exploded. "Have you managed to go utterly and completely mad? I leave London and here you are, making eyes at the daughter of a woman who's desperate to see her married off."

Simon didn't look particularly perturbed as he leaned back against the cushions. "You just described half the mothers present tonight."

A reply, angry and sarcastic, bubbled up. Blair caught himself, taking a deep breath to calm himself. "Why are you cozying up to Lady Eastleigh? Old Forebridge—"

"Is a parsimonious bastard who resents having to pay for a season. Some say he behaved the same way when his daughters made their bow."

"The rumors—"

Blair stopped, uncertain if he wanted to complete the sentence. The idea his father insisted he marry as soon as possible was appalling, but worse was his proposed bride being the subject of sniggering whispers. He wanted to tell this to Simon, seek his friend's advice.

Augusta Eastleigh had cut off that avenue by snaring Simon in her web. Now, any discussion would lead not to counsel but disagreement.

His friend would not take kindly to such words spoken about a woman he held in any sort of esteem.

Taking a deep breath, he changed course. "You know your own mind, of course. Given your lack of enthusiasm for pursuing any woman until now, I wonder why you suddenly find yourself in Miss Eastleigh's company."

Simon shrugged. "She's bright, quick, not unattractive, and I find I can hold an intelligent conversation with her. I must marry at some point and cannot marry where I will, so why not consider her? Better than finding myself yoked to someone such as Miss Wilmont or one of the Misses Hibbert. Be glad you are not in such a position."

Blair winced. "Have you noticed she's sharp-tongued?"

The words escaped before he could stop them, but Simon only chuckled. "She told me the two of you had sparred."

Blair grumped as he shifted on the seat. "How black did she paint me?"

"She said you were rude and disagreeable. I asked her to be charitable because of your distress over your brother. The two of you were oil and water on the floor. Lady Eastleigh did her best not to comment, but she was not happy with what she saw."

She'll be less happy with me when she learns what's planned. "Am I supposed to grovel when next we meet?"

"Be polite. That's all I ask." Simon cocked his head to one side. "Why did you ask Miss Eastleigh to dance? You seemed eager to leave. You grumbled at the idea I owed a lady a dance. Then, next thing I see, you're on the floor with her yourself."

Blair's eyes dropped to his hands, a bit surprised to discover his fingers had curled into claws. Slowly, deliberately, he forced them to relax. "I don't know what I was thinking," he said. "I was a fool to come out tonight because I'm not in a fit state to be around people. I needed to get away from the house, though."

"It's that bad?"

Relieved at the change of topics, Blair said, "Hamish is lucky he didn't lose the leg, though there's still a danger infection might take hold." He stopped not wanting to think of the possibilities. "He's best away from the battlefield and rough medicine, in any case. I wonder, though, if we'd have fared better staying on the coast instead of making the crossing. The water was a bit choppy, but given the effect on him, you would think it a gale. I tried to delay, but staying in Portugal was something he refused to consider."

He let the tale of the journey spool out, Simon listening silently as he told of Hamish's reluctance to leave his company, even with his commander's leave. Then, once the journey had been taken, his agitation at any hint of delay. That agitation had kept them moving on, Blair worried at making his brother's condition worse with the worry. Only when they reached Spelling's Coffeehouse did Blair pause in his story.

Once comfortably settled with a meal on its way, he took up the tale again. "I fear this will end his career. Even if he recovers, even if he keeps his leg, he will likely never be the same again. Might not be able to sit a horse properly or move without the stick. I have Parliament, James the estate, but Hamish's life is the army. I'm unsure what he'll do without it."

There. At least that much had been said and Blair could breathe once more. "Is he allowed visitors?" Simon asked.

Blair shook his head. "Not yet. He needs to recover from the journey first. See if being with the family improves." A tankard of beer appeared in front of him and he drank gratefully. "We've engaged a nurse, but I'll wager when I get home, Father will be sitting with him. This aged him. He's worried for Hamish and the estate."

Another deep swallow, and he set the tankard down, sighing. "I was a fool to come out because I'm not any fit company. I needed to talk, though, needed to get away for a while."

"Why did you not send a note? I would have skipped the assembly, had you come to the house. We could have missed all this palaver."

Simon had no idea how much Blair wished they had. He might have voiced his complaints about Augusta with no idea of his friend's involvement. "And not meet Miss Eastleigh? I should make her acquaintance if you are thinking of her as a wife. Still think you're a fool for pursuing her."

"Try making her acquaintance without the disagreements. I think you'll understand why I'm considering proposing. Not that it's settled yet."

Blair was happy to drink to that. No, things were not settled. But if his father had his way, things would soon be.

"I'm not certain we want to attend Lady Wilmont's dinner party," Lady Eastleigh said, reading from one of several envelopes delivered in the morning post.

"Again?" Eastleigh slathered some butter on his bread. "Does she ever do anything except dinner parties?"

Augusta snagged the butter once her father was done. Just the three of them at breakfast, as usual. Lord Forebridge preferred to be served in his chambers, rather than share the table with his daughter-in-law. She didn't mind, but enjoyed this quiet time when she and her parents could behave as they did at home, rather than forced to exhibit "London manners."

"Lady Wilmont had enough of large parties after what happened at her daughter's ball, I'm told," Lady Eastleigh said, putting the note to one side. "We missed a juicy little scandal there."

"You said there was no reason for us to be in Town in December," Augusta pointed out. "Father isn't in Parliament, so he didn't need to be here for the Regency Bill. Much more enjoyable spending Christmas at home."

Lady Eastleigh smile fondly at her daughter. "It was. Your last Christmas at home. Come December, you'll be a bride with your own establishment. My little girl, all grown up."

She reached out to touch Augusta's cheek fondly, and Augusta did her best to smile. The pride and love on her mother's face warmed her, but her stomach still flopped at the thought.

With a sigh, Lady Eastleigh turned back to her correspondence. "I think we'll pass on the Wilmonts this time. Unless you possess a burning desire to watch Miss Wilmont preen as if she were the toast of London."

"I will bow to your decision," Eastleigh replied.

With a smile, Lady Eastleigh turned back to the invitations , arranging their social calendar to the maximum effect. Forebridge would want to know the latest plans to promote Augusta when they faced their daily interrogation as to how things progressed.

Another reason Augusta wished this affair was over and done.

They had nearly finished when Forebridge strode into the room. "I imagine this is your doing, madam," he said, brandishing a sheet of notepaper aloft. "Did you not bother to tell the girl it's impolite to abandon a gentleman to whom she promised a dance because someone else offered?"

Lady Eastleigh's face hardened. "Let me guess. Lady Knowle sent you a note."

"I'm glad she did. I warned you; I will not stand for more scandal tainting this family's name."

"I believe Lady Knowle misinterpreted the situation," Augusta said. It appeared the daily interrogation was to be now instead of after breakfast. "That is, if the gentleman in question is Mr. Wilverton."

Forebridge's attention moved to her, and every muscle in her body tensed. She never liked being under her grandfather's scrutiny, knowing he saw error in every move. "You're saying Lady Knowle is lying?"

Harsh words and a harsh accusation. "She did hear Mr. Wilverton protest that I had promised him a dance. I had not. He uttered this falsehood in attempt to prevent me from dancing with Lord Blair MacDonald, as he tries to interfere with any gentleman who pays me attention."

She could guess what would come next. Why did Wilverton say such a thing if he had not been promised? Was she leading him on in some way?

Forebridge did not demand an answer to the expected questions. "Rutherglen's boy?" He looked back to Lady Eastleigh. "You didn't tell me she knew Rutherglen's son."

"Perhaps because they were only introduced last night," Lady Eastleigh replied. "He just returned from Portugal."

A slow grin spread across Forebridge's face. "How fortuitous. You had a look at the young man."

Augusta sensed a trap and chose not to comment Blair had

annoyed her. "He is a very attractive gentleman," she replied, unwilling to commit to more.

"And single. His father wants him to marry."

Lady Eastleigh was out of her chair in an instant. "You said we had until the end of the season. Lord Chalton—"

"Hasn't come up to snuff, nor has anyone else." His gaze swung back to Augusta. "Any of your suitors given you an indication they want to speak with your father?"

She thought of Wilverton. "No, sir. They have not."

For a moment, Lady Eastleigh's lips tightened, then she gave the briefest of nods. From his chair, Eastleigh said, "Are you delivering this as a fait accompli, Father?"

"Yes." He paused. "Not quite. Rutherglen and I still need to hammer out the marriage settlement, which will take longer than I would like. The man's second son is back from Spain and injured, which means his attention is elsewhere."

"With nothing settled, I think you should leave *my* daughter's future in my hands." Eastleigh did his best to look cool and collected, but his fingers tapped a rhythm on the table, sure signs his own temper bubbled below the surface. "Can we at least agree on that?"

Forebridge considered, letting the silence stretch on long enough Augusta was certain she would scream in frustration. "You have until the ink is dry on the settlement. Bring me a proposal from Chalton or anyone else halfway acceptable before then and I'll break off negotiations. Once Rutherglen and I reach an agreement, the girl will be married to his youngest son."

"Her name is Augusta." Lady Eastleigh's voice issued from behind gritted teeth.

He spared her the barest glance. "I'm told it is."

With that, he walked from the room, not bothering to close the door behind him. Lady Eastleigh stood stock still for a moment, hands clenched at her side. "Out," she said to the servants. A deep breath, and she continued in a kinder tone. "Thank you, but we will ring when you may clear the dishes."

Augusta didn't miss the looks the footmen exchanged before departing, closing the door behind them. "He promised," Lady Eastleigh hissed at her husband. "He promised we would have until the end of the season."

"Since he agreed to finance this expedition," Eastleigh said, "he believes it is within his rights to change the terms. You knew he might do that, Soph."

He turned toward Augusta. "I'm sorry. I understand you would prefer Chalton, but please tell me you didn't find Lord Blair unreasonable."

"He was not at his best," she said. Her parents appeared genuinely concerned, but she did not think rehashing the argument would serve any purpose. "Lord Chalton said he was upset about his brother."

"At least his family cares about one another, it appears. More than this one." Lady Eastleigh resumed her place at the table, picked up her piece of toast, stared at the bread for a moment, then put it down again. "No sign of Chalton asking?"

Augusta shook her head, provoking a sigh. "You know what's going to happen," Lady Eastleigh said. "Chalton will get wind of things and he'll play the gentleman and withdraw to leave the field clear for his friend."

"This might prove the impetus Chalton needs to ask for Goose's hand," Eastleigh countered, "Let's try to think positive." He reached out to take her hand. "We're going to try to make things work out. I promise."

Augusta returned his smile, though she imagined there was as much false bravado to her smile as to her father's.

CHAPTER 4

Blair felt exhausted as he made his way downstairs to breakfast. He returned home last night at a surprisingly respectable hour, only to find his father still in Hamish's room, watching his second son sleep. Some quiet persuasion had convinced the Marquess of Rutherglen to seek his own bed, but Blair had found himself sitting for a time before leaving his brother to the tender care of the nurse.

Now, he stifled a yawn as he entered the dining room, only to try to catch himself at the sight of his sisters. "Good morning, Blair," Caitlin said, sounding far too grownup for her sixteen years.

"Good morning to you as well," Blair replied, seeking his own chair. "And you, Finola. I thought the two of you still dined in the nursery."

The scowl on Caitlin's face showed exactly what she thought of that. "Miss Richards said if we behaved, we would be allowed to eat downstairs as a reward for being quiet. Hamish needs quiet."

Finola, her mouth filled with toast, nodded her agreement. Two years younger, she was at an awkward age, some baby fat in her cheeks still lingering. Blair glanced toward the footman who stood against the wall, waiting for instructions. "Have they behaved?"

The footman allowed himself a smile. "Most properly behaved, as young ladies should be."

Blair grinned at the answer. The girls had most of the staff wrapped around their little fingers. "Then you earned your treat, and I am happy to join you."

They did their best to retain decorum, but both were desperate for details about his trip and Hamish's condition. Blair had found little time to speak since his return, though he embraced both tightly when he arrived. "Hamish is still very ill," he said, "though better than he was on the journey, I believe. If he is to get better, he will need quiet."

Caitlin and Finola nodded solemnly in agreement. That message had likely already been drilled into them, for he saw no sign of them chafing under such restrictions. Hopefully the quiet, clean sheets, and the best doctor his father could find would work its magic and once more the house would be filled with the cheerful bustle that usually marked the family.

He prayed they would see the day soon.

The girls were nearly finished when Rutherglen himself appeared, looking more than a little worn about the edges. Still, he had a smile for his children. "Been keeping Blair company this fine morning?"

"Yes, Papa," Caitlin said. "He told us about his journey to Portugal."

Finola nodded, curls bouncing with the gesture. "It sounds most horrible."

Rutherglen cast Blair a chiding look. "I was telling them how dusty everything was when I was traveling through Portugal," Blair replied.

"Horrible," Finola repeated.

Tension eased from Rutherglen's shoulders as he chuckled. "Now I must ask you to retire to the schoolroom. I imagine your governess has lessons for you this morning."

Neither girl looked eager to go, but Blair sensed his father had conversation he did not wish them to hear. "What would you say to a walk along the Serpentine this afternoon? In a few days, perhaps we can pay a visit to the Tower menagerie."

"Will we get to see Miss Maria, the leopardess?" Finola asked.

Blair tried to restrain a grin. "Along with Master Bobby and Miss Fanny the lioness." He forced himself to appear stern. "That is, if you behave and do not cause your governess to give an ill report."

Both Caitlin and Finola promised they would be perfect models of propriety, made their curtsies and departed. "Thank you," Rutherglen said once the girls had gone. "I fear I indulged them somewhat in your absence. They dined with me most meals. I know 'tis not the fashion, but the house was lonely with you gone."

"According to them, Miss Richards allowed them downstairs for breakfast as a treat."

"Perhaps she thought the household would return to normal with you and Hamish back." Rutherglen sighed. "I fear there will be no normal, not for some time."

"I'm hoping being in one place will help him improve," Blair said. "He did not travel well."

"No, I imagine not. Worse, the moment there is any improvement, he will wish to return to his duties. He said as much yesterday."

Another heavy sigh. "Thank you for offering to take your sisters to the Serpentine. They will do their best to be behave, but I suspect the enforced quiet will prove hard on them. Other things require your attention. Parliament, of course, and I imagine the Regent will expect your attendance now that you've returned."

"Aye, but my first priority is the family. His Highness understands that." He grimaced. "Though he does expect me to be present for this grand fete he is giving next month. My job is mostly to tell him how wonderful his ideas are."

"Rulers are fickle figures. Always remember that, my son."

Rutherglen gestured to the footman, who fetched him a plate filled with a modest selection of food. "I wanted to continue our discussion of yesterday. We did not finish."

Blair put his fork down. "I thought I had made my position clear." The last thing he wanted this morning was a repeat of the angry argument, uttered in harsh whispers because both were cognizant of the man lying upstairs.

"You did not allow me to explain my reasoning. I was hoping you would agree to listen before refusing. Hamish broke off his understanding with Miss Sanders."

"I heard some rumbling of a delay in setting a date," Blair said, "but Hamish mentioned nothing of a break."

"I only learned the last time he was home. When I asked, Hamish told me he didn't want to risk leaving a young widow and child. I hoped he would come to his senses, find a way to mend the breach. Before you returned from Portugal, I received a letter she has now married."

A creeping sense of dread filled Blair's bones. "Does James know?"

"He does. He made some vague gestures about coming to London and finding a wife, but when I pressed him on the matter—"

Rutherglen broke off and rose. "Let us continue this discussion in my study."

He turned from the table, only to turn back and grab his plate and utensils. "No sense in wasting the food."

"You could ask the servants to leave," Blair said as they made their way toward Rutherglen's study.

"Leave them hovering outside the door, wanting to clear the things away? That would be the excuse they gave. Better this conversation occurs somewhere more private."

His father's words did little to calm Blair's concern. At the same time, he couldn't help his curiosity at the possibility of learning why his eldest brother was adamant against marriage.

Once they were in the study, with the door shut, Rutherglen settled behind his desk, tucking into his breakfast. Blair waited until he could no longer restrain himself. "What did James say when you pressed him?"

"That—" Rutherglen looked down at his plate, scowled and pushed it away. "That the bloody fool managed to catch a dose of the pox and found himself impotent."

Blair opened his mouth, only to shut it again. Not what he anticipated. No, not at all what he anticipated. "Which means no possibility of children."

"That's what the physician he saw to treat this malady said."

Rutherglen rose and began to move about the room, wandering restlessly. "He actually tried to comfort me. He told me, 'Don't worry, Father. You still have Blair.'"

The implications weighed on Blair. "First him, now Hamish," Rutherglen continued, still pacing. "It's a bloody mess." He stopped, pivoting toward Blair. "This is why I want you to marry. I must think of the estate and our tenants. No grandsons, everything goes to your cousins. They're likely to squeeze the place dry for every penny and not care whom they might hurt along the way."

Just as he had yesterday, Blair wanted to rise to his feet and shout a refusal. He couldn't, though. "I didn't realize," he said.

"Of course you didn't, and you had every right to grow angry. This is your brothers' responsibility, but here we are."

"You'll sell me off to Forebridge's granddaughter."

"Do you think this is what I want for you? I always thought you'd choose a wife to serve as a political hostess, someone to enhance your standing. I wouldn't look askance at a prime minister in the family, but I must think of the estate."

Blair sat silent, remembering what Chalton had said. *I must marry at some point. Continuation of the line and all that.*

Chalton would laugh once he discovered Blair's predicament. Until he discovered who the intended bride was. "Hamish may still recover, and I doubt Miss Eastleigh will take kindly to the idea. 'You might never be a marchioness, but a possibility your son will, *if* my brothers don't do their duty'. I doubt that will suit her at all."

Rutherglen frowned. "You shouldn't judge her before you meet."

"I met her. Last night."

Rutherglen brightened. "And?"

"She is possessed of a biting, shrewish tongue and does not think highly of me at all."

With luck, his father would accept the match was not to be and send word to Forebridge "with all reluctance" the match was off. Luck was not with him. "She is Sophia Eastleigh's daughter. Did you expect the girl to be a milksop? How did you manage to earn the sharp edge of her tongue?"

Squirming, Blair wondered how to frame this. "Lady Eastleigh doesn't want me for the girl, anyway. She's determined to snare Simon."

"Chalton?" Rutherglen frowned. "That might be a complication. I understand he's your friend, and you wouldn't want to get between him and—" A pause. "Did you try to warn the girl off him? You appointed yourself his protector after the unpleasantness with Miss Shelby."

"Unpleasantness? His father did everything he could to keep Simon and her apart. Miss Shelby cared for him, was willing to elope, but her father hurried her into a marriage with another man. After that, if you think I'll let him be caught by a fortune hunting harpy of dubious parentage, you're sadly mistaken."

Rutherglen did not respond, fixing him with the steady gaze Blair had dreaded as a child. The one which warned he'd blotted his copybook badly and there would be consequences. "I think I understand why Miss Eastleigh spoke roughly to you," he said at last, "I brought you up to behave better, Blair. Make your apologies to her. Act in a civilized manner and do your best to determine if she would make a suitable wife. If not, you *will* find another young lady to pay court to. Miss Eastleigh or someone else, it is time for you to marry. Do I make myself clear?"

"Perfectly." The word ground out between clenched teeth.

Their eyes remained locked on one another for a long moment. Rutherglen turned away, breaking the tension. "Is Chalton serious about marrying her?"

Saying yes would be an easy escape. His father would likely not push the match if his friend was determined to propose. "He seems to have fallen rather casually into this, and the idea of marriage is only just starting to raise its head. He had not met her before I left for Portugal."

"Consider this. Marry the girl, you'll not only help secure the future of the title, you'll rescue your friend."

The joke was weak, and they both knew it. The words, however, warned his path was set.

It was a relief to escape upstairs. Poking his head into Hamish's room, he found his brother awake and sitting up as he scowled at the tray resting on his lap. "May I come in?"

Hamish brightened. "Please. Anything to distract me from this gruel I'm being fed."

"Calf's Foot broth is considered to be most restorative," Mrs. Petherbridge, a woman of indeterminate age with her hair firmly hidden beneath a starched cap, told him primly. "The doctor hopes to increase your strength without upsetting your stomach."

"My leg's the trouble, not my stomach." Still, Hamish took a spoonful, scowling all the while.

"I think not being bounced around on the road will do more to help you than anything else," Blair joked, taking a chair by the bed.

"Not being tossed about on the Channel is better," Hamish replied. "Lord, that was a rough crossing."

Blair chose not to argue. Hamish's skin had darkened with exposure to the sun while in the field, but there was a paleness underneath the hue which worried. "How are you this morning?"

Hamish made a face, dipped the spoon in the broth once more, then dropped it back into the bowl. "I'm done for the moment," he told the nurse.

"You need to eat more," she warned.

"I will. Once I talk to Blair."

Disapproval in every line, the woman picked up the tray and carried it to the desk which stood against one wall. Hamish watched her move before turning back to Blair. "Truth be told, I feel awful. Can't sleep because of this damn leg. I want to turn on my side, but can't because of the way it's bound. The times I do manage, the pain keeps me awake. You remember how I was on the road."

Blair wished he didn't. "Rest when you can, then. You always managed short naps. Especially in church during the sermon."

The chuckle he received in response was heartening. "Aye. That I could. Thank goodness I don't snore."

"Wellll…"

More laughter which ended in a cough. Wordlessly, the nurse brought him a glass. Hamish drank deep, then handed it back with a nod. "How do you like being home? Anything exciting in Commons?"

Blair blinked. "I didn't think about it to be honest. When I left, we were dealing with the bullion mess, and I don't know where that stands. I should find out when we're sitting next. Now that the Regency Bill is passed, we're not meeting and debating every day. At least, not when I left." He sighed. "Another thing I need to check. Oh, and Father has some crazed idea I need to carry on the dynasty, that he can't count on either you or James."

He tossed the words offhandedly, only for Hamish to wince. "Sorry about landing you in the soup. He's not happy at the idea I broke things off with Miss Sanders. Given how things are in Portugal, I didn't like the possibility of leaving a widow with a small child."

"Father would ensure she was cared for, since the boy would be heir after James."

"*If* the child was a boy. Would she live the rest of her days like a nun while the boy is brought up to be the future Marquess of Rutherglen? What if she fell in love again? A new husband would want his wife in his own home, but would he enjoy having a young stepson who outranked him?"

Hamish sighed, turning his head away. "All theoretical in any case. Clarissa wrote to say she's marrying someone else. Since James won't step up—"

"Not won't. Can't."

Hamish perked up a bit. "I want to hear that story." He glanced toward where the nurse stood. "Though preferably when Mrs. Petherbridge isn't in the room. I imagine the tale's somewhat rude."

The nurse smiled. "I can assure you I don't shock easily. It might be best, though, if Lord Blair lets you finish eating and you can try to get some rest. The doctor will be here later, and you would like to be at your best."

Less than ten minutes, and Hamish was already looking worn. His hope was being in a comfortable bed, cared for and not having to travel would be a tonic. If anything, his brother appeared as tired as he had during their travels. "I'll take my leave. I'll come back later, and we'll try to shock Mrs. Petherbridge."

Hamish said he would hold Blair to that, while Mrs. Petherbridge favored him with an indulgent expression. No, he wagered she would prove difficult to shock.

Blair, though, felt more unsettled than before, wondering if his father truly had cause to worry.

CHAPTER 5

The evening being musical, footmen circulated with trays of punch in the grand salon of the Gresham townhouse, as the guests greeted one another. Augusta played the dutiful and demure daughter, trailing a step behind her parents. The social convention allowed her to stay back and let her attention wonder as Lord Manville offered up the latest tidbits of gossip to Lady Eastleigh. "Rumor is Lord Rutherglen's lost faith in the possibility of his heir marrying."

In an instant, Augusta's attention fixed on the conversation. "You don't say," Lady Eastleigh replied, her voice light, but her smile fixed about the edges.

"No one knows why, though all my little birds are working hard to learn what they can. I also know Lord Hamish broke off an understanding before being wounded. All the dynastic hopes may rest on Lord Blair's shoulders."

His gaze slid past Lady Eastleigh to land on Augusta. "Hasn't he been paying attention to Miss Eastleigh of late?"

Lady Eastleigh waved the idea away. "He danced with her the other evening, after they were introduced, that is all. They only met because Lord Chalton introduced them. He has been very attentive.

There is Lady Phipps and I simply must speak with her. Pray excuse us."

She whisked August and Eastleigh away. "Why make certain I knew Lord Rutherglen is worried about his son's marriage?" Lady Eastleigh said as soon as they were out of earshot. "He's ferreted out some rumor and is trying to learn more."

"I agree the effort seemed obvious," Eastleigh said. "I can't see Father spreading the news, though. Not without a firm settlement"

"Such news might easily discourage some suitors, especially Chalton, which would suit your father." Lady Eastleigh turned back to Augusta. "You are to be charming and attentive to the earl as he asked for you to accompany him this evening. Your father and I will sit a short distance behind, allowing you some semblance of intimacy. Do what you can to encourage him because time is of the essence."

Hardly conducive to a relaxing and enjoyable evening, but Augusta understood the importance of her mother's words. If she had not accepted them before, she did now. In an effort to distract herself, she surveyed the other guests, finding no one unfamiliar to her, at least by sight. She preferred these smaller gatherings to assemblies. Wilverton had complained of not being invited when he called that afternoon. Perhaps this would prove an evening to enjoy.

Then she spied Lord Blair hovering near the room's entrance. He watched her with the same intensity as the night they met. What was he thinking now? Did he know about the match? Was he as unhappy about the idea as she? Did he look upon her as a necessary evil to secure the future?

Or was he biding his time? There was the possibility if Chalton learned of a pending engagement between them, he would withdraw, ceding his friend the claim. All he had to do was wait for Chalton to appear and—

As if summoned, Chalton approached. "Here I am, and before the music starts," he said, with a respectful bow.

"So you are," Eastleigh said. "Augusta has been watching the door for the last few minutes. Haven't you, Goose?"

Augusta felt her cheeks warm as her father chuckled. At the moment, she allowed the misrepresentation stand, as Chalton smiled at her. "How could I be late when I had such a pleasant companion waiting for me?"

"Then enjoy yourselves," Lady Eastleigh said. "Take a turn around the room before the entertainment starts. You'll find that more enjoyable than standing here."

She made a shooing gesture and Chalton offered Augusta his arm. "Is all well?" Chalton asked as they began to stroll. "You looked somewhat pensive when I arrived."

While she was watching Blair. "A stray though. Nothing of import. Being in London presents some challenges."

"London presents challenges for a great many folk," Chalton replied. "Which is why it is important to find those you can rely on."

Before she formed a response, Chalton said, "Speaking of those you can rely on, here is Lord Blair. I believe he may have something to say to you."

Augusta tensed as Blair approached. "Chalton," he said, acknowledged with a bow of his head. "Miss Eastleigh."

His half-bow was courteous in every way. "Lord Blair," she replied, letting a hint of wariness color the words.

The three of them stood silent for a moment, until Chalton gave Blair a look. Blair took a deep breath, every inch the man doing as he must but not caring for the task. "I must apologize for my behavior the other evening. Other matters plagued me, and I unfortunately channeled that upset into our conversation. In short, I was inexcusably rude. I will understand if you do not wish to forgive, but I hope you will at least allow me to show myself in a better light."

No, she didn't feel like forgiving him. She didn't care to grant him a second chance, either, but she could not refuse the gesture with Chalton standing at her side. "Let us begin again," she said. "We should try to see a better side of one another."

That at least was true. With her grandfather set on making Blair her husband, best to find some common ground with him or face an unpleasant future. Perhaps her efforts would spur Chalton on; he wanted her to be on good terms with his friend. If he were not serious, would he care?

Blair fell into step next to her as she and Chalton began to stroll again. Lovely. Hard to achieve her mother's goal of intimate conversation with a third person marching beside them. Were they going to be reduced to inane small talk. Would Blair try to cut her out of the conversation?

"Didn't expect to find Mrs. Hibbert here," Blair said. "Not the sort of event I would expect her to enjoy. Fewer opportunities for her daughters to shine since Lady Gresham doesn't ask her guests to contribute their musical talents."

Mrs. Hibbert was indeed greeting their hostess, who didn't appear as pleased to welcome this guest as she had others. "She's probably hoping the intimacy of the evening will allow her quarry less of a chance to get away," Augusta said. "With fewer unmarried ladies present, much easier to promote her daughter's charms."

To her surprise, Blair laughed. "Well played," he muttered.

He still laughed as Mrs. Hibbert approached. "My dear Lord Chalton! Lovely to see you once more, but sad to find you on your own for the evening."

"I am not alone," Chalton said. "I have Miss Eastleigh as company, and Lord Blair."

A bit surprised, Mrs. Hibbert looked toward Augusta and Blair, then back again. "I thought—"

"Lord Blair is without a partner," Augusta said before Mrs. Hibbert could share her thoughts. "Perhaps he might escort one of your daughters."

Blair flinched visibly, as did Mrs. Hibbert. "No, no, my daughters are spoken for. I merely expressed my concern that he might find himself lonely."

She bobbed a bit of a curtsey and moved on. Augusta snuck a glance at Blair, who met her gaze with concern. Word was leaking out, though from whom, she did not know. Lady Eastleigh would be quick to blame her father-in-law, but could Rutherglen have said something to someone?

"Did you have to offer me up as a sacrifice?" Blair asked, a teasing note in his tone, breaking the tension.

"I wagered she would not be content to pair one of her daughters with you," Augusta replied. "A calculated risk."

36

"Why would she think you were with Blair?" Chalton asked, looking puzzled.

"Willful misunderstanding," Blair said. "She wished you to be available for her daughters, and ignored the evidence of her eyes. Very much within her character. The musicians are taking their places. Shall we find seats?"

He took the lead, moving toward the chairs arranged for the guests. Lady Eastleigh would have likely preferred Augusta suggest to Chalton they find a seat on one of the couches along the wall, but Blair focused on the best vantage point. She did not think Chalton would take kindly to abandoning his friend.

One thing was certain, though. Lord Blair was no happier about the situation than she. Nor did he appear to want to tell his friend what was in the offing. Augusta had to wonder why.

Sitting next to Augusta was not what Blair had in mind. Truth be told, he didn't plan to sit near Simon, either, who found such evenings a bit of a bore. Shortly after the music began, he wouldn't be able to resist making comments, which drove Blair to distraction. Hopefully, she would not exhibit the same tendencies.

After sending Mrs. Hibbert on her way, it felt appropriate to find seats for the three of them together, which meant he was stuck. Sitting next to her wouldn't help the rumors which had begun to circulate. That was Forebridge's doing, he wagered. He couldn't imagine his father diverting his attention from Hamish's condition long enough to inform anyone of the news.

To his relief, Augusta paid close attention when the music began . She did not exhibit the rapt expression some women adopted to mark themselves as some kind of aficionado of the arts. Her head nodded in time with the music at moments, smiling over the particularly skillful handling of a passage at another. Just beyond her, Simon did his best to focus, but the somewhat glazed expression warned boredom was already setting in.

When the piece ended, the guests offered polite applause, followed by the murmur of conversation. At the front of the room, the musicians were conferring. They allowed a few minutes, enough time for the guests to exercise the need to talk, but not so long as to lose them completely. Augusta, not surprisingly, turned to speak with Simon, leaving Blair on his own. He couldn't resist glancing back along the rows to find the Eastleighs sitting close behind. Lady Eastleigh looked pleased with what she saw, but when her eyes moved to him, she frowned. She had warned him to stay away, yet here he was and there was nothing she could do. He doubted the situation made her any happier than he.

The musicians struck up another tune, and the crowd fell raggedly silent. Once more, Augusta focused on the music. Soon, though, Blair heard a quiet murmur as Chalton addressed a remark to her. She responded, but only briefly before her attention turned back to the music. Blair couldn't help smiling. She didn't care to be interrupted while she was listening either, no matter what her instructions might be.

Once more, polite applause was offered at the end of the piece. While the musicians re-arranged their music, a woman moved toward them, pausing to confer with their leader. "This must be the surprise Lady Gresham hinted at in her invitation," Blair said to Augusta. "Madame Solange is a coup; she doesn't often perform at private gatherings."

She broke off her conversation with Simon to ask, "Why not?"

"She claims her schedule is too full, but I think the lady is wise enough to recognize limiting her performances raises her exclusivity, which in turn raises her fee."

"Don't get him started," Simon said. "Lord Blair is a fanatic about opera."

"Chalton is a philistine about such things. Best get used to the idea now. You are familiar with opera, are you not, Miss Eastleigh?"

A slight hesitation before she answered. "I've not heard it sung."

"Then you are in for a treat," he said, his suspicion overcome with the possibility of creating yet another devotee. "With luck, she'll favor us with the Queen of the Night's aria from *Der Zauberflöte*, but any selection she wishes to sing—

He stopped, holding up a finger as the woman stepped forward, and leaned toward Simon. "Let's allow Miss Eastleigh enjoy this, shall we?"

Simon rolled his eyes, but he stayed silent as Madame Solange began. For Blair, this alone was worth everything else he must put up with this evening. The chance to be transported for a while on by the glorious music. Except, he found his attention divided. He couldn't help sneaking glances at Augusta to see if she enjoyed herself.

She did. Now her expression was rapt, nothing false to find, only the discovery. When the last note died away, even before they had finished their applause, she turned to him, eyes sparkling. "Is all opera like this?"

"No," he admitted, "but many wonderful performances and scores help overcome the lesser ones."

"I wish Grandfather had agreed to a box for the season," she said. "He did not feel it a useful expense, though."

"My father always keeps a box," Blair replied. "He's even allowed my sisters to attend, though they are not yet out."

Again that smile, warm and real. "How lucky for them." Remembering her duty, she turned to Simon. "Did you enjoy the singing, my lord?"

He offered up a sheepish expression. "As I said, I'm not an enthusiast."

"As I said, he's a philistine," Blair shot back.

Augusta laughed again, but fell silent as the next number began. He found it pleasant to sit next to someone who appreciated the artistry on display. Even if she tried to trap his best friend into marriage.

By the time the performance ended, Blair found himself in a better mood than he been in over a month, and more than willing to show some goodwill toward his fellow man. Or woman, as the case might be, trailing behind as Simon escorted Augusta back to her parents. With the music done, the party began to break up, guests making their farewells to their hostess. "Did you enjoy the evening, Lord Chalton?" Lady Eastleigh asked.

A slight grimace on Chalton's part. "Musical performances are not my favorite I'm afraid, but this was a social obligation. I was pleased to have your daughter as company. She made the time pass more quickly."

Not what Lady Eastleigh had been expecting, most likely, but she covered. "Then I am glad she kept you entertained. I know such things are always better with a partner.

"Lord Blair also enjoyed her company," Simon said. "He is always eager to introduce someone to the joys of opera."

Lady Eastleigh looked from Simon to her daughter. "Lord Blair was kind enough to explain some things to me about Madame Solange's performance," Miss Eastleigh replied.

Now the gaze slid from Augusta to him. "Did he, now? I should thank you then, Lord Blair. Please, give my regards to your father. Are you ready, Lord Eastleigh?"

While Lady Eastleigh might give away as little as possible, Lord Eastleigh was less adept in that arena. He also seemed more amused, a hint of a grin on his face as the family departed. "You were being pleasant with Miss Eastleigh tonight," Simon said.

"I thought you wanted us to get along. She accepted my apology and we're making a fresh start."

"Excellent. Not certain I appreciate you selling her on opera. I don't know if I can face years of evenings in a box, trying to do my best to stay awake."

Blair chuckled at Simon's wry expression because it was expected. Still, he worried at the signal marriage to Augusta might indeed be on the table. He had a simple way to stop this. One word about his father's plan and Simon would withdraw. It would be kinder to say something before his friend became too set on the idea and suffered disappointment once again when news of the proposed alliance made its way beyond just whispers. Not to mention the upset and hurt that Blair had allowed him to carry on knowing of the possibility.

A word. Simon wouldn't be surprised after their conversation the other evening about Hamish. Was he willing to marry the girl, or at least consider it, to save his friend?

"My advice to you?" Blair said. "Practice the art of sleeping with your eyes open."

No, he wasn't ready to walk that path. Not yet. But Simon had just given him an idea that would make Rutherglen happy.

CHAPTER 6

The butler entered the drawing room, a note on the usual silver tray. Augusta paid no further heed beyond noting his entrance, focused on the conversation between Lady Fortesque and her grandfather. Forebridge never came down when they were receiving calls, which made his presence unsettling.

The clearing of a throat and she looked up to discover the butler next to her chair. "This just arrived, miss. The messenger said he was to wait for a reply."

Conversation ceased, attention focused on her. Willing her hands to be steady, Augusta reached out to take the folded paper from the tray.

My dear Miss Eastleigh, the note began, *I hope you will not think this an impertinence. Given how much joy you took in Madame Solange's performance, I would be greatly appreciative if you and your family would agree to join my family in our box one evening when she is performing. I would find great pleasure in the chance to introduce you to the full glory of what the opera can be.*

With my deepest respect,

Lord Blair MacDonald

She couldn't help it. Augusta's reaction upon seeing his name was, "What?"

"Is something wrong, my dear?" Lady Eastleigh asked.

Damn. She hadn't meant to say that aloud. "A note from Lord Blair MacDonald. He would like us to attend the opera with him and his father."

"Damn foolish thing, opera," Forebridge grumped from his chair. "Most men attend to watch the dancers. Who are no better than they should be, mind you."

Next to Lady Eastleigh, Lady Fortesque laughed. "I remember when we both were younger, you found the opera very entertaining and hied yourself off to enjoy its pleasures at every opportunity."

"Which is how I know about the opera dancers," he shot back. "Not a place for a respectable lady. Certainly not one who bears my family name."

Augusta couldn't believe he had given her an out. "I suppose, since Grandfather does not approve of opera, I must decline his polite invitation. It would not be right to accept in the face of such disapproval. I will send a note to thank him for his kindness, along with our regrets."

She rose to move toward the secretary desk in the corner, but stopped as Forebridge said, "Did he say he wished you to join him *and* the Marquess of Rutherglen?"

"Yes, Grandfather."

To her surprise, Forebridge chuckled. "Maybe he's spoken to the boy. I'll tell Rutherglen we'll be happy to make it a party."

Impossible to miss he included himself. "I should send a note in response," she offered, a but unsure as to which way his mood would shift.

"Tell him you are seeking permission and thank him for his kindness. That should be sufficient." When Augusta did not move, he glowered. "What are you waiting for? Go. Write."

She retreated to the desk, aware her mother glared daggers at Forebridge. Lady Fortesque begged her leave within a few moments most likely sensing the undercurrent of tension.

The instant their guest was out the door, Lady Eastleigh exploded at her father-in-law. "When I suggest that we go to the opera, you prattle about loose women, but the moment a gentleman suggests Augusta share a box, you're instantly determined she should attend."

"*You* want to go to opera to put yourself on display, madam, just as you do at every event you attend. This is different. This signals Rutherglen told his son of our plans and the lad's not resisting."

Augusta was unsure this was the reason, but she said nothing, pulling a sheet of paper from the desk's supply and beginning to write the few words required. Forebridge continued, his hands steepled before him. "Before you swear he isn't what you're looking for, let me remind me that the third son of a marquess is not something to be sniffed at, since there are skeletons in the closet."

"There are no skeletons." Lady Eastleigh's arms were stiff at her side. "You think there are because your stiff-necked pride that won't allow you to admit Richard is her father. If you're going to heap scorn, heap it on me. Don't involve my child."

"I told you, I'll foot the bill for one season. One. What do I have to show so far? A large number of bills for all sorts of female frippery and no proposals. You keep promising, but deliver nothing."

"The Earl of Chalton is paying Augusta much attention. He asked prior to the evening at Lady Gresham's that he be allowed to escort her. What is that but interest?"

"I don't find that encouraging at all. Gossip is he's still mourning the girl his father wisely prevented him from marrying. Perhaps he's looking to the future, but if he is, I doubt he'll propose to anyone this season. Blair MacDonald is a decent match. He should be encouraged. Don't you dare try to upset things because they don't suit your plans. It suits mine."

He turned toward to the desk. "How long does it take for you to write a note, girl?"

Augusta put down her pen and blotted the paper. "All I need to do is inscribe the address."

"I want to read what you wrote first."

Her mother would want her to refuse, say she was perfectly capable of writing her own notes without his supervision. She also knew to do so would trigger another round of arguments. Without a word, she crossed the floor, laying the paper in his hand. Forebridge scanned the lines, then handed it back. "You at least write with a fine hand and pleasant words. Just enough to show you are interested, but nothing which might be too forward."

He levered himself out of the chair. "Most fortunate I chose to be here while you visited with Lady Fortesque. You might have written the wrong sort of note in response."

Strolling toward the door, he paused on the threshold. "I've not been to the opera in some time. I find I'm looking forward to the evening."

"He's determined to be rid of you and doesn't give a fig about your future," Lady Eastleigh said when he departed.

Augusta returned to the desk and sat down to seal and write Lord Blair's name on the exterior of the folded paper. "Can we not revisit how much you and he despise one another, Mother? It doesn't help ."

"How can you be so unconcerned?" Lady Eastleigh moved toward the desk. "Do you not understand how this sets the course of your life?"

"I understand. I 've heard nothing but for the past several months. You impressed on me how important I find a titled husband with a large fortune. Grandfather just wants me married off respectably and doesn't care who the groom is."

The letter sealed, Augusta blew on the wax to cool it. Flipping the folded sheet over, she picked up the pen once more, but paused. "Funny, no one bothered to inquire as to what I might like."

Taking up the pen, she wrote Lord Blair's name, deliberately turning her gaze away from her mother. She didn't know who she was angrier with, her mother or Forebridge. She grew weary of being a pawn in their continual game of one-upmanship.

When she had done, she laid the note to one side and looked up to find her mother had settled in the small chair near the desk. "Do you care for someone such as Mr. Wilverton?" Lady Eastleigh asked quietly.

"Mr. Wilverton?" Augusta shook his head. "I'd rather Lord Blair any day than Mr. Wilverton. Someone of his station, a plain gentleman with no title and a modest estate, no." She sighed. "I'm glad Father keeps finding a way to avoid meeting with him. I fear Grandfather would not be pleased if I turned down any proposal."

"Never underestimate your grandfather's innate snobbery. Is there no gentleman who catches your fancy, even if he's not someone I would favor?"

Her mother's face filled with concern, but there was also doubt, as if she'd somehow caused this situation. "No one at home, and no one here who strikes my fancy in particular. Lord Chalton is the most interesting gentleman I've encountered, but I worry Grandfather is right, that he is not ready to commit to a marriage."

"You mean, not yet. We still have time." Lady Eastleigh held up a hand. "Before you object, remember your alternative."

She glanced at the note. "I suppose you must encourage Lord Blair. He does not seem to be the type of man to interest you, but your grandfather will expect you to be kind. I just hope the gentlemen don't cancel one another out."

Augusta was unsure what she wanted, except to not find her grandfather playing matchmaker at the end of the season.

Climbing the stairs to the foyer for the boxes at the Queen's Theatre, Haymarket, Augusta took a deep breath, then another. She wanted to enjoy this evening, see if the performance on offer was as magnificent as the performance at Lady Gresham's. With her mother and grandfather enduring a frosty truce in addition to wondering what was behind Blair's invitation, relaxation was not likely.

Blair and Lord Rutherglen were waiting for them when they finished their ascent, accompanied by two young ladies dressed in their best, though neither looking to be out of the schoolroom yet. The marquess was the first to greet them. "Good to see you, Forebridge. Eastleigh, Lady Eastleigh."

He bowed courteously over Lady Eastleigh's hand before turning to Augusta. "Miss Eastleigh. How charming you look this evening. Isn't she charming, Blair?"

"Charming, indeed." Blair's words held more enthusiasm than she expected. She did not know what to make of that or his expression. Or the way it made her shiver. God help her, had he resigned himself to this match?

She made the expected curtsey and rose to find he watched her with that expression which seemed to weigh and measure every part. "Allow me to present my sisters, Lady Caitlin and Lady Finola MacDonald," he said, eyes not leaving her.

The two girls stepped forward to make a curtsey, doing their best to appear proper and sophisticated. "They're not out," Rutherglen said, "but I don't think it hurts to give them a chance to learn how to behave at such things. Will serve them well in a few years." He smiled fondly at the two girls. "I'm proud of how they carry themselves."

Any attempt at sophistication melted away into pleased smiles at their father's words, the obvious closeness of the family filling Augusta with warmth. Watching how Blair regarded the girls couldn't help but soften her. He couldn't be completely callous if he was that fond of his younger siblings.

Didn't mean he would make her a good husband, though.

Rutherglen suggested they move into the anteroom of the box itself, away from the crowds outside, where a footman waited with light refreshments. "How are you enjoying London, Miss Eastleigh?" Rutherglen asked. "I imagine most young ladies are enthralled with their first season, and Caitlin would love to hear your experiences."

Lady Caitlin's eyes were bright and shining, and Augusta chose her words carefully. "I find Society exciting, but also overwhelming at times. There's so many people, and fierce competition for beaus."

"Competition?" Finola asked. "Don't they flock to you when you appear?"

Augusta couldn't help laughing. "You must remember only so many gentlemen are available, and one must consider if one's parents think they are fit suitors. There are questions of station and lineage and, yes, fortune. Many a poor man will seek a rich wife, while a poor beauty will do what she can to secure a wealthy man to help her own family and any sisters who are yet unmarried."

The last was her mother's story, but she felt no shame in the telling. The girls would soon learn of gentlemen who sought to woo them because of their fortunes and connections, not giving a thought to their own person or what they might feel. Even now, Augusta could see both Caitlin and Finola working over her words.

"But—" Caitlin began, then stopped. A touch to her elbow by Blair, an encouraging glance, and she found her words again. "How do you know who is interested in you and who might be interested in your fortune and connections? Don't they all use nice words to make you think they care about you?"

Who indeed? This one is clever. "Best to have an older friend or relative who can offer advice about the gentlemen's history. Are they deep in debt, things of that nature. They look out for your interests."

"That is why I will be asking your Aunt Cecilia to come to London for your season," Rutherglen said. "She may not have experience of the Ton, but she has a way of ferreting out information I think will make clear which gentlemen should hold your interest and which should not."

He turned to Forebridge. "I must say, Miss Eastleigh is well-spoken. A credit to your family."

Forebridge snorted, but he didn't refuse the compliment, Augusta noted. He also didn't argue when Rutherglen indicated they should take their seats in anticipation of the performance starting. Rutherglen offered Lady Eastleigh his arm, while Lord Eastleigh did the same to Caitlin and Finola. Forebridge followed, leaving, Blair and Augusta to bring up the rear.

"Shall we to it?" Blair said, offering his arm.

She should take his arm and move into the box where they would all paint a pretty picture for everyone present. By tomorrow, word would be about town the two families had been seen together.

Still, she hesitated. "I wonder at your sudden enthusiasm for my company, sir. Yes, I accepted your apology and we passed a pleasant enough evening at Lady Gresham's, but your invitation was unexpected."

"You said your grandfather didn't approve of you at the opera, I thought I would extend an opportunity where he found it impossible to say no."

His arm was still extended, waiting for her acceptance. "Did you intend to give him and your father the impression this arrangement they're suggesting is something you're in favor of? Then why not say something to Lord Chalton? I believe he would withdraw gracefully if he knew the plans."

Given the struggle on his face, her question had unsettled him. "They're going to move forward with this whether we will or no," Blair said. "They both see this as a solution to a problem. It's up to us to make the best of things."

"You'll give in so easily?" She frowned. "After everything you accused me of the night we met, you'll marry me because your father says you must?"

She stepped closer to him, closer than a young lady properly should. "What are you not telling me, sir? What secret are you hiding for your father to move swiftly?"

"Because my eldest brother can't father children, apparently, and Hamish doesn't want to marry because of the war," Blair blurted out, the words forceful enough for Augusta to step back a pace. "Because we all know Hamish could get himself killed when he returns to the battlefield—*if* he recovers from these wounds—all dynastic hopes now rest on me. Just like Chalton, I must marry, whether I will or no."

The raw anger and hurt in his voice shook her. This was a dangerous thing, something which could swirl into a pool of resentment, poisoning any chance they might have of finding common ground. Worse, a glance towards the box itself warned they were being watched, his words not quiet enough to escape notice.

Stepping close once more, she said in a careful voice, "I am sorry. Truly, I am. But best for all if you escorted me to my seat."

"I fear I have lost my taste for entertainment."

"I understand this is the last thing you wish at this moment. I know what it is to smile when all you wish to do is rage. But if you leave now, Lord Forebridge will blame me for your departure and things will not go well, for myself or my mother." She paused. "*Please.*"

She dare not say more and she hoped her words were enough. Given how Blair looked at her, she doubted it.

Then, the moment passed, and he clear his throat, standing a little taller. With a hollow smile on his face, he once again offered his arm. "Shall we go in, Miss Eastleigh?"

Matching the tone of that smile with one of her own, she laid her hand atop his arm. "We shall, Lord Blair."

CHAPTER 7

With Augusta settled in her seat, Blair found his own. He didn't miss the concern on his father's face, or Lord and Lady Eastleigh's. Forebridge appeared annoyed, but his gaze was directed at his granddaughter, not Blair. Just as Augusta had said.

He'd made a right mess of things. No way around that. But she pushed and he reacted. Something about this woman would not allow him to be peaceable. Somehow, she disassembled his efforts to appear as calm and unruffled as a gentleman should, no matter what disasters might befall the family.

Why had it felt good to say the words as plainly as he had? That was the wrong question. Why had it felt good to say the words to *her*? He had no reason to open himself up to Augusta Eastleigh. Even if his father succeeded in pushing this betrothal through, many men kept their true feelings from their wives.

Wives. He let his gaze shift from the stage to her. She sat with her spine erect, the whole of her attention focused toward the front. Unlike at Lady Gresham's, though, Blair found no enjoyment or transportation here as the orchestra played the overture. Like him, she was presenting a face to the world.

Word was going to spread. Any number of folk had seen them,

and they would be a subject of comment since Forebridge chose to attend. Blair could not remember any event where Forebridge had attended if his daughter-in-law was present. The two families together gave the impression some type of union was in the offing. Which meant Simon would hear. And ask.

He doubted he would find any sort of story that would make him appear any less of an ass. Worse, Simon would ask the pertinent question: was Blair going to agree to marry Augusta, or try to find another bride?

Which meant he needed to commit. Problem was, which way?

At the interval, as the others began to chatter, Blair chose not to move from his seat or join in these conversations. This hadn't gone the way he planned. The idea had been for himself, his father, the Eastleighs and their daughter. Then Forebridge had invited himself. Then Rutherglen declared the girls should attend because he thought they might enjoy Handel's *Oreste*. With everyone crowded into the box, this was nothing less than the announcement of a union.

With his luck, Simon would learn within a day. Blair knew he should have said something that night, ascribing his words to unhappiness at parental meddling. Simon would have counseled patience, and tried to convince Blair she was possessed of sterling qualities. Augusta was, he admitted, both attractive and intelligent, and would shine as a hostess for whomever married her. Why him, though?

He survived the first interval without having to engage, watching as Augusta listened attentively to her elders and chatted with Caitlin and Fiona. She bent her head close to her mother's for a bit of private conversation, shaking her head at whatever Lady Eastleigh had to say. For just a moment, her smile dropped to reveal a somber, thoughtful expression. Then Rutherglen spoke and she turned towards him, the mask back in place.

Rutherglen wouldn't recognize the mask, but Blair remembered the light in her eyes when she turned to him after Madame Solange's first song. Was she wondering what Simon would do when he heard the gossip, worrying all her plans would come crashing down?

During the second interval that his father turned to him, asking quietly. "Why did you near shout at the lady? Why are you avoiding speaking with her now?"

Blair did his best not to squirm. "She vexed me, and I lost my temper. Just as I vex her. Neither of us want a part in this mad plan you and Forebridge cooked up."

"Not if you keep shouting at her." Rutherglen's voice was tight. "Are you even trying? If you don't want to marry the girl, best tell me and we'll consider other choices. Leaves her free to make other choices —though I imagine Forebridge will be the guiding hand in any decision."

He leaned closer in. "You're the one who suggested this evening. I took it as a sign you made your choice, and find it cruel to lead everyone on with false hopes. Don't think I didn't notice you've not spoken to her after we heard raised voices. Speak with her now if you possess any sense of decency."

Blair was unsure about decency, but he understood when his father's suggestions were a command, and rose from his seat. "Might I have a word with your daughter, Lady Eastleigh?"

Lady Eastleigh looked ready to refuse. Not because he wasn't on her approved list, he wagered. Still, a sideways glance towards Forebridge and she nodded her assent. "Stay within sight," she warned as he held out his hand to assist Augusta in rising.

Which meant precious little privacy. Perhaps that was best. He would watch his tongue with others close. That is, if he figured out anything to say.

Standing a spare distance from him by the door to the box, Augusta eyed him warily. "They will be happier if we speak," he said, not certain how else to begin the conversation.

"They would be happier if we did what they asked without argument," she replied. "Unfortunately, their desires are in conflicting desires and I do not believe you have any intention of following their direction. Before you suggest I would be happier if I didn't, allow me to remind you I don't have that option. My grandfather is set on this match. He will not take kindly to the idea you arranged this evening with no true intent."

This was not vexation or annoyance because he upset her plan.

53

Blair saw a simmering anger in her eyes. "We barely know one another—" he began.

"Do you think most couples in society know one another when they approach the altar? Young ladies are warned not to present their true self, but craft an image to attract a gentleman. Gentlemen do the same, do they not? They make themselves pleasant and amiable, only revealing debts, cruelty, and callousness after a woman is in their control."

He did not know how to react to these words. Her voice was pitched not to carry, but every line of her body radiated tension for any to see. He wagered a look would find both Lady Eastleigh and Rutherglen watching closely, Forebridge also.

He did not look, unable to tear his gaze away from those green-gold eyes which bore into his. "Just as a woman can hide a shrewish temper behind a pretty smile," he countered. "Or a desire for fortune and position behind protestations she would love a titled man if he was poor."

"The fortune hunter pretending to love a woman for her true self and not the sovereigns she possesses."

"Speaking of desire and longing while staying within the bounds of society. Then turning cold once the vows are pronounced."

"Attempting to control her every move like she was a piece of prime horseflesh, before promises have been made."

Blair opened his mouth to reply but closed it again. Her breath had quickened, proved by the rapid rise and fall of flesh above the neckline of her gown. A glance down and he found her fingers curled tightly into fists. "Who has done such a thing to you?"

"Why ask?" she replied. "You made it clear you don't care."

She turned her gaze away with a deliberate movement, focusing on the stage. "I believe the musicians are gathering once more. We should take our seats."

Augusta did not wait for him to offer his hand, but made her own way back to her chair, sliding into it with easy grace. Back rigid, she faced the stage, not turning when Lady Eastleigh reached out to lay her hand atop her daughter's. They had been watched. His sisters seemed puzzled, not understanding what was happening. He didn't look forward to navigating their questions.

Worse, though, were the gentlemen. Both Eastleigh and Ruther-glen appeared displeased, though he wagered their reasoning was different. Forebridge, though, wore an angry expression, and Blair was struck by how similar that expression was to Augusta's. Then, he shifted his glare to his granddaughter, and Blair realized things would go badly once they were away from company. Just as she had predicted.

This was unfair. They weren't suited to one another, no matter what the elders wanted. That didn't matter to Forebridge, though. He wanted this match and any failure would be laid on Augusta's head.

The music began once more, and Blair took his seat. He didn't want this match, but neither did he mean to do harm. Gossip would still spread through London, though what the topic was, he was no longer certain.

Unsurprisingly, Forebridge unleashed a torrent of fury once they were in the carriage. Augusta was wondered he managed to wait until then. "You are supposed to charm him, move this match along. Instead, you unleash your tongue on him, and we know where you got that."

He glared at Lady Eastleigh. "Didn't you teach the chit how to be pleasant to gentlemen, entrap them in her web? You have the talent, because you used those wiles on my son."

"Father, please don't say such things about my wife. Why are you blaming Augusta, anyway? Clearly Lord Blair didn't want to be there or speak with her."

"He seemed eager enough when we arrived," Forebridge snapped in response. "Something changed, and I'm certain she's at the root."

"He doesn't want the match," Augusta said. "He was very plain about that. He extended the invitation because it would please his father. He didn't care if it pleased me."

She responded with more force than usual, but she was tired, and her eyes burned with unshed tears. She would not cry in front of Forebridge, not if she could help it. He would interpret her tears as weakness and use them as a weapon.

"I don't care if it pleased you, miss. Your job is to ensure he's willing to go along with the match. You smile, you dissemble, you say the words that make him think you will be a biddable mate. After you're wed, he can always find company elsewhere if you're not to his liking."

Lady Eastleigh had wrapped her arm about Augusta's shoulder, and her mother's fingers pressed into her flesh. "You make it sound like a market transaction. Augusta is not some breeding stock you're selling to the highest bidder."

"That is her only use to me. Rutherglen needs an heir and expects his son to get him one. I want the girl settled and gone so at least one reminder of my son's folly is not before me. Before you prattle on about love and affection, Richard, might I remind you I still hold the purse strings and there are two more brats you'll be wanting to bring out in a few years' time."

"You wouldn't deny them husbands." Eastleigh said, shocked.

"No, I wouldn't. I don't want them as a drain on the estate. They can be found husbands without this folderol. No presentation to Queen Charlotte, no string of expensive dresses. Your son, of course, will need to be launched properly to meet a girl with sufficient fortune. But the girls? They're of little use to the family."

Forebridge turned to Augusta. "Since my wishes do not appear important to you, let me add this incentive. You will make things right with Lord Blair or Chalton had better be ready to propose. If not, I'll find you a husband myself and ones for your sisters when the time comes. Do you understand?"

Augusta nodded, understanding far too well. She didn't dare speak now, the burning in her eyes becoming almost unbearable. Forebridge leaned forward. "Don't think tears will make me change my course. Ask your mother what happened the last time she tried that trick on me."

She would not ask. Not now when he could enjoy the discomfort he caused. Instead, she kept silent as the carriage came to a stop in front of the townhouse. Without a word or backward glance, Forebridge left the carriage. "Richard——" Lady Eastleigh began once he was gone.

"What do you expect me to do?" Eastleigh asked. "Yes, he controls the purse strings. Don't think he won't tighten those if he feels like it. He's perfectly capable of denying a season to the twins. He's already grumbled about the cost of bringing two girls out at once."

With a sigh, he turned toward Augusta. "I hate to ask this, Goose, but do you find anything about Lord Blair pleasing?"

His face, his form, his easy competence on the dance floor. These were things she could answer but they would only give her father false hope. "It's not an issue with me finding him pleasing. He doesn't want this marriage because he doesn't want to be yoked to a woman just because his father says. He's looking for a reason to scuttle the match, and he'll likely resent me if we are forced to marry."

"Which is why we need to get Chalton up to the mark," Lady Eastleigh said, her voice urgent. "You need to do everything you can to convince him this is the match he wants, and you need to do it swiftly. I'm afraid your grandfather would take pleasure in ramming this through, and if it doesn't work, he may be spiteful in his choice of a match. None of us want that for you."

"Try not to argue with Lord Blair if you can," Eastleigh added. "You might buy yourself some time if you don't struggle where your grandfather can see."

He took a deep breath. "We can't sit here all night. Get her settled in bed, Soph, then you and I will talk, see what we can come up with. We will do our best to make this right, Goose. I promise you that."

Augusta managed a smile, wiping tear tracks from her cheeks. Her parents' words gave her some comfort, but she feared there was nothing they could do. Chalton might be her only hope.

CHAPTER 8

Rutherglen was quiet during the trip home. Too quiet for Blair's liking. Somehow, they managed to get through the evening without any further hot words, though the parting proved been somewhat awkward. Except for Forebridge. If anything, he seemed even more intent they should be moving forward with negotiations on the marriage settlement.

Once inside the townhouse, his father bid Caitlin and Finola good evening, then shooed them upstairs to bed. Only then did he turn to Blair. "What the hell were you thinking? I thought your suggestion to invite the Eastleighs was a sign of your willingness to pursue the match. Instead, the two of you barely speak a civil word to one another."

"I told you she had a tongue on her." Blair didn't want this conversation.

"Did you think I would pair you with some simpering milksop? You'd run mad within a month and then where would we be?"

"Where we are now, with you trying to get to me to agree to marry a woman who doesn't suit me."

"Is that she doesn't suit you? Or are you angry at her because I need you to marry?"

"Yes, I'm angry! I'm angry because you came up with this fool plan without thinking anything through. You're putting all the dynastic expectations on my shoulders, but what if Hamish marries after he recovers? What if he fathers sons? They would inherit the title before my children."

"Hamish may still die." Rutherglen's voice was hoarse. "He may lose his leg. That happens, I fear he will give up."

"Don't be ridiculous. This is Hamish. He would never——"

"How many men have you seen come back from the wars with missing limbs, son? It changes them. Even if they survive the shock of the operation and the risk of infection afterwards, they're changed because they are no longer who they once were." He shook his head. "Do you think I want to be worrying about this while your brother lies ill upstairs? I would rather have been at his bedside than the theater tonight. But I also owe a duty to the estate and our tenants. They depend on our family to steer a course that will not put them in peril. I want Hamish to recover and give me some grandchildren. I'm aware how perilous our situation can be. I inherited because my older brother died young. There are siblings you don't remember because they died before you were born."

Blair offered no response. Something lay beneath his father's words, something he wasn't catching.

Rutherglen turned away, toward the stairs, but stopped halfway and came back. "I'm sorry this is on your shoulders, Blair. But James caught the pox and the outlook for Hamish is still grim. There is no one else to turn to. Now, if you cannot stomach Miss Eastleigh, I'll break with Forebridge, tell him your attention is engaged elsewhere."

He held up his hand before Blair could speak. "Don't give me your answer now. We're both tired and upset. Sleep on it. In the morning, ask yourself if you don't want to consider her. Think who else might suit you and I will make overtures." He sighed; weariness etched into every line of his face. "I'm going to look in on Hamish. I'll bid you goodnight."

With that, he was away up the stairs, leaving Blair to contemplate his next move. To be honest, he had no idea what it would be.

. . .

When Blair came down to breakfast the next morning, his mood was no better than the night before. Sleep had eluded him, trying to make sense of this situation. Easiest would be to tell his father he couldn't see himself spending the next thirty years or more with Augusta, and find someone more amenable. Not a milksop, certainly, but someone less forthright with their opinions.

Caitlin and Finola were present, as had become the norm, and Blair found himself grateful for his sisters' presence, as it was unlikely Rutherglen would raise the issue of a decision, giving him a reprieve until the girls departed for their morning lessons.

Half-listening to their chatter, he turned his attention to the pile of letters next his plate. Not surprisingly, some were letters from members of the county, most likely requests related to parliament. The closer they came to the end of session, the more such letters appeared, and he sorted them into a stack for review. Invitations went in another. Which left a note in a hand he didn't recognize. Curious, he opened that first, finding only a few lines inscribed on the sheet inside

To Lord Blair MacDonald.

The Earl of Chalton asks me to inquire if you will be available to meet with him at noon today as he has a matter of some importance and delicacy he wishes to discuss with you. If you cannot attend upon him then, please provide a more congenial time and his lordship will make every attempt to accommodate you. Otherwise, his lordship will expect you at the appointed time.

Your obedient servant,

Thomas Malling

Secretary to the Earl of Chalton

Blair's first reaction was to wonder why Simon's secretary would send him such a formal note instead of Simon writing himself. Then it hit him: he had heard.

Damn. The gossips worked quicker than he expected. Scanning the note again, he recognized the polite phrasing to cover what was undoubtedly ordered in fury. His only hope was that by the time he arrived, Simon would have calmed somewhat. Not that he counted on such a thing.

"You're quiet this morning," Rutherglen said from the other end of the table.

Folding the note, Blair set it to one side with a deliberate casualness. "An appointment for noon which I forgot. I'll depart after breakfast." He hesitated. "On the matter you wished to discuss, may we speak later?"

Rutherglen nodded. "Take the time you need. I want you to be certain in your answer."

Caitlin and Finola looked from their father to their brother and back again, curiosity writ large on their faces. Blair had no intention of satisfying that curiosity, and neither did his father, he suspected. Finola looked fit to bursting, and she offered a few openings in which either gentleman could drop information, but by the time Blair rose from the table, she had received no satisfaction.

He left the house with more than enough time to make it to Simon's establishment. This walk would be the only chance to organize his thoughts and he knew he needed the time. Had he underestimated Simon's regard for Augusta? Or was his friend angry Blair appeared to do what they always avoided: paying court to a woman the other held an interest in. Blair had been the first to pay court to Eleanor Shelby, but it was Simon who fell for her, and he stepped aside.

Simon had spoken the truth when he said he must marry, but Blair assumed it would take longer for the pain to ease. Wouldn't be the first time he'd been wrong.

He could hear the church bells tolling noon as he knocked at the door of Simon's home. "I've been summoned by your master," he said cheerfully to the butler. The man did not crack a smile, but took Blair's hat and cane, and passed them off to a footman before escorting Blair to the drawing room.

The choice was to sit comfortably or stand until Simon appeared. Blair paced, still marshalling arguments in his head. When he heard the door open again, he turned, ready to greet Simon as if nothing was wrong.

Something most definitely was wrong, given the annoyance on Simon's face. "If you are going to court Miss Eastleigh, you might have mentioned it to me. Is that the reason you stayed close at Lady Gresham's? You usually hie yourself off somewhere among the music lovers, but, no, not this time."

"Did I appear to be courting Miss Eastleigh?" Blair countered, sensing reasoned arguments would not hold much sway.

"Then why were you at the opera with her, accompanied by your family? I might believe it evangelism for the opera. But Forebridge, who won't go anywhere Lady Eastleigh is? What would you have me make of that?"

"That my father and Forebridge cooked up an insane plan neither myself nor Miss Eastleigh want any part of."

Not what he planned to say, but it had the effect of quieting Simon for a moment. "My father wants me to marry because of Hamish, and he's fixed on Miss Eastleigh as my bride for some reason. Most likely because Forebridge is eager to be rid of her, he will make a decent settlement. At least, I think that's what he believes."

"You agreed to go along with this? After everything you said about her?"

Simon was no longer loud, but anger lingered in his voice, enough to warn Blair to go carefully. "I didn't say I agreed. I said it's what my father wants. We've found out why James won't marry, by the way. He apparently caught the pox somewhere and is now impotent. I don't think Father's come to grips with the idea he'll likely go mad and die young. With Hamish, I think the doctors told him something he's not shared with the rest of us. Now he's resting all his dynastic hopes on me."

He gave a short, sharp laugh. "You see, I do understand the pressure on you to marry, suddenly and unexpectedly."

"Your father's a reasonable man. Tell him you're not interested."

"Because my very reasonable father is not being at all reasonable now. If not Miss Eastleigh, I'm supposed to pick some other fair maiden and right quick."

Blair paced away. "I wanted to tell you all this the first night I saw you after my return. I was going to tell you it was her, and how the choice showed how frightened Father was."

He turned back. "Seeing you liked her, I didn't think I could speak freely after the wrangle she and I had on the dance floor."

He stopped, hoping Simon would understand. That Simon might find a plan or suggestion to lead him out of this mess. He found no sympathy or help in his friend's face, only a slow burn. "You stayed silent, knowing all the while this was hanging over your head."

"It's also been hanging over her head, I might point out."

"You have more options." The words were barked. "Tell your father to find someone else. She does not enjoy that luxury. Forebridge wants her married and with as little bother to him as possible. He thinks he's found a solution with you. Did you ever stop to think how he'll react if you throw her over? I'll wager you'll receive precious little blame."

Augusta pleading with him to take her in to her seat, or things would go ill for her. The way Forebridge focused on her after they argued. Had he made things worse?

"There is another option," Simon said, "one Lady Eastleigh has been working hard toward."

"You can't seriously suggest you'll marry her? I'm the one who's supposed to slip my neck into the halter."

"Do you think I am going to let a sweet, intelligent lady marry someone who views her as a fortune hunter of dubious parentage? You made your position clear, Blair. What's more, you obviously resent the idea of being matched with her. Or have you experienced some change of heart I don't know about."

He could claim yes, get Simon to withdraw, then withdraw himself. It would free both of them. Augusta could go to the devil. Which Simon would probably hate him for. If he thought too much about it, Blair might hate himself. "No change of heart. I still do not think she and I are suited."

Simon nodded, his lips pressed tight. "Do not worry yourself. I'll not see her wed to someone who despises her or tolerates her, which might be worse. I must wed, and Miss Eastleigh is as fine a choice as any I see in London. Before you raise your objections, I understand what I am getting myself into and what sort of mother-in-law I will gain. I believe she will be worth the trouble."

Blair wanted to say so many things, but any combination of words would only start an argument he feared would provide no return. That fear proved true when Simon said, "I'm disappointed. I thought you better than this. I'll say your worry about your brother is to blame, but I think we should not speak for a while until we are both in a better place."

He moved to ring for the servants. "Lord Blair is leaving," he said when the butler appeared in the door." Fetch his things."

The butler bowed and withdrew, leaving the door open for Blair to follow. "Simon…"

A wavering of doubt on Simon's face for just a moment, but the mask descended again. "We both need time. Without that, I fear our friendship will end."

There was nothing else Blair could do except to bow and soon find himself on the sidewalk in front of the house. He should be happy with at least one of his troubles solved. While he and Simon might be at odds at the moment, at least there was a willingness to try and find a way back.

None of this stopped him from feeling hollow.

CHAPTER 9

Augusta couldn't help fidgeting as she waited for Chalton to arrive. He had been attentive the last few days, enough she believed her mother's hopes might be correct. Just last night, he hinted broadly he had something to ask her which he hoped she would consider. For a moment she thought he would make his intentions known, but he left her with only the hint.

With a proposal, many of her troubles would disappear. Forebridge would be disappointed at not having his own way, but he wouldn't find the Earl of Chalton a step down. Her mother would be happy, and she wouldn't need to worry about Blair MacDonald.

"There you are, Miss Eastleigh. I have done my best to obtain a dance with you since I arrived, but you are somehow never available. That is unkind of you."

Nor would she need to worry about Mr. Wilverton. Naturally, he would choose a moment when her mother was deeply engaged in conversation and unlikely to notice any frantic signals begging for a rescue. "I am afraid my mother is determined I meet certain people," Augusta said, craning her neck to try and catch sight of Chalton. "Rather a crush this evening, is it not?"

"I didn't believe London could contain this many idle people."

He accompanied his words with a priggish sniff. She wanted to send the man packing. Given he ignored being cut by both her mother and her, likely only a betrothal would convince him of her lack of interest.

"I was hoping your father was present," he said when she chose not to reply to his comment. "I sent him several notes, but he has not done me the courtesy of responding."

Another sign the man had willfully ignored. "Many things occupy his attention."

"There is a pressing matter, and given certain whisperings I hear, I should speak with him as soon as possible, let him know there is an alternative."

The time had come to be blunt. "Did it occur to you, sir, I might not wish an alternative. Or there might be a reason for my father's silence?"

Wilverton frowned. "Lord Eastleigh does possess a reputation for flouting some of society's convention. This is why I need your help."

"I don't wish to give it. You refuse to understand my father did not respond to your requests for a meeting because I will not accept your proposal. I tried to tell you this gently, but it is the time for more frank talk than a young lady should give."

His immediate response was to blink. Then, an unpleasant scowl spread across his features. "This is your mother's influence, for I cannot believe Lord Forebridge would countenance such behavior. Clearly, your husband will be tasked with guiding you back to the correct path. You will need to be separated from her to accomplish that."

"I hardly think—"

"I cry your pardon, Miss Eastleigh, but is this gentleman bothering you?"

Augusta had never been so happy to see Blair MacDonald. Wilverton, on the other hand, didn't bother to conceal his annoyance. "You are intruding on a private conversation, sir."

"Which seems to be distressing the young lady." A pause. "Sir." He turned back to Augusta. "Shall I escort you back to your mother?"

Who stood three feet from them. "That would be much appreciated, Lord Blair."

With that, they turned their backs on Wilverton, covering the short distance between where they stood and Lady Eastleigh. As they waited her for her to acknowledge their presence, Augusta said, "Is he gone?"

Blair turned his head slightly. "Not yet."

"I fear he may linger until I dance with someone or Mother is forced to be unspeakably rude to him."

"Then allow me a chance to speak. I should beg your forgiveness for my behavior at the opera. I invited you because I hoped to give you an opportunity to enjoy something new. I fear I ruined the evening by being unpleasant. For that, and any difficulty I might have caused, I apologize."

She did not want to have this conversation, but if she broke away, Wilverton would use the opportunity to pounce. Something in his manner had gone from annoying to unsettling and Blair was her best protection at the moment. "I will confess I had ulterior motives for the invitation," he confessed. "I wanted to show my father we were not suited for one another and thought observing us together would support that view."

"You invite me to enjoy something I just discovered which you also secretly hoped to use to scuttle the betrothal." With a struggle, she managed to keep the incredulity from her voice. Almost. "I would think such an invitation would convince him we had common ground."

He grimaced. "My plans are misfiring of late, and I'm not certain why. The move was a foolish one. Surely you don't want to marry a complete stranger just to please your grandfather."

She turned to face him. "It's not a matter of 'pleasing' my grandfather, sir. He controls my future and is determined I will marry and quickly. I do not like his scheme, but my only alternative is to produce a suitor who is willing to make the offer. There is only one man I can confidently say would do this, and I would rather beg my bread than marry him."

"Hasn't Chalton spoken to you? Or to Lord Eastleigh?"

She couldn't help laughing at his puzzled expression. "No, and I would not be surprised you had a hand in that. He gives me hints is on the brink, but not said the words. Without the words, my choices are you and Mr. Wilverton. You made it clear you have no desire to marry me or to even make my acquaintance, but I will marry you if I must. That is my lot. Now, if you will excuse me, I will attend upon my mother."

The curtsey she dropped was not as deep as etiquette demanded, but Augusta no longer cared. She didn't want another hollow apology offered only because his father had said something. The Marquess of Rutherglen seemed a kind and amiable man. Why couldn't his son be the same?

Blair did not move, watching as Augusta maneuvered herself into a position next to her mother where she was not readily accessible by either himself or any other suitor she might wish to avoid. His conscience prickled at her words, and as much as he tried to tell himself she attempted to play the wounded party, he couldn't swallow that line of reasoning.

"I take believe the rumored betrothal between you and her is not yet set."

Wilverton had moved closer, his face smug. "I would say it is none of your business, sir," Blair replied.

"I say it is very much my business, sir, as I intend to marry the lady." Once more, Wilverton's chest puffed with his own importance. "I believe she will provide excellent connections for my future."

The reasoning behind Augusta's decision to accept his invitation to dance the night became clearer. "I believe Lady Eastleigh has other plans."

"I know she does. I need to find a way to overcome them. Since she pins all her hopes on one man, do not think your suit will be looked upon with favor, sir. She is a sly one, Lady Eastleigh is. She will do everything she can to obtain her goal with no consideration for propriety."

Did Wilverton understand he was being insulting, or was this his nature? Blair did not know, but neither did much to engender a fine opinion. "Lady Eastleigh cares for her daughter's future, as a mother should."

A snort. "Miss Eastleigh's future would be best served by being removed from her mother's influence as soon as possible."

Why did he argue instead of walking away? Yet, he could not help himself. "I would take care. If you continue in such a manner, you will not endear yourself to those who care for her."

"You would—damn."

Wilverton scowled at the sight of Simon bowing over Augusta's hand, then offering his arm to escort her to the dance floor. "You distracted me, Lord Blair. I wished to claim a dance before Lord Chalton importuned her. I will not make that mistake again."

The man stalked away without even the courtesy of a nod. Blair chose not to take the move as an insult, more inclined to relief at his absence. At least he kept the man away from Augusta for a few minutes. He could do her that favor, if nothing else.

He was about to turn away himself, when Lady Eastleigh caught his eye. To his surprise, she smiled and bowed her head to him, mouthing "thank you." At least one person appreciated his effort.

Augusta couldn't help the hope rising in her chest as she and Chalton took their places on the dance floor. She had never considered herself a romantic, but the idea she might be facing a proposal made her a bit giddy, her future opening up before her.

Problem was, Chalton looked somber and unhappy. Then, just as the musicians picked up their instruments, he said, "Would you care to promenade? I promised you a dance, but I would rather stroll for a while."

Strolling was good. Strolling was much more conducive to making a proposal. "I think that is a splendid idea, my lord."

They escaped the floor before the first notes and began to meander slowly about the room. It did not take long for him to lead her to a place near the windows, allowing them the barest modicum of privacy. "I hold you in great esteem, Miss Eastleigh," he began.

This is it! "As I hold you, Lord Chalton."

He tried to smile, but the gesture was weak. "I esteem you and am honored to count you as a friend. I must thank you for the help and company you bestowed on me these past few weeks."

Her heart sank. She might not be experienced in the art of love, but she recognized an apology when she heard one. "I know you mother hopes for a proposal and I had planned on speaking with your father. But..."

He drew a deep breath. "I regret I cannot bring myself to do it. My heart is still too entangled with another's, enough I fear it would not be fair to you. With such hesitation in proposing to a woman who would make me an excellent wife, how much regret and hesitation will I feel by the time I get to the altar?"

"Perhaps the asking would help settle your mind?" she offered, not wanting to think of what would happen if her grandfather learned of this.

"You deserve better than a reluctant bridegroom."

"That is what I may face." She wasn't above begging, not with the alternatives. "You know Lord Blair is reluctant. That is one reason he..."

She stopped before she could say, "didn't want to tell you," but she had not mentioned the plan to him before this evening. Given the coolness between the men the past few evenings, she thought that might be the case, but she was not certain. Swallowing, she tried another tack. "He apologized to me once more for his behavior."

Chalton raised an eyebrow. "Did he now?"

"I suppose I should thank you for insisting. Or perhaps Lord Rutherglen."

"I didn't ask him. In fact, Blair and I have not spoken since the morning after you were seen at the opera."

"Then he did not try to dissuade you from proposing?" She didn't want to think about the implications of this. Not now. Taking a deep breath, she said, "I must ask a favor. Please don't let my mother know you aren't going to propose. When she hears, she'll try to find someone else to match me with. Lord Blair and I have our differences, but he is a far preferable candidate to some of the gentlemen and—"

He caught her hands. "Do not worry. I will not give the game away. Besides, if she learned I was not going to propose, she might not allow you to dance with me anymore, and I would regret that. I do count you as a friend and find it a pleasure to spend time in your company."

Offering his arm, he said, "We should return. Too much longer and she'll be ordering the wedding breakfast."

Augusta did her best to smile, though her mid was still racing. *What now?*

Upon delivering her into Lady Eastleigh's care, Chalton did not choose to linger despite every indication on Lady Eastleigh's part he was more than welcome. The moment he was away, she demanded, "Well?"

Choosing her words carefully, Augusta replied, "He did not propose. But we spoke most seriously."

To her relief, that seemed to satisfy her. Chalton had been right; Augusta could almost hear her mother planning the menu for the wedding breakfast.

With a sigh, she turned back to face the ballroom. All she had done was buy herself some time, and not much at that. Two days, perhaps three, and her mother would guess the hoped for proposal was not coming. The question was, what would she do then?

These thoughts occupied her brain as she watched the guests mingle. On the surface, everyone appeared to be enjoying themselves, but she saw the signs of stress here and there, and wondered if her own were visible to others. Spying Chalton along the side of the room, even he looked sadder than she would have thought, as if something he valued was now lost. She knew it was not her.

A gentleman spoke to him, but he shook his head, declining. After a moment, he turned and made for one of the doors, seeking solitude away from the crowd. Emily Hibbert, oldest of the two Hibbert girls, followed him.

She could be taking herself to the retiring room as many young women did. Something warned that was not her destination. Her steps were too purposeful, and her eyes fixed on Chalton. Was there a retiring room in that direction?

A glance over her shoulder revealed her mother occupied with conversation once more. Taking a deep breath, Augusta made a decision and moved to follow Miss Hibbert. Her fears were probably baseless, and she would find nothing. Otherwise…

Augusta moved a bit quicker.

CHAPTER 10

Leaning against one of the walls, Blair wondered if he made another mistake coming out tonight. He didn't feel right indulging in frivolity while Hamish still lay ill. He tried to explain this to his father, but Rutherglen had fixed him with a baleful gaze and asked, "Have you apologized? Made a decision? No? Then I suggest you go speak to the lady."

This would have been easier if such a thing could be done in an afternoon call. Lady Eastleigh, though, would ensure he stayed strictly within the time limit allowed gentlemen calling upon young ladies and watched every move. He had made his apology here, even if he did not find her receptive. Likely his father would blame him for that as well. At least Lady Eastleigh had been appreciative, even if only for keeping Wilverton away for a few moments. Was that the fate awaiting Augusta if he refused the match? Surely no; Simon had made his intention clear the last time they spoke.

Watching them speak, Blair didn't think things were going as either hoped. There was a mystery to unravel, not that he could question either party.

His gaze lingered on Augusta as he pondered, watching as she told her mother something which seemed to please Lady Eastleigh. He also noted the less-than-pleased expression on Augusta's face when she turned away. Had Chalton asked? Or had his courage failed him at the last moment? Whatever had happened, she seemed lost in her own thoughts. Until something caught her attention, and she began to move purposefully.

Curious, Blair straightened, watching as her steps quickened. What was behind such movement, and why did she appear determined? What was she looking at? He followed her gaze as best he could and found Simon retreating from the ballroom.

No. He didn't want to think she'd pull some low trick to catch her quarry in what the gossips would call a compromising position. Such gossip had been behind the Abernathy marriage and someone desperate might think the gambit worth a try.

No, he wouldn't think that of her. He had said unkind words, but he would not impute such behavior to her.

He wouldn't...

Blair let his own feet begin to move as he followed her.

Once she left the ballroom, Augusta almost lost sight of Miss Hibbert. A number of guests milled about in the corridor, but the sight of a pale gown disappearing into a room, the door closing after, guided her steps.

Hoping against hope she would stumble on someone else's liaison, she pushed the door open and stepped inside. Chalton was forcibly removing Miss Hibbert's arms from around his neck, looking none too happy. The triumphant gleam in Miss Hibbert's eyes died as she turned toward the sound of the door opening. "Do you mind?" she asked in an acid tone. "Lord Chalton and I were having a private discussion."

"Too private," Chalton said. "I am very glad to see you, Miss Eastleigh."

"I think I came just in time." Stepping forward, she grabbed the other girl's arm. "We leave now, we might be able to get away without being noticed.

"Annoyed you didn't think of this first?" Miss Hibbert shot back, pulling her arm free. "We all know Lord Chalton is a man of honor."

"Who would never lure an unmarried lady to an assignation which would mean her ruin if discovered. Come with me."

"Go away," the girls hissed as Augusta reached for her arm once more. "You are not wanted."

"Please stay," Chalton said. "You're much appreciated."

Miss Hibbert jerked her hand out of Augusta grasp and slapped her. The sound resounded through the room, causing everyone to freeze. "You're not making this easy," Miss Hibbert said. "Just go and I'll pretend you were never here, only Lord Chalton and myself."

All the rumors of Mrs. Hibbert being determined to trap a title at any cost were true. Or at least for this daughter. She reached out to grab Miss Hibbert's arm a third time, no longer worrying about being gentle. "I think we had both better get back to our mothers."

"Let me go!" Emily squawked. "You have no right to—"

Everything devolved into a struggle, Augusta trying to drag Miss Hibbert toward the door, Miss Hibbert doing her best to remain in place. That was when the hair pulling began.

Blair found his worst fears confirmed when he saw Lord Manville and Lady Knowle heading toward one of the side rooms, both wearing a look of anticipation on their faces. They didn't pull their old trick of peeking into empty rooms in hope of finding something amiss. At this moment, they appeared certain of their destination. Unsure what he could do if Simon and Augusta were caught, he still hurried after them. Perhaps if he threw himself across the door...

He wasn't quick enough to stop the pair's entry, but close enough behind to see the scene in front of him in all its glory. Augusta struggling with Miss Hibbert, hands buried in Augusta's hair as she tugged wildly. Simon, meanwhile, did his best to separate the ladies, though success escaped him.

No, not a romantic assignation. At least, not one which had gone anticipated.

"Quite the little row you're having." Lady Knowle sniggered unpleasantly. "Another sign the generation these days doesn't know how to behave."

"I agree," Manville said. "The most interesting events this season happen in rooms people shouldn't be wandering into."

"Trust me," Simon said, "this is not what you think."

He used the words to pull Augusta and Miss Hibbert apart, though Miss Hibbert couldn't resist getting a kick in, eliciting a sharp "Ow" from Augusta. The action produced more sniggering. "I think I want to hear this tale," Lady Knowle said. "It looks to be most entertaining."

Blair offered up a silent prayer that Simon would spin a story to satisfy the two worst gossips in the *Ton*. There was no avoiding a bit of scandal with this. The question was, could he frame the situation in such a way he avoided finding himself forced to make an offer of marriage to one of the ladies. Especially since Miss Hibbert looked ready to spin her own version of the story.

"I was on my way to the card room," Simon said, his voice strong, "when I heard a scuffling in here. Concerned, I investigated and found Miss Eastleigh and Miss Hibbert arguing." He paused. "More than merely arguing, I'm afraid."

"So it would appear." An unholy gleam lit Manville's eye. "Were you able to ascertain the reason behind the argument between the young ladies?"

Simon looked embarrassed. "I'd rather not say."

The perfect answer, but it left the narrative open. Miss Hibbert opened her mouth, but Augusta interrupted. "Miss Hibbert importuned me to speak with her. When I agreed, she informed me I was to stay away from Lord Chalton, that he was hers and I should not even consider continuing a courtship with him."

"You lie!" Miss Hibbert hissed. "You lying little tart." She kicked again at Augusta, but missed her target and caught Simon in the shin. He grimaced, but said nothing.

"You did not tell Miss Eastleigh she was to stay away from Lord Chalton?" Lady Knowle chuckled. "What an interesting tale."

"She *should* stay away from Lord Chalton because he's supposed to be courting me," she spit out. "Instead, she keeps making eyes at him, and at Lord Blair. It's not fair."

The foot stamp accompanying these words provoked Lord

Manville to hide his smile behind his hand. "You're saying the ladies were quarrelling, Lord Chalton?"

"There was hair pulling." Simon spoke as if every word was being pulled out of him. "I was doing my best to separate the two ladies when you found us."

"But you declared your love for me!" The words came out of Miss Hibbert in an explosion. "This...creature interrupted us. Of course I was going to object."

"I was not declaring my love for you." Simon's voice was cold, and he took a step away from Miss Hibbert, toward Augusta. "Whatever you might claim, that was not my intent. Lady Knowle, might I impose upon you to escort Miss Hibbert back to her mother? I would do so myself, but I fear the words I would say at this moment would not be ones appropriate to being uttered in a ballroom."

Any lingering doubt Simon lured either lady into the room for an illicit tryst existed were scuttled with his words. "I will be more than happy to accommodate her, Lord Chalton." With a curtsey, Lady Knowle stepped forward and took Miss Hibbert rather firmly by the arm. "Come, my girl. Best get you back to your mother."

"I would be most happy to escort Miss Eastleigh back," Lord Manville said as the two departed, stepping forward to extend his hand. "I doubt she would want to delay your progress to the card room any longer."

Augusta looked at Manville's hand, then beyond him to where Blair stood. She was not fit to be seen in company, her hair tumbling from her pins about her shoulders, gown askew with the lace on one sleeve dangling. One cheek blazed red with the mark of Miss Hibbert's hand, and a call for rescue in her gaze.

Stepping forward, he said, "Perhaps Miss Eastleigh should be escorted to the retiring room where she can make some repairs to her appearance and her mother sent for."

Manville turned his head just enough to scowl at him, a child deprived of a sweet he craved. "Then perhaps you will be good enough as to inform Lady Eastleigh. We wouldn't want her to learn such news from a servant, would we? Come, my dear. Best not to delay."

Reluctance in every gesture, Augusta laid her hand in Manville's and allowed him to lead her away. Blair turned toward Simon. "What the hell were you—no, don't tell me. I'll go fetch Lady Eastleigh. The less time Miss Eastleigh spends answering Manville's questions, the better for both you. Just stay there. We'll talk when I return."

With that, Blair departed to give Lady Eastleigh the news. She wouldn't be happy and he couldn't blame her. Ironically, his father might find this a reason to scuttle the betrothal. If he did, Blair didn't want to think about the consequences to Augusta.

"Now, girl," Manville said the moment they away. "Why don't you tell me what really happened?"

"That would require me to speak ill of Miss Hibbert," Augusta replied.

"Do you think she will hesitate to speak ill of you? I'm certain she's spinning Lady Knowle a merry tale. One, I imagine, at odds with yours. Did you interrupt her and Lord Chalton, or did she interrupt you?"

He was fishing for a scandal, not caring what harm it caused others. "Miss Hibbert demanded I leave Lord Chalton alone," she said, doing her best to ignore the glances of other guests as they passed. "I refused and she grew agitated, swearing I stood in the way of him declaring his love for her. I tried to leave, but she grew even more agitated, took hold of me, and we began to struggle."

She gingerly touched her hand to her head and grimaced. "That's when she pulled my hair."

Manville made appropriately sympathetic noises, but she doubted he believed her. "Why, pray tell would you allow yourself to end up in a private interview with the lady if you believed her to be unreasonable?"

"She caught me by surprise," Augusta said. "I was on my way to the retiring room when she said we needed to speak. She gripped my arm and insisted. I tried to pull away, but she was determined. I decided better to converse with her rather than cause a scene."

The detail that would seal this tale popped into her mind, and

Augusta leaned in. "You know how Lord Forebridge despises scenes. I didn't wish to anger him by creating one over something as simple as refusing a conversation that should not, by rights, cause comment to anyone."

Manville nodded sagely. "A wise move. If she was that determined to speak with you, best to not have the conversation in front of everyone."

The way he patted her hand made her skin crawl, but Augusta put on a brave smile. "She insisted you leave Lord Chalton alone?"

"She has marked him out as hers and does not appreciate interference. I would understand if Lord Chalton was showing her attention, but he does not." Augusta took a deep breath, deciding to share a modicum of truth. "The first time Lord Chalton asked me to dance, I believe he did because he was attempting to escape her and her mother rather than any inclination to partner me. It is embarrassing to admit, but I believe it to be the truth."

There was a juicy enough story to hopefully satisfy his requirements. That it would be at odds with whatever Miss Hibbert was currently telling Lady Knowle would only make the story more appealing to him. As long as she and Chalton remained firm, though, she suspected they would escape unscathed within society. Escaping unscraped once Forebridge heard of the incident was another thing entirely.

"And after such a chance meeting, he comes back again and again." A chuckle accompanied by another pat on the hand. "A fine tale of romance. Do not let Miss Hibbert bother you, Miss Eastleigh. Clearly, she failed to capture the man's heart. I would suggest, though, you avoid finding yourself in such a situation again. A scene in the corridor would be better than what just occurred."

The man was practically salivating. Still, Augusta put a smile on her face as they reached the retiring room. "Thank you for the advice, Lord Manville. I will endeavor to avoid Miss Hibbert in the future."

"Should she come looking for you, you may always consider me a protector if one is required."

She dropped a curtsey, lowering her eyes demurely to hide her disbelief at the offer, which came with strings as reliably as the sun rose in the east. Then she entered the retiring room to put herself in the hands of the maids to see what repairs could be affected and await her mother's arrival.

CHAPTER 11

It didn't take long for Lady Eastleigh to come sweeping through the door of the retiring room. "Why did Lord Blair bring me news of a fight between you and Miss Hibbert?"

For a brief moment, Augusta considered trying to send some signal her mother should be cautious while the maid tacking the lace on her sleeve was nearby. Then she realized her mother would not lead with that if she thought discretion necessary. Since Manville and Lady Knowle were probably spreading the news even now, she likely didn't think discretion worth the effort. "Because Miss Hibbert and I had a disagreement which turned ugly. You can see the results."

Pursing her lips, Lady Eastleigh pulled a chair closer considering. "That's going to leave a bruise, I'm afraid." Turning to the maid, she asked, "Is there perchance some doves-foot in the house?"

The maid frowned. "I don't believe so, but the housekeeper has water fern cream. Let me just finish this" she took two more stitches, then tied a knot and broke the thread "and I'll fetch some."

Lady Eastleigh smiled beneficently and waited until the girl departed to speak again. "I'll get to the idea of the fight in a moment, but why did Lord Blair bring me the message? Why did he not escort you back to me?"

"Escorting me through the ballroom looking like this was Lord Manville's original intent. Lord Blair suggested I should go directly to the retiring room. He tried to escort me, but Lord Manville insisted. He wanted to question me on what happened."

"Which means we best turn to the fight." Lady Eastleigh gave a long-suffering sigh. "Tell me what happened."

Conscious of others in the room, Augusta spun the tale which had grown up between what Chalton and she had said. Lady Eastleigh looked as if she thought as little of the tale as Lord Manville had. She did not question too deeply, only asking, "It was Miss Hibbert who struck first?"

"Struck, pulled hair and kicked." Augusta reached up to touch her cheek, wincing slightly. "I should consider myself lucky she didn't bite."

"I would not want to explain that to your father. Let us be grateful for small favors."

The maid returned, carrying a small pot of cream in her hand, followed close behind by their hostess. "My dear Lady Eastleigh. I was appalled when I heard Lord Manville's tale. How could this happen?"

"I would like to think it is the excitement of a young girl in her first season," Lady Eastleigh said, putting on a mournful expression. "But I fear Mrs. Hibbert did not teach her daughters the choice belongs to the gentleman. Attacking those he favors is not the way to attract him."

She smiled at the maid. "You are so kind. Could I trouble you to do what you can to make my daughter's hair at least a bit tidier? I'll apply the cream."

The maid handed the pot to Lady Eastleigh and moved to stand behind Augusta, frowning as she tried to sort through the fallen locks. "Really, Lady Causter, I must compliment you on the quality of your servants. They are most helpful."

A nod in acknowledgement of the compliment. "You are too kind, Lady Eastleigh. I am still distressed by this, though. I regretfully asked Mrs. Hibbert to depart, as both Lord Manville and Lady Knowle insist her daughter was the aggressor." She turned toward Augusta. "I would take this as a warning, Miss Eastleigh, not to venture into spaces where a young lady should not be found."

Meaning the gossips had been gleeful enough in their description of the event, responsibility was being laid squarely on Miss Hibbert. Otherwise, Augusta and her parents might have been also asked to leave. "I will heed your wise advice, Lady Causter. I would not wish to find myself in a repeat of the situation."

The response satisfied their hostess, and she left them to finish their repairs. Lady Eastleigh did not say a word, but finished applying the cream. Her eyes, though, warned she wanted the full story later.

The repairs were done quickly, and with more skill than Augusta had hoped. "You have talented hands," Lady Eastleigh said, pressing some coins into the maid's hand. "Thanks to your skill, I think my daughter will be able to rescue at least part of the evening. Come along, Augusta."

Augusta did as she was bid and followed her mother from the room as the maid offered a deep curtsey. "Money well spent," Lady Eastleigh murmured as they left. "She's much more likely to speak kindly of us if anyone should be gossiping. Never forget to tip the servants, Augusta, especially those employed by others when they do you a kindness. It always enhances your reputation, because they will speak kindly of you to their betters."

She paused and took a breath. "Now, dare I hope you can wheedle another dance out of Lord Chalton? Even if he didn't want to make a scene, people will talk if he does not come to speak with you."

Augusta disliked the idea of finding herself on display for the benefit of the Ton, but she saw the wisdom in her mother's words. "I suspect he will come to speak with me." *If only to ensure our stories align.*

The words earned a nod of approval as they returned to ballroom, only to find Eastleigh waiting for them. "Manville's spreading some terrible gossip Goose was in a brawl with Miss Hibbert."

"Is he at least saying that Miss Hibbert started it?" Lady Eastleigh asked.

"Yes, but—"

"We will speak when we get home," Lady Eastleigh said in a

voice so soft Augusta could barely hear, then added in her more normal tones. "Really, I would think Mrs. Hibbert would teach her daughter better manners before foisting her on the ballrooms of London. She objected to the fact Lord Chalton prefers Augusta's company to hers. I hope many hostesses will see what unsuitable company they are, and we will not be burdened with her presence again."

She punctuated these words with a snap of her fan opening, and Eastleigh sighed. "Let this go, for Augusta's sake. He'll be furious if you don't."

No need to say who "he" was. "We should have rented a house like we usually do," Lady Eastleigh grumbled. "Then we wouldn't have to face him every day."

"You know he wouldn't let us have our independence and foot the bill for Augusta's season. I'm afraid living under his roof is the only way."

Lady Eastleigh muttered something under her breath which sounded like a description of Forebridge in the most impolite manner possible, but she didn't continue to argue. For that, Augusta was glad. She didn't want an argument.

What she wanted was a chance to speak with Simon. There was still a scandal brewing and she had no desire to see it explode.

To Blair's relief, Simon was waiting when he managed to return. "Lady Eastleigh has been informed and looks for all the world as if she is ready to burn the world down," he said as he closed the door to ensure at least a modicum of privacy. Unless the gossips came looking for scandal once more. With luck, the fight was enough to sate their appetites tonight. "What in the blazes was that all about?"

"Miss Hibbert attempted to trap me in a situation where I would be obliged to propose. Miss Eastleigh, for whatever reason, appeared and tried remove her, not allow us to be caught alone. Miss Hibbert took exception and I tried to separate them. Then Lord Manville and Lady Knowle appeared. A little too damn conveniently, I might point out."

Blair blinked. "From where I stood, I thought Miss Eastleigh was following you."

Simon shook his head. "She must have seen Miss Hibbert move and suspected something. Thank goodness. When she arrived, Miss Hibbert was backing me into a corner and wouldn't allow an avenue of escape that didn't require me putting my hands on her."

It was a strange tale, stranger than the one Simon had offered when the trio was caught. "When you said you discovered the ladies fighting—"

"I was thinking as fast as I could." He scowled. "I regret throwing Miss Eastleigh to the wolves, but two ladies arguing was better than admitting to being alone with one who'd swear I invited her to an assignation."

It was, but Blair suspected things might not be better for Augusta once her grandfather heard. "Saying Miss Hibbert attacked her was brilliant," Simon continued. "Reduced everything to a small tempest which will cause comment for a day or two only. I am beholden to her for the risk she took on my behalf."

"You should go speak with her once she's back in the ballroom. Will look better for her, if you're concerned for her well-being."

"I had thought of calling tomorrow to thank her privately," Simon said, sounding oddly reluctant. "I suspect you're right. Not a dance, perhaps, but being seen with her would support the story, since I will be going nowhere near the Hibberts."

He cocked his head to one side. "You're awfully concerned given all your comments about her."

"She bore no fault in this," Blair said. "I think you were deliberately set up. Lord Manville and Lady Knowle seemed to know exactly where to go because I was right behind them." He paused. "I couldn't get ahead of them, keep them from going in the room. Is it possible they were given a specific location?"

The words sent a shiver through Simon's body. "I didn't want to believe Mrs. Hibbert could be this determined. She's tried it once, she could again. I need to be careful."

"Once your betrothal to Miss Eastleigh is announced, that should stop things."

"Or drive her to more desperate measures. There's a problem. I'm not proposing."

Blair frowned. "Does she know?"

"I told her this evening. I was going to, but I can't. The more I thought it, the more I thought of Eleanor."

Lady Eastleigh would be furious. The past two weeks had shown she pinned her hopes on a proposal. Which meant Forebridge would see no reason why an engagement between Blair and Augusta shouldn't move forward as swiftly as possible. If he refused, the man would find someone else, based on what Augusta had said.

"You're being awfully silent," Simon said. "Isn't this what you wanted?"

It was. Only, he found he worried more about the impact on Augusta rather than Simon's escape. "I feared you were rushing into things, despite not being over Miss Shelby."

"You were right on that score, as much as it pains me to admit." Simon stepped forward. "Now that I've admitted I will not propose, what are you going to do? Marry her grudgingly or throw her to whatever fate awaits her if the agreement between your father and Forebridge falls through?"

The words were a challenge, pushing him closer to making the decision his father had been pressing him for. Negotiations had already begun, he knew, and Rutherglen would soon insist on an answer before he fully committed. "I don't know," he admitted. "I fear the two of us are trapped, which is no good way to make a marriage."

Simon let loose a sigh. "At least you're being honest. You could do worse, Blair. She bright and resourceful. Loyal, too. She saw what was happening and didn't stop to think of what it might mean to herself. She tried to help me. Surely those qualities are worth something."

He was making the case for her, and a damn sight more effectively than Rutherglen. "I think she despises me somewhat."

"Because you acted like an ass. Try not doing that."

Easy enough for Simon to say, but he chose not to argue as they returned to the ballroom. For one thing, they seemed to have crossed the chasm that parted them, but Blair couldn't help sensing things were still strained. Didn't help Simon was right.

Hanging back, he watched as Simon made to where the Eastleighs stood. Given how Lady Eastleigh greeted him, Augusta had not shared her news with her mother. He couldn't blame her for that. He had no doubt Lady Eastleigh would refuse to give in to Forebridge's plan, but try to find some other gentleman.

Augusta had admitted she did not care for some of her mother's choices.

She'd been right she had little choice in the matter, forced to wait for a proposal or hope those in whose charge she lay would act with consideration in choosing her spouse. He held sway in the matter, by choosing whether or not to agree to a match between them.

He was unused to holding someone's future in his hands. He wasn't at all certain he liked the idea.

CHAPTER 12

Blair gave the maid a bit of a fright when she came in to open the window shutters in the study shortly after dawn. Not surprising, given she had no reason to expect to find a gentleman there. He reassured her nothing was wrong, and he had merely woken early. As such, he had no objection to her getting on with her work. No, she wouldn't disturb him, he would continue reading his book and if neither of them said a word, the housekeeper would be none the wiser. If there was trouble, the girl was to send the housekeeper to him.

She got on with her work, and he did his best to focus on the pages. Unfortunately, he had no more success than when he crept downstairs before light had touched the sky. In the end, he let the book come to rest in his lap and half-closed his eyes, letting his thoughts wander.

Simon had decided against proposing to the girl. He wondered briefly if Augusta's actions might provoke a change of heart. There was something attractive about a woman who was willing to take such a risk. There were any number of women in London who would have been more than happy to leave the earl to his fate after being rejected or spun it directly into a situation where he owed her for risking her name and reputation.

From where he stood, watching as Simon very publicly inquired if Augusta was well, stating that he wished for a sooner arrival to spare her grief, she showed no inclination to take advantage of the situation. Lady Eastleigh had to be a bit more direct, hinting broadly that if he wished to take Augusta aside for more private conversation, she would not object.

Augusta, however, had offered her thanks for his quick thinking, but did not press him. There had been smiles and a squeeze of the hand, but nothing more.

Was it possible what existed between them was friendship, and Augusta valued it enough she would not use such against him for her own gain? He remembered her actions the night they met, subjecting herself to a whisper or two to give Simon a better chance escaping Mrs. Hibbert's pursuit. Nor had she shown any sign of collecting on the favor then owed.

Which left Blair wondering how badly he misjudged her. That question didn't help answer the other one, the one his father would surely press him for an answer on once more. Given the dictum he must marry, would he be willing to consider her as a bride?

A noise in the hall stirred him from his thoughts. There was a low murmur of voices along with the sound of the heavy front door closing. With a frown, Blair rose from his chair to lay the book aside on the small table which held the candle he brought downstairs with him. It was barely ten, far too early for even intimate visitors. No one would be calling unless...

Striding to the door, he stepped into the hall, expecting to discover the doctor had been summoned. To find his eldest brother pulling his gloves from his hand and handing them off to the footman was a surprise. "I thought you were supposed to arrive Thursday."

James MacDonald, heir to the Marquess of Rutherglen, Earl of Strathern by courtesy, rolled his eyes. "Hello to you, too, Blair. I can always count on a warm greeting."

He flicked at a spot of mud on his jacket, scowling at the splash. "Father's letter concerned me enough I pushed the horses. How is Hamish?"

Blair gave his brother the latest news. "The worst thing," he concluded, "is that he's not getting better. He's got every attention, but things don't improve."

"Is he better or worse than when you left the Peninsula?"

"Worse," Blair admitted. "Travel took a toll on him. We had to wait several days once we landed in Dover. He couldn't continue, no matter how hard he insisted. I think we left Spain too soon, but Hamish got it into his head that if they wanted to send him home, then he should go, come hell or high water." A pause. "Stubborn git."

James chuckled. "That's Hamish. Stubborn to the end."

He sobered as the import of his words sunk in. "Is it as bad as the letter said?"

"Enough Father is spending part of his time worrying the future of the line needs to be seen to."

James waved the concern away. "You know Father. He needs something to worry about. Probably doesn't want to worry about Hamish because he doesn't want to face what might happen. You know how it is. I'll smile at some eligible ladies now that I'm here to make him happy."

"I know what you told him."

The words wrought an instant change. "What do you think I told him?"

When Blair didn't reply, James drew himself up. "Spare me a lecture on morality or I'll go wash some of this mud from me. I've no desire to hear another of those."

"I'm no minister of the kirk to say you are wrong. I am angry. Since you did this damn stupid thing, Father's looking to me to take care of the dynastic responsibility. No, he's not waiting until he knows if Hamish will recover because Hamish broke it off with what's her name he's been courting forever."

"Miss Sanders," James supplied. "You know her."

"Her name is not the point," Blair said through gritted teeth. "The point is he doesn't think Hamish will marry any time soon even if he does recover. He's panicked and this is the form his panic is taking. I never wanted this responsibility."

"Neither did I."

The words were quiet, quiet enough to cause Blair to stop. "I'm going to do my duty, take care of the estate, But the idea of settling down with a woman only because she is 'appropriate'..." He shuddered. "I wanted to make the choice in my own time, perhaps someone local who knew the estate, the people. When it appeared Hamish was going to marry Miss Sanders, I thought it would take the pressure off me. Then Hamish got it into his head he didn't want to risk leaving a widow."

He offered a lopsided grin. "Sorry, old boy. Looks like you're stuck with it. Who is Father trying to pair you with?"

"Augusta Eastleigh."

James stared at him in shock for a moment, then started laughing, the sound echoing off the walls. "Forebridge is not the friend Father things he is if he's trying to palm off a woman he doesn't believe is his flesh and blood."

"I'm not certain Forebridge has any idea how bad it is with Hamish. Will you stop laughing? You're going to wake everyone up."

Blair pushed his brother toward the study and more privacy. "Few folk outside the family have been told the extent of Hamish's injuries," he said as he closed the door. "It's not something Father wants bruited about town, not until we're surer of the outcome."

Strolling toward the sideboard where his father kept a decanter of whiskey, James took a glass and poured himself a healthy measure. Blair couldn't help scowling as he considered the hour. "You told Chalton, of course."

"Who do you think I turn to when I have trouble?" Blair said. "He's not going to talk, but he is going to listen."

James snorted, then raised the glass to his lips. Taking a long sip, he let forth a contented sigh. "Is your friend telling you to marry the Eastleigh chit? Has he ceased his perpetual mourning for a woman he can't have?"

The jibe pricked, a needling Blair found put himself on the defensive. "Simon thinks highly enough of her he was considering marriage."

The glass had been lifted for James to take another drink and he almost choked. "That's rich," he said once the coughing cleared. "Having rejected a gentlewoman of respectable family because he

90

deemed her not elevated enough, Old Chalton would spin in his grave at the idea of his son marrying a woman with such a story attached to her. Here's to the ultimate act of revenge."

Blair said nothing. There was much he wanted to say, but he bit his tongue, wondering how his older brother had come to this state. James finished off the glass and turned back to the decanter. "Are you going to do it? Marry her? Or find a way out of it?"

Was this what he sounded like to Simon when Blair had tried to convince him of the folly of courting Augusta? Little wonder they'd fallen out. To his knowledge, James had never met her, though it was clear he knew the gossip. As far as his brother was concerned, she was tarnished goods from birth.

Glass full once more, James lifted it in a toast. "I'm wagering you're going to marry the girl. Father can always depend on you to step up when Father wants something. I wish you joy with her."

"Do you really mean to be drunk when you see Father? Or Hamish?" Blair could feel anger simmering below the surface. Clenching his fist as he tried to control himself, he asked, "I'm certain Caitlin and Finola will enjoy seeing you in such a state."

"It takes more than this to get me drunk these days." He put the glass down, though not before draining the contents. "He'll never say it, but Father would rather you were the eldest. I'm a disappointment, as has been made clear to me more than once. Problem is, I never had a choice. I didn't get to choose the army or the church or find a seat in Parliament. From the moment of my birth, my destiny was foretold. Heir during his life, marquess after Father's death. Marry, get more children and lock my eldest son into the same cycle. Trust me, I'd trade places with you in an instant."

There was bitterness in the words, James' fingers stretching toward the glass once more, only to pull back at the sound of feet clattering on the stairs. The door to the study was flung open as Finola rushed in, followed more sedately by Caitlin. "I told you James was back!" Finola announced as she hurled herself at her brother.

He caught her with a laugh, wrapping his arms tightly about her. "Oh, ye've been missed, lass. Home is quiet without you raising a ruckus. Look at you, Caitlin. You're turning into a proper lady before my eyes."

Caitlin blushed a little, but she didn't hesitate to step forward to claim her own hug. James looked happier when listening to his sisters' chatter. Perhaps because they didn't worry about the future of the line or demand things of him the heir must do. Such things would come, but for now they simply were. That appeared to be what he needed.

Miss Richards had followed in her charges' wake and was endeavoring with little success to invoke some decorum when Rutherglen entered. His coat appeared hastily pulled on, probably at the sound of his daughters rushing downstairs. The expression on his face was one of palpable relief at the sight of his eldest. "Thank the lord you're here, though we didn't expect you for a few more days."

"I came by horse, not carriage," James said, disentangling himself from the girls. "Given the urgent tone of your letter, I changed my mind about using the carriage after I sent the response. If it wasn't almost summer, I might have kept to that, but I made better time on horseback."

Rutherglen nodded. "Wise of you." He took a deep breath. "Hamish didn't pass a good night. The doctor should here soon."

The room grew silent. All knew this boded ill. "Is Hamish…" Finola began, then stopped, swallowing.

"I hope not, child. His condition has worsened somewhat and I'm glad all the family is here." He glanced at James. "He's been sleeping fitfully. I know you've not had the chance to wash the dust of the road from you, but would you like to come upstairs, see if he's awake?"

"I would like that." A pause. "Thank you, Father."

Rutherglen nodded and the two men left the room, leaving Blair with Caitlin and Finola. Both looked at him beseechingly, as if asking he find some way to fix this situation, they found themselves in. He wished he could but had nothing to offer save to suggest they see if Cook had breakfast ready.

Rutherglen and James didn't descend while they were eating, so Blair supposed Hamish must be awake. Either that or the two men were talking, hopefully without arguing. Thinking back, he realized the relationship between father and son had become more fractured over the years. He hadn't understood it was because his older brother was unhappy with his lot. That unhappiness was leading to his destruction and there seemed little any could do to stop it.

Or was there?

He ruminated on the question through the rest of the meal, glad when Miss Richards led Cailin and Finola back upstairs for lessons. It was not the course he expected to take, but part of what James had hurled at him was true. When Father needed him to, Blair had always stepped in to fill the breach. Which meant he had a call to pay.

Augusta and her parents had spent the morning braced for the moment Forebridge learned of the previous night's escapades. There'd been plenty of chatter within their hearing at the assembly. Certainly, there had been more outside earshot. One didn't engage in hair-pulling among the Ton without comment being made.

The question was not if the news would wind its way to Forebridge. The question was when and in what manner. "Mostly likely one of his friends who will put everything in the worst possible light," Lady Eastleigh complained as they finished their morning meal.

"Someone could express indignation at Miss Hibbert's behavior," Eastleigh offered, though he seemed more hopeful than certain.

"There's a great deal of indignation that should be expressed at Miss Hibbert's behavior. But when have such things stood in the way of good gossip?" She sighed. "At least Lord Chalton was very solicitous. Hopefully, he'll pay Augusta a visit today. That should show your father. Maybe he'll stop trying to upset everything and let us get on with it."

Augusta did her best not to squirm in her seat, but it grew harder when Lady Eastleigh continued. "With luck, being in private will inspire Lord Chalton to finally pose the question. You should put on your best day dress, my dear, so you'll be at your loveliest. Just in case."

Satisfied with the instructions, Lady Eastleigh lifted her cup. "I for one will certainly not object if he overstays his time if it produces an engagement."

Augusta was going to have tell her mother the bad news. Better now, before she further anticipated the afternoon events. Yet, she hesitated because knew the reaction would not be good. Worse, when her mother discovered she'd delayed in relating the news, there would be an explosion. When Forebridge heard, his instinct would be to push harder for the betrothal to Blair. Or to someone else if Blair still refused to cooperate.

Realizing she was trapped, her fate hanging on the actions of others was not a pleasant feeling.

She finished her breakfast in silence, then went upstairs to change as her mother insisted, and asked her maid to re-do her hair, anticipating that would be the next instruction. It bought her time when she didn't have to be in the middle of plans and machinations.

When Augusta did descend to drawing room, it was to the sound of arguments. "This is your fault, madam. This is the result of how you raised her. Bad enough you bring infamy on the family, but you couldn't be bothered to teach your daughter how to act in polite society, so she'll follow in your path."

"Augusta was attacked," Lady Eastleigh countered. "You don't care about that, do you? No, because you don't care about anyone, certainly not your son and his family."

For a moment, Augusta considered retreating, but knew it would do no good. Perhaps her presence would cause her mother to hold her tongue. She did, however, close the door to muffle the noise for any visitors who might arrive.

The noise caught Forebridge's attention, his head swinging toward her. "What were you thinking, getting into a tussle with a jumped-up nobody? Did you bother to stop and think of your family and our reputation?"

Stick to your story. Taking a deep breath, Augusta said, "I agreed to speak to Miss Hibbert because she first accosted me where others could see. I worried that if I did not agree to speak with her privately, she would make a scene. I did not expect her to strike me."

Forebridge pursed his mouth. "Shows at least some sense. But to drag Lord Blair into this? I swear, girl, if you upset this match, I'll—"

He stopped abruptly at the sound of the butler clearing his throat. "What is it?" he demanded.

"Lord Blair MacDonald is here, wishing to pay a call on Lady Eastleigh and Miss Eastleigh."

Lady Eastleigh's face was sour as Forebridge grinned. "Is he now? This is the first time, is it not? Show him in."

As the butler departed, Forebridge turned back to Augusta. "You'll be kind to him and show him interest. Your mother may have her sights on Chalton, but MacDonald's my choice. Do I make myself clear?"

She managed to say only, "Yes, sir," before Blair was announced and she turned to meet her fate.

CHAPTER 13

The first indication Blair had he hadn't thought this visit through was when he found himself faced with not just Augusta and Lady East-leigh, but the Earl of Forebridge as well. *Perhaps I should have sent a note.*

No. A note might give the wrong impression, though his presence would undoubtedly do the same thing, given the gleam in Forebridge's eye at his arrival. Finally paying a call after the discussions between his father and the earl would only leave one impression after last night.

"It has been some time, Lord Blair," Forebridge said, coming forward to offer his hand, never mind Lady Eastleigh was hostess. "I hoped you would call on us after your return."

"I should apologize for delaying so long," Blair replied. "Other considerations kept me away."

"You're here now, which is the important thing. Come, sit down. Don't you usually provide refreshments or some sort for visitors?"

This last was addressed to Lady Eastleigh. "It is not usual," she said through gritted teeth. "If Lord Blair is in need of refreshments, I can certainly ring for the servants."

"Not necessary, but I thank you." Blair waited until the ladies took a seat on the sofa, then settled in a chair himself. "I wished to pay my respects to Miss Eastleigh. I fear she found last night's events distressing."

Forebridge, still standing, snorted, earning a glare from Lady Eastleigh. It was the tensing of Augusta's shoulders which caught Blair's attention, though. There was much unsaid here. "I think I have recovered somewhat," she said, "and thank you for your concern."

"So terrible for Miss Hibbert to behave in such a matter," Lady Eastleigh said. "Don't you agree, Lord Blair?"

He wagered she knew the truth, just as she would suspect he had been informed by Simon what had happened. "I do agree. Miss Hibbert took advantage of Miss Eastleigh not wishing attract undo notice to put her in an unfortunate position. Which was not her fault."

This last was aimed indirectly at Forebridge, who offered some sort of uncommitted noise again before saying, "There are things which require my attention. Good to see you, sir."

Blair rose as the man left, not at all grieved by his absence. He came in hopes of some semi-private conversation with Augusta, something made impossible by the presence of both her grandfather and her mother. Not that it would be easier without other guests to distract Lady Eastleigh's attention. He could only hope others would arrive soon.

Lady Eastleigh asked him about the health of his father. Blair responded his father's health was excellent, and he had hopes they might meet at the opera another night. "That is, if Miss Eastleigh still has a taste for the opera."

"One performance which is not at its best should not deter one," Augusta said. "Repeated performances of the same tone, however, are a sign perhaps you should find other distractions."

Should he read what he thought she was saying into her words? Had his behavior gone too far to find common ground between them now? "Then let us see if we can arrange another evening, one I hope you will find much more to your liking."

He earned the glimmer of a smile. Lady Eastleigh appeared puzzled by the exchange. "I'm not certain we will be able to accept such a kind invitation. Our diary is—" She broke off, looking toward the door. "Yes?"

"I beg pardon, my lady," the butler said, "There is a difficulty with the housekeeper, and she begs your indulgence."

"I am receiving guests."

The servant looked apologetic. "I am sorry, my lady, but I was told this is *most urgent*, you must come at once, and Lord Blair will understand. I am to leave the door open and wait outside while he and Miss Eastleigh continue their conversation."

No difficulty guessing no crisis with the housekeeper existed and who these instructions had come from. Lady Eastleigh rose, her face a study in annoyance. "Excuse me. I shall endeavor to return soon."

Blair rose and nodded in acknowledgement, having no doubt she would do exactly that. When she was gone, he asked, "May I join you, Miss Eastleigh?"

Augusta nodded, and sighed as he sat next to her, still leaving a respectable space between them. "I really should apologize for my family. It is kind you came to inquire how I was doing, and most unfair to find yourself in the middle of their schemes."

"Given what our families are attempting to do, should we be surprised? I wanted to tell you I am grateful and in your debt for the help you gave Chalton last night."

She laughed. "I know how much difficulty he's had with Mrs. Hibbert. She was how we first came to dance together. We had some pleasant talk when Lord Abernathy introduced us and when we met again, he asked me to dance to avoid being maneuvered into dancing with one of the girls."

"He didn't tell you that?"

"The third time he asked to partner me, I asked. I saw her lurking about and wondered." Augusta smiled. "He was embarrassed and apologized for using me. I told him I understood as Mrs. Hibbert had behaved dreadfully each time I had the misfortune to encounter her. Our friendship grew from there."

She glanced away for a moment. "I had hoped our friendship might become something more. Given my circumstances, how can you blame me?"

When she turned her head back, her expression was serious. "You may stop worrying. He told me he will not be speaking to my father.

You must make your own decision, but you need not fear you must rescue your friend."

Taking a deep breath, Blair accepted he was about to cross the Rubicon. "Another thing I wished to speak with you about. There are reasons my father wishes me to wed. Sound reasons. My brother is ill, more ill than we've said. What's more, my eldest brother appears to have turned into a wastrel and a fool. My father's not just trying to find me a wife; he wants me to ensure there is a next generation. My son could become Marquess of Rutherglen one day."

Augusta's eyes grew wide. "Does my grandfather know this?"

Blair shook his head. "I doubt it. I wonder if he would be as enthusiastic if he did. I mean this as no slight against you," he added. "Merely an observation."

"An astute one."

She smiled at him, and he found he liked it. Shifting his seat to close the gap between them, he asked, "We started badly, but is there the tiniest possibility you might not find being married to me too horrible? Could we at least try to see if we could consider tolerating one another for the rest of our lives?"

At least she's not laughing in my face, he thought as she stared at him with surprise.

Augusta was not certain how to react to his question. Would marriage to him be horrible? She could find worse looking husbands, for Blair was handsome. He often shown himself to be arrogant and full of his own importance. Yet...

"You once made it clear the very thought of being married to me was a horrid fate we should both want to avoid. What made you change your mind?"

She did her best not to sound too surprised, but it was difficult. His manner was different than before. The last time he apologized, it'd been grudging, a small boy under orders. Not this time. "I'll confess when I saw you moving across the floor, I thought you were going after Chalton. I missed Miss Hibbert completely, somehow. Yes, I feared the worst, not because you sought his fortune, but because I've come to recognize the...difficulties of your situation. I'm certain at the moment Chalton appeared a better choice than me. Given the way I behaved, I couldn't blame you."

Blair offered her a lopsided smile which softened his words. "When I realized what you were doing, I was stunned. You were willing to potentially sacrifice yourself for a man who, I found later, had told you he would not propose. Of course, you had no way of knowing Lord Manville and Lady Knowle were likely told something that would interest them was going on there."

"You did think I might try to trap him into marriage." Try as she might, she couldn't keep the hurt from the words.

"You would handle it much more smoothly, if you intended to trap Chalton into marriage. Something which didn't involve maneuvering him into place to be found by two known gossips at a certain time."

"At least you give me credit for that." She laughed. "What would I do?"

A shrug. "Something much more discreet. While a hasty marriage might cause whispers, no public scandal writ large across an assembly. I believe someone heard the tale of Lord and Lady Abernathy's discovery and thought it a brilliant plan. Theirs was accidental, trust me."

She laughed again but stopped as his face turned to a frown. "That is an unpleasant looking bruise. Does it hurt?"

"It's tender when touched. I try not to."

"May I?"

He held up his hand, indicating her face. A moment's hesitation and she nodded, trying not flinch as his fingers touched the line of her jaw, turning her head to give him a better view. "Miss Hibbert left quite a mark," he said softly.

"I have another on my shin where she kicked me. I trust you'll understand why I won't show you."

"That would be the moment for your mother to return, wouldn't it?" His fingers lingered, warm against her skin. She let her head return to where she could look at him directly, but those fingers did not withdraw. Instead, they cupped her cheek, carefully avoiding the bruise. Funny, but she always found his blue eyes cool. Now she saw an unexpected warmth. "She does have an excellent sense of timing."

"You haven't answered my question," he said.

"What question?" They leaned toward one another. The movement was not planned, but still felt natural.

"Would you consider trying to see if we could tolerate one another."

"I think I might." She let her eyes start to close, relaxing into the moment. They were playing with fire, but she didn't care.

"I'm glad that's taken care of."

At the sound of Lady Eastleigh's voice, they pulled apart abruptly, the moment gone. Augusta did her best to appear as if all had been proper, but she recognized the look in her mother's eye which warned she knew something was up. A long silence as Lady Eastleigh looked from Augusta to Blair, then back again, the mask of the gracious hostess falling into place, she settled in one of the chairs. "What are you other interests besides opera, Lord Blair."

It was the most innocuous of questions, but one which kept his attention focused on her and not Augusta. If he began to address something to her, Lady Eastleigh drew his attention back.

Other visitors began to arrive, breaking up the conversation. Blair yielded his place on the sofa to one of the visitors, and Lady Eastleigh took the opportunity to say, "Kind of you to call, Lord Blair. Do come again. We receive visitors every Tuesday. After all, you are a friend of Lord Chalton's, therefore we also should count you as a friend."

Blair didn't argue with the dismissal, but Augusta longed to call him back. She couldn't really, not without causing whispers. When he bowed to take his leave of her, she said, "In answer to your question, sir, I think I would care to try the opera again."

It was silly, speaking in some code neither of them had agreed to, but the light in his eyes showed he caught her meaning. "I would like that, Miss Eastleigh. I would like that very much."

Then he was gone. Augusta was uncertain what to think. But she felt more hopeful than she had this morning.

. . .

Blair was barely out of the drawing room when Forebridge approached. "Glad you came calling, showing an interest in the girl. One must, after all. At least, until after the wedding. Can I take this as a sign the settlement talks can move forward?"

There were many things Blair could say in response to Forebridge's words. None of them were particularly flattering and all would provoke outrage. "You can, sir. I will ask my father to move things along. You must understand, though, other things weigh on his mind."

"Yes, your brother. Sad business. But he should be well soon and able to dance at your wedding." Forebridge chuckled at his own joke, not taking note how Blair tensed. "I'll confess I worried last night's incident might put everything in a muddle. She's a passably good girl, beneath it all. Get her away from her mother and a man can mold her into the wife he needs, as long as he exercises a firm hand. She's a dab hand at managing a household, I'm told. Handles most of it at home, anyway, because my daughter-in-law doesn't understand how to save a penny."

Blair would swear Forebridge was trying to convince him of the finer points of a horse or herd of cattle he wanted to sell. Both Simon and Augusta had told him he didn't need to worry about doing a rescue because Simon chose not to propose. He was still bent on a rescue, though, because he couldn't bear the idea of Augusta being bundled off to someone who didn't give a damn about her.

He just wasn't sure when he started to give a damn.

CHAPTER 14

"May I say you look happy this evening, Miss Eastleigh."

Augusta couldn't help smiling somewhat coquettishly at Chalton. "Are you suggesting I appeared unhappy on other evenings?"

She was rewarded with a chuckle as they circled away from one another. They had not seen one another for nearly a week, Lady Eastleigh insisting on a temporary moratorium on events until the bruise on Augusta's cheek had begun to fade. Tonight, a light dusting of powder and cream, along with some artfully placed curls proved sufficient to cover the traces, and Augusta deemed fit for company once more.

As the dance brought them back them back together, she said, "I am happy."

"Interesting you look happy and Lady Eastleigh appears more stressed."

While Augusta spent evenings at home with a book, her mother had not, doing her best to control the story and hoping someone else would slip and catch the gossip's attention. "I fear she's worried. The settlement negotiations are moving ahead quicker than she would like."

She caught the frown he tried to hide. "I had heard progress was slow."

"Are they? Any progress is too swift for my mother."

Chalton considered her. "You don't seem upset at the idea of marrying Blair. What changed your mind?"

Her cheeks began to warm as she thought of the conversation shared on the couch, and the halting words allowed since, Lady East-leigh playing strict chaperone on the two calls he made since. "He is being kind. We're trying to get to know one another, not that my mother is making it easy."

They moved down the line to take their place for the next figure. "You're not in need of a rescue?"

The laugh which escaped her was easier than before. "Not at the moment. I thank you for the concern, my lord."

"Of course I'm concerned. I prefer to see my friends settled and happy." A pause. "I can count you as a friend, can I not?"

"You may. And not because Blair is your friend. I enjoy our dances and our conversations. I hope they can continue."

"I believe I can accommodate that, even when you are Lady Blair."

They finished the dance in good spirits, and he escorted her to where Lady Eastleigh waited. The corners of her mouth were tight, but she put on her best smile at their approach. "The two of you looked wonderful on the floor. Did you not think so, Lord Blair? As if they were made for one another."

Blair, standing to one side, nodded. "They do make a handsome couple. Should I be jealous, Chalton?"

"Always," Chalton replied. "Miss Eastleigh is the best partner I've had in London for some time."

"I am glad you enjoy her company," Lady Eastleigh said. "So flat-tering in your attentions. I swear, you can make me dream."

Some of Augusta's happiness dimmed at the obvious attempt to introduce an opening for Chalton to make his intentions clear. The moment approached when she must tell her mother any hope of Chalton proposing was gone. She didn't care for the deception, but she also didn't relish the panicked efforts that would ensue once Lady Eastleigh learned the truth.

"I think I would like to inspire some dreams within Miss Eastleigh myself," Blair said. "As such, I am claiming the next dance." He turned to Lady Eastleigh. "If there are no objections, madam?"

For a moment, Lady Eastleigh looked as if she would offer an objection, but then Wilverton, whom Augusta had been doing her best to ignore, stepped forward, ready to claim her hand if Lady Eastleigh should decide against giving Blair permission. "Of course not, Lord Blair. Why should there be?"

With that, Blair bowed and offered his hand to Augusta. Together, they moved out toward the floor. "I should have sympathy for Chalton," he said as they took their places. "No, let us move farther down the line. That will put us a bit out of your mother's sight."

"Why would—" Augusta began, then stopped as she counted the couples. "You're hoping we'll be the odd ones out."

"At which point we can step away gracefully, and talk instead of dance. You don't mind, do you?"

"Without Mother hovering over every word? No, I don't mind at all."

They shifted twice more, and found themselves at the bottom of the set, where they must stand waiting through the first figure. The music began, they paid their respects to one another, then Blair pulled her out of the line and toward the refreshment room. Even mostly empty, they were not inappropriately alone as anyone could enter and footmen lined the room, ready to assist the guests as needed.

For forms sake, he fetched her a glass of punch, which neither of them chose to drink, but it did make a fine prop to hold. "More pleasant than a dance?" he asked.

"I enjoy dancing, but I think it is wise we talk."

Why did they suddenly feel awkward? When they had a chance to speak in private at Forebridge House, things had felt surprisingly easy between them. When her mother had kept strict watch, she put any rough edges down to the constraints they found themselves operating under. Without Lady Eastleigh's presence, though, the edges were still there.

"The bruise is recovering nicely," he said at last, breaking the silence they had lapsed into.

"Mother wouldn't let me come out until it was less noticeable. She was insistent on that point. I think the only reason Grandfather put up with it is because he found the entire mess with Miss Hibbert embarrassing and he's more confident of his plans with your father.

"I wish my father was more confident," Blair said, a scowl crossing his face. "He's not particularly happy with Forebridge at the moment."

Even as she tensed, he added, "Don't let it worry you. I'm certain we'll get everything handled. I don't think Father's eager to find me another bride."

"Don't even joke about that. If things don't work out——"

"If they don't work out, it will not be because of my father."

"Oh, because you can't see any of the fault——" Augusta stopped and took a deep breath. It'd been easy to fall back into their old pattern of sniping at one another. She didn't like that. "What is bothering you?"

His brows drew together at her words. "What makes you think something is bothering me?"

"There is your brother. How is he doing?"

A long sigh, then a quick glance toward the door, where others had come in. A hand under her elbow and he guided her farther away, toward one corner. "The news is not good. There's some sign of infection in the leg. The doctor is doing his best to keep it at bay, but if it gets worse…"

There was no need to elaborate. Augusta knew her upbringing had be somewhat sheltered, but she remembered when one of tenants had suffered an injury that had festered despite best efforts. For both farmer and solider, the loss of a limb meant the end of their livelihood. "I would like to meet him at some point." She smiled. "Since I'm likely going to be his sister-in-law, it'd be nice before everything is settled. Only if he's well enough, though."

"That sounds like a wonderful idea. Something at home where Hamish won't exert himself too much. Your family, my family, perhaps a few other friends." He smiled at her. "The Abernathys. Show him he missed the mark with his matchmaking."

"I think he was being kind as Lord Chalton and I were seated next to one another. How would our meeting have gone if I did not know your friend?"

Blair frowned. "I don't want to think about it. I told Father several times that I didn't know if I wanted to go through with this. I *resented* it."

His words unsettled her. "And now?"

"Now, I want to see where things go." Looking toward the door once more, he said, "I believe the dance may be done. I should escort you back to Lady Eastleigh. I don't want to tempt gossip."

Augusta had no argument with that, and after disposing of their mostly undrunk glasses, she let him lead her back to her mother. To her surprise, Chalton was still speaking with her. "There you are," Lady Eastleigh said brightly. "Lord Chalton kindly kept me company while you danced." She tapped him teasingly with her fan. "A young man such as yourself should not be sitting the dances out when young ladies need partners. Augusta will need one for the next dance, for example."

Her mother was getting desperate. "I would be happy to take a short rest," she said. "Perhaps I should sit the next dance out. There will be supper later, but perhaps something cooling to drink?"

"An excellent idea." Lady Eastleigh turned toward the gentlemen. "Will you join us, Lord Chalton?"

"I'm afraid there is something I must discuss with Lord Blair," Chalton said, offering a slight bow. "I would enjoy a second dance with Miss Eastleigh later in the evening, however. As, I believe, would Lord Blair."

Lady Eastleigh's mouth pursed as if she sucked on a lemon. "I'm certain Augusta would be happy to accommodate both of you. Now, if you'll excuse us, gentlemen."

She whisked them away as Wilverton stepped forward to offer an arm, clearly intending to do his best to escort them. Lady Eastleigh behaved as if she did not see him. As they moved, she said, "You and I have much to discuss, my girl and I don't care to wait until we get home."

From Lady Eastleigh's expression, Blair worried the conversation about Simon had come and there'd be no way for Augusta to avoid it. One look at his friend's face warned he was in for a similar discussion. "The card room?" he suggested.

"As good a place as any as any. We'll be expected to keep any conversation quiet so as not to disturb the players." He fixed Blair with a sober gaze. "You also understand it means I won't be able to yell at you without causing talk. We both understand Miss Eastleigh doesn't need any more of that."

Blair chose not to admit he was counting on exactly that as they made their way to the card room. It was filled with gentlemen—and a lady or two—who preferred the turn of fortune to the dance. The stakes would be small here, for no hostess would stand for great losses to happen under her roof, but the games taken seriously nonetheless.

One of the corners was empty, giving them the semblance of privacy, same as he enjoyed with Augusta a few minutes before. He would prefer to speak with her.

Leaning in, Chalton asked, "Now you're happy you're going to marry Augusta? What are you up to? I told you, I wasn't going to ask her to marry me, so no need to martyr yourself with a rescue."

"Like you, it appears I'm in need of a wife." As Simon started to say something, he continued, "James isn't going to do what's necessary for the estate and we don't know what will happen with Hamish. My father's panic aside, someone's needs to ensure the future of the line and that someone appears to end up being me."

Simon said nothing for a long moment, then turned to gesture to a footman. "Is there something stronger than whatever they're serving for the ladies?"

The servant nodded and departed, returning momentarily with two glasses of port. Simon took both glasses, then handed one to Blair. "To those of us who bear the burden of future generations," he said lifting his glass. "I'm sorry it's come to you."

Blair lifted his glass in reply and they both drank deep. "At least you understand," he said. "Both my brothers apologize for landing me in the soup, but I don't think they get it. Hamish I can understand. A soldier's life is dangerous, and I suppose he thought James would eventually come around."

He sighed, then leaned in, not wanting his voice to carry. "James says he never wanted the responsibility and got himself a case of the pox he claims made him impotent, so no heir from him."

Simon's eyebrows rose, and Blair couldn't help squirming a little. "I know. That's the big reason behind Father's panic. I may be the only chance left." He couldn't help laughing. "I'm not the spare. I'm the spare spare. That I would find myself in this position…"

He broke off and took another swallow. "You're at least looking at someone you developed respect for," Simon said, "and whom you know keeps her wits about her. Both are assets. There are worse women your father could decide to pair you with. You must treat her right. If you don't…"

The threat hung in the hair and Blair didn't doubt the truth of it. "We're feeling one another out. She has qualities I didn't recognize before. I think I can understand why you were caught by her, enough to consider marriage. Now the stumbling block is Forebridge. Having been the one who pushed for this, Father's complaining he's proving parsimonious, trying to push as much of the cost on Father as he can. I shouldn't be surprised, given what he thinks of Augusta—Miss Eastleigh, but it's worrisome. The last thing I want is Father losing his temper and breaking off negotiations."

"Do your best to mend the fences. For now, though?" Simon raised his glass once more. "I'm glad for you. Be happy."

He finished the glass and set it down on a nearby surface. "I just wished I was."

CHAPTER 15

Augusta found herself once more back in the refreshment room, and once again holding a glass of punch she was not going to drink. This time, though, she was sitting on a chaise in the corner, her mother close enough to speak without being overheard. "We've been dancing about this for over a week. Why isn't Lord Chalton proposing?"

She could frame her answer a hundred ways. None of them would please her mother, and only make things worse if lies of omission were later exposed. "He isn't going to propose."

"What do you mean, he isn't going to propose?"

Catching herself, Lady Eastleigh cleared her throat, casting a quick glance around the room, glaring at a footman who had turned his head in their direction. "I thought we were supposed to be kind to other's servants," Augusta said.

"Not if they're eavesdropping on a private conversation." The words were sharp but uttered at a quieter level than before. "How do you know he won't be proposing? He's certainly been attentive enough. After watching the two of you together, everyone is awaiting the announcement."

This was not the moment to point out the only people aside from her family who were waiting were those who lived on gossip. "He told me. He tried to bring himself to speak with Father, but at the last, he couldn't."

Rarely did she see her mother stunned, even more rarely by something Augusta had said. Lady Eastleigh blinked as her mouth hung open. "He told you this?" she managed at last in a strangled voice.

"Lord Chalton and I are honest with one another. I think that is the best way."

Lady Eastleigh did not move, still staring. Her face began to flush, though, and her knuckles white around the glass she held, fury in her eyes. In private, the air would be ringing. Now, everything was held within, the fearsome storm was brewing, not apparent to anyone who did not know her. It was a talent Augusta doubted she would ever learn.

At last, Lady Eastleigh's mouth shut, only to open again a moment later. "You are not to dance with Lord Chalton again. I don't care I said he may partner you a second time. You are not to engage with him any longer."

Her tone brooked no comment, but Augusta knew she must. "This is why I didn't want to tell you. I knew you would react like this."

"How did you expect me to react? We worked so hard toward this moment. That was my one desire for this season in London, to see you settled with a man who will take proper care of you. Your grandfather is going to be over the moon at this news. He'll wash his hands of you and make me eat crow for the rest of my life because he won."

"What if I don't mind marrying Blair MacDonald? Can't you be happy for me? Please don't say because you don't want Grandfather win."

Lady Eastleigh was quiet for a long moment, staring down at the glass she still held. At last, she raised her eyes. The fury was still there, but also sadness. "I don't want you to live the life I have, worrying if our funds from the estate will be cut because Forebridge gets himself into a snit of some imagined slight or fault. To fund this season, I had to grovel to that man, give up more control than I thought wise, because he wouldn't help us otherwise. Sometimes I wish I hadn't."

She raised the glass to her lips and took a deep sip, only to scowl as she lowered the glass again. "Why can't they come up with better punch than this? This is not a children's party. Yes, he's negotiating a settlement with the MacDonalds, but he won't be generous. Lord Blair finds himself on the wrong side of a family argument, whatever you bring to the marriage might prove all you have to live on. Worse, he's a third son; you're not guaranteed of your own establishment, but forced to make do with room in the family home. You'll play lady of the manor until his elder brother marries, and heaven help you if she's jealous of the friendships you formed or the regard you're held in."

Leaning a closer, she dropped her voice. "I love your father and have never regretted making the decision to elope with him. We reached Scotland just ahead of his father. Even then, with us wedded and bedded, he still tried to get the marriage annulled. I sometimes wonder if he's the one who started the rumor I was pregnant by someone else when we eloped."

The talk was blunt, blunter than Augusta thought her mother would be willing to utter at an event. "Many times I wished we were able to live more comfortably, with less worry. The men I encouraged all have control of their fortune, so will be able to provide for you in a fitting manner and you will not be forced to squeeze every penny. Can you be sure of that with Blair?"

It was on the tip of Augusta's tongue to say there were things her mother and her grandfather didn't know, that the situation was more complicated than either of them thought. The words lingered, and yet she stayed silent. Blair had told her certain things in confidence, so it was not her tale to tell. What's more, while the news might calm her mother's mind, she had no guarantee Lady Eastleigh wouldn't throw the knowledge in Forebridge's face during an argument.

Just as she didn't trust Forebridge to scuttle the match if he found it too advantageous to her. Time in London had shown her he might want her to marry high enough to not embarrass the family, but not *too* high.

Before she found a way to express herself, Lady Eastleigh sighed. "At least you told me. Yes, you should dance with Chalton again if he's willing. Too many eyes are watching after the incident with Miss Hibbert. A refusal would send the wrong signal. We need time to decide who else we should encourage. I came to count on Chalton so much, I'm afraid I let things slide and some gentlemen slip away. We need to reel them back again. Doesn't help the old goat keeps telling me how negotiations are going."

This at least Augusta could speak to. "Lord Blair says the negotiations are not proceeding swiftly. He says Lord Rutherglen is not happy with Grandfather."

"Not surprising. He's likely showing his parsimonious side, trying to give as little as possible." For the first time since they sat down, Lady Eastleigh smiled. "It does, however, buy us time. You need to keep both Lord Chalton and Lord Blair dancing attendance. Don't tell me you don't like encouraging them if you're not going to marry either," she said as Augusta opened her mouth to object. "A woman must do what she can to secure her own future. I'm determined to see that future is secured."

Her head turned, followed by a nod of acknowledgement to the party who had entered. "Enough talk for now. We'll discuss this once we're home. Best to return to the floor; you don't want to keep the gentlemen hanging, do you?"

With that, she plucked the cup from Augusta's fingers and gestured to the footman to take both glasses away. Then, she rose and steered Augusta toward the other ladies, greeting them as if nothing were the matter. A few words, and they moved back toward the main room. Augusta couldn't help reflecting there was a time when she would welcome the idea of negotiations not going smoothly. Now the news left her unsettled.

"Do you think Hamish is well enough to enjoy a musical evening?" Blair asked his father the next morning. "Hire some musicians to play a small concert? I was thinking we might ask the Eastleighs to attend, along with a few other guests. And Lord Forebridge of course."

Rutherglen lowered the paper he was reading, and Blair noticed the smudges under his eyes. "I do not think, given how your last musical scheme went, such an invitation would be appropriate. It would cost Hamish considerable effort to make his way downstairs to greet people. He would not benefit by you and Miss Eastleigh ending up in a fight."

"That's not my intent," Blair said as his father raised his paper once more. "Miss Eastleigh and I have come a way since then. I said I was willing to marry her. Shouldn't that signal a change?"

"You told me this after James arrived, which I find somewhat suspicious timing." Down the paper went once more. "I wonder if you gave in solely from a sense of duty. If you did, how much resentment do you hold toward her? Besides, Forebridge doesn't enjoy music. The only reason he was willing to go to the opera is the dancers."

Peering around the sheets, he added, "For all his moralizing against loose women, he was involved with one of those dancers after his son eloped. Some said he was besotted enough to consider marrying her."

Blair blinked. "Really?"

A heavy sigh. "No. He did say he might because he wanted to get another son. Why consider such a woman rather than a girl of good family, I don't know. He doesn't think straight when he's angry, and he was very angry at that moment."

His father's tone was one of annoyance, a sign his patience was stretched thin. Everyone's tempers were on edge. Hamish put on a cheerful face, but the doctor was grim each time he paid a visit. It was as if the infection in Hamish's leg would be beaten back for a short while, only to creep forward again.

Resolutely pushing that reality aside for a moment, Blair said. "I understand Forebridge might not enjoy music. Miss Eastleigh does, though, and I want her to meet Hamish. James, too, I suppose. Better that happen now than after a betrothal is announced."

This time, Rutherglen folded the paper before laying it aside. "Do you now? Doesn't have to be a musical evening. They could come calling on a day when he felt up for visitors."

"Where etiquette demands they stay no longer than fifteen minutes, and a visit to the sickroom of a gentlemen she does not know would not be considered appropriate." He flicked a piece of lint from his sleeve. "I spoke to Mrs. Petherbridge this morning. She believes having a chance to come downstairs and be among people would be most beneficial to Hamish. She says he's getting restless and a change of scene would do wonders."

"Hmmm. I suppose she may be right. The doctor won't like it. He doesn't seem to want Hamish to move at all. If we host a small gathering, we'll be expected to give them supper. Do you really thing we should put Hamish through that?"

"He can join us after. As the doctor has insisted on a special diet, he can't eat the meal you'll be providing, so he's eating with Caitlin and Finola. They can eat in his room, and that will provide a change of scene. Then, before we leave the dining room, he can be moved downstairs and settled. Save him embarrassment, too."

"If the girls are with him, he'll look as if he chose to keep them company with his meal. You are talking an intimate gathering if you're looking at the girls being here." Rutherglen leaned back in his chair. "You' changed your mind about her? No more roadblocks? No second thoughts?"

Blair shook his head. "If you and Lord Forebridge can find your way to getting the settlement done, no reason we couldn't be married before the end of June. We'll need to be in London for the Regent's fete, a perfect moment to present her to him." He frowned. "I probably should dance attendance at some point. Just between this and Hamish, both have slipped these past weeks."

"We have all let things slide. The times are difficult. After the fete, you should take her to Whiterose."

"Not home to Rutherglen Castle?"

"Nay. Whiterose is old, but in good repair. It will make a bonny love nest for the two of you, give you a chance to get to know one another. Parliament will be prorogued, so no responsibilities to call you back to London. That is, of course, if we finish this negotiation. Forebridge is being difficult. I don't expect the world, but the man should give a little. He's trying to do things as cheaply as possible, almost as if he wants to scuttle the progress. He would send her to us in her shift if he could."

The words worried him. "I want you to understand," Blair said carefully, "If I must marry, then my bride should be Miss Eastleigh. As you pointed out, she has many excellent qualities. Even if Hamish does recover and marries, she will be a great help to me in my career."

The air of satisfaction which settled around Rutherglen was something of a relief to Blair. For the first time in over a week, his father looked as if some of the weight had been lifted from his shoulders and knew his words had helped. "I'm glad to hear. Perhaps it is not being done in the way either of us might wish, but it is good to see it done. May she bring you much joy."

A smile which vanished as other worries settled on his father's shoulders. "You're right to say 'if' with regards to Hamish. I don't know how this will go. The nurse is doing her best, but he isn't getting better. I wish we could send him away from London, into the country air. To Whiterose, in fact, it being so close. In his condition, though..."

Blair remembered the journey from Portugal, the days he insisted they needed to stop because the travel was too difficult for Hamish, despite his objections. Would it have been better to take him directly to someplace such as Whiterose instead of coming to London?

No. That would have added at least a day, if not two, to a journey that was already difficult. London had been closer and excellent doctors to hand. Just as, for those very same reasons, Hamish would likely not be moved again until he recovered, or was carried from the house.

Father and son sat in silence for a long moment before Rutherglen roused himself. "Yes. A musical evening. It won't put as much stress on him as some of the other things we might try. You're right Miss Eastleigh should meet him. Can I leave you to handle everything?"

"Certainly." Blair pushed away from the table. "Let me tell Hamish. I'm sure the news will help lift his spirits."

He'd almost reached the door when Rutherglen spoke again. "If the worst happens, do you think Miss Eastleigh will be satisfied with a quiet ceremony and a small wedding breakfast? Or will she want to put things off for six months until we're out of our heaviest mourning.

Fighting down the sudden surge of panic he felt, Blair replied, "I think a small wedding would be better than a delayed one. I'm certain Miss Eastleigh would understand the need. We could leave for

Whiterose almost immediately after. Even the Regent would understand why I would not wish to attend his fete under those circumstances."

With a nod from his father in agreement, Blair made his way out of the room and toward the stairs, his mind churning over what had not been said. That if they begged a delay, even for a death within the family, Forebridge might not react well. If he grew too angry, negotiations might collapse, the last thing Blair wanted.

CHAPTER 16

Hamish was awake and even sitting up when Blair entered his room, though he didn't look comfortable. The reason for that was obvious, as Mrs. Petherbridge was undoing the current bandage in preparation for a new dressing. "Have I come at a bad time?" Blair asked.

"No, my lord," the nurse replied. "Your help, though, would be appreciated." She glanced up. "Unless you would find it too difficult."

"Who do you think changed the dressings on our trip home? Where would you have me stand?"

She directed him to a place near the foot of the bed and asked him to lift Hamish's foot, so the leg was elevated. "Gently," she said as Hamish uttered a small grunt of pain. "This will allow me to remove the dressing quicker."

Hamish nodded. His fingers were gripped tight in the sheets, but he did not utter a word as Mrs. Petherbridge worked quickly. With Blair's help, she was able to use both hands to remove the dressing with having to pause to lift the leg, slowing only as she reached the innermost layers. Here, she took care to make certain the bandage came away without ripping away any scabs which had formed. Still, she made swift work, frowning as she took in the discharge which stained the linen.

As the last of the strip fell away, Blair required no medical knowledge to recognize things were not healing as they should. The skin around the wound was red and angry, covering a much larger area than when Blair had last seen. The wound itself looked no better, spots of red flesh without a thick, yellowish discharge. For a moment, he regretted the breakfast he had eaten before coming upstairs.

Mrs. Petherbridge show no signs of flinching, instructing him to put the leg down as she fetched a basin, cloth and jug. "What's the news of the bride hunt?" Hamish asked. He winced as she applied water to the wound, smoothing away the discharge.

With difficulty, Blair turned his attention from the wound to Hamish's face. "Not as well as I would like. Father is in negotiations with Lord Forebridge, but the man is being difficult. He apparently thinks we should be happy with the idea he's willing to let us marry into the family."

"With his stance the girl might not be his granddaughter?" Hamish shook his head. "The family's not that grand and their connections not so fine. How is Father's temper doing?"

"I think he's growing weary of the game."

Something in his voice caused Hamish to stare at him a bit more intently. "You're not happy about that. I thought you didn't want to be yoked to Miss Eastleigh."

Clearly, no one would allow him to forget that fact. "I was perhaps a bit too hasty. She's not what I thought she was. What I assumed her to be. She possesses excellent qualities that should not be ignored. Also, she likes music."

Hamish started to reply, but instead hissed in pain. "Are we nearly done?" he asked through gritted teeth.

"Almost. I need to apply the cream the doctor prescribed." She glanced at Blair. "Please continue. The lady enjoys music?"

He doubted she was interested in the woman the brother of her patient was considering marrying, but he recognized the request to continue distracting Hamish as she worked. "She does. She enjoys opera, though she was not familiar with it before she arrived in London."

"Surprised Father doesn't make that a requirement to marry into this family," Hamish said. Beads of sweat were dotting his brow and his fingers curled more tightly into the sheets. "Does she play an instrument?"

"I'm not sure," Blair confessed. "We've had no opportunity for her to display her talents, and I haven't asked. She enjoys a concert. Not with the attitude some ladies take to make themselves look cultured. No one could be as enthusiastic at Madam Solange's performance as she was and be putting on an act."

"Lord Blair, if you would lift Lord Hamish's foot again, please."

Dutifully, Blair did as he was bid, though he was more careful this time. Still, he saw the wince. Re-bandaging the leg was much swifter than undoing the wrappings, Mrs. Petherbridge's hands moving carefully and efficiently. "I'm going to speak with the doctor when he comes," she said as she secured the linen. "I'm wondering if some Tetter Berry powder might not help with the discharge."

"You think it will help?"

"I do, but I must defer to the doctor. Lord Hamish is, after all, his patient. You may put his leg down and thank you for your help, sir."

Blair lowered Hamish's leg as carefully as he could, but was rewarded with another hiss of pain. "I'm fine, I'm fine," Hamish said. "Come sit down. I'm tired of craning my neck to look up at you."

Blair settled himself in the chair at the side of the bed, but as he did, he noted the frown on Mrs. Petherbridge's face. The wound had her concerned, more than would be normal, he wagered. "So Miss Eastleigh's enthusiasm for the opera changed your opinion of her," Hamish said, and Blair turned his head back toward him.

"That and other things," he admitted. "There are depths there I had not grasped. We are doing our best to find our way with one another, and I convinced Father to invite her and her family for an evening of music in order for her to meet you."

Hamish's eyes lit up at his words. "Excellent! I swear, I am so tired of being stuck within this room that I would willingly listen to the rudest musician on the street if it meant the chance to see other people. Who are you hiring, because you and father won't risk relying on the talents of our friends when there are musicians close to hand."

"We just decided to arrange this." Blair felt lighter, glad of his brother's enthusiasm. "We've not yet settled all the details. A small party, something intimate."

"There are some names I wish you to add. Just one or two, but friends who'll be happy to find I'm doing well."

Blair doubted the wisdom of the idea. Still, he smiled and said, "Give me their names and we'll issue the invitations." After a moment's pause, he continued, feeling his way toward this. "We were thinking you might come downstairs after supper and be waiting in the reception room. Father and I feel that wouldn't put too much strain on you."

As he feared, Hamish's face darkened. "Why don't you want me included in the dinner? If the idea is for me to meet this Miss East-leigh, shouldn't I be a part of the entire evening?"

"Don't be foolish," Mrs. Petherbridge said. "Do you wish to waste your energy sitting up exchanging small talk and eating rich food you shouldn't? Yes, you're eating heartier food, but what you would have at such a gathering is not suitable at this time."

"Damn it, woman! Next you'll be saying I shouldn't attend at all but be content with what whisps of music might waft up from below.

The anger behind Hamish's words were surprising. His brother was sitting up straighter, fists clenched, as if daring his nurse to tell him no. "I'm tired of being in this room and seeing nothing but the four walls. I'm tired of no one but you for company. My sisters come in and I can tell they don't want to linger because they've been told any noise could do me harm. Who told them that? Who told them?"

Mrs. Petherbridge did not reply, standing straight and calm as Hamish ranted. At one point, Blair reached out to put his hand on Hamish's arm, hoping to calm him, only to have the hand shrugged off. Still Mrs. Petherbridge waited calmly, no emotion crossing her face.

Hamish tired quickly and he collapsed back against the pillows, his face drawn. Only then did Mrs. Petherbridge speak. "I don't believe it wise for you to attend the supper portion of the evening because you will tire yourself out and be forced to miss the music. However, we bring you downstairs while supper is in session, you'll be able to settle in your chair and take a short rest before the party joins you. You'll be able to enjoy the music, focus on those people you wish to see, and endure fewer wearisome inquiries about your health. You may also have whatever sweet is passed to end the evening. No, I won't tell the doctor because we both know he'll forbid it."

She looked toward Blair. "Best if you and your father don't share that information with him either. I believe if we are careful, seeing other people and enjoying a pleasant evening as much as he can will only encourage his recovery."

Taking a deep breath, she added, "Will you be able to sit with him until I return. I should empty the basin and dispose of the cloth. They're unhealthful things to have in the sick room in his condition."

When Blair said he would be happy to, Mrs. Petherbridge dropped him a curtsey and fetched the items she was to take away. At the door, she paused to say, "I did not tell your sisters to be quiet. They bring a smile to your face, and as long as you do not find the noise disturbing and if they don't jump on the bed, I would think their presence would help keep your spirits up."

With that she was gone, closing the door behind her. "She's a gorgon in many ways," Hamish says, "but she does her best to ensure I'm comfortable. Tries to be gentle when she changes the dressings, but damned if sometimes every little movement feels as if a thousand knives were slicing me open."

None of that sounded good, but Blair chose not to speak. Hamish understood the situation, which led to the question: who was putting on a good face for whom?

Gesturing Blair to pull his chair nearer, Hamish said, "Since we're actually alone, you can finally tell me about James. I get the sense you didn't want to share this story with outsiders."

"Has James been up?"

"Aye, several times. Mrs. Petherbridge was present always, and if he's done something particularly stupid, he wouldn't say a word."

Unsure how long the nurse would be gone, Blair took a deep breath, . "He's gotten the pox. Worse, he's gotten the pox bad enough he's impotent."

Hamish stared at him for a long minute, then let his head drop back, staring at the ceiling. "Damn."

"Exactly. How the hell did he manage to get himself in that situation? Were the matter were not so dire, I would swear he was lying to get Father off his back."

"He's made certain he's not going to get anything else at this point. Impotent?"

Blair nodded. "With just enough honor not to pass it along to a young lady so he can give the appearance of doing all the right things dynastically."

"But where? This is James. Can you picture him spending money at a bawdy house?"

"No, which is the strange thing." Blair laughed. "He told me he didn't want the title. He'll do his best by the estate and our tenants, but he wished he could trade places with me."

They sat in silence for a while, each ruminating on the conversation. Hamish shifted and winced. "It's not getting better," he said. "Mrs. Petherbridge does her best to watch over me, and make me comfortable, but I know things are getting worse."

"What makes you say that?"

"She does her best to block my view of the wound, trying to ensure I don't see. Except this time, she prioritized my comfort when she asked you to raise my leg up. I saw enough wounds on the battlefield."

There was little for Blair to argue with. "Father is worried."

Hamish snorted. "*I'm* worried. I'm not ready to leave this world yet, but I don't want to lose my leg. That would mean the end of my career. Don't know what I'd do after that."

"Comes that, you likely won't be in a position to make the choice. Father will. He'll choose your life over your leg."

A roll of the eyes. "Sounds like something some maiden aunt would embroider on a pillow. You're starting to think you might enjoy having Miss Eastleigh as your bride?"

The change of topic was a welcome one. "I'm finding I may like her. Which is a good thing, I suppose."

"Could it be love?"

Blair's first urge was to throw a cushion at his brother, which he resisted. "I have not considered it," he admitted. "I find her attractive, I worry about her, but I'll confess to not thinking about love."

He fell silent for a moment, pondering the question. "I think love could come."

"Treasure that," Hamish says. "Don't let it go. For everything I said, I wish hadn't done what I did. I regret that, in trying to be noble, I didn't allow myself the chance of happiness. I assume the worst would happen and acted accordingly. I didn't give a thought to her feelings, either, because she was hurt by what I did."

He shifted to meet Blair's eyes. "If you have any feelings for this girl, don't delay. Marry. Don't put things off, even if I…"

The words trailed into silence for a long moment before he continued. "Don't let things you have no control over stop you."

Mrs. Petherbridge chose that moment to reappear, effective ending the conversation. "I spoke with cook. She's made barley soup with a thick beef broth. Some might consider that fit for only the servants, but I think it will do you better than the thin gruel. Also fresh baked bread."

Hamish smiled weakly up at Blair. "See how I'm treated? Everything is going to be fine."

The three of them knew it wasn't, but they were going to keep hoping until hope was gone. If wishes might make things come true, then by heaven Blair was going to wish harder than he ever had since he was a child.

CHAPTER 17

"That's not the way I see it at all."

Augusta couldn't help glancing toward Blair. He had to notice the testiness in his father's tone in response to the position Forebridge had been putting forward. She was used to people losing patience with her grandfather, but this was the third time during the supper they had disagreed. Given what Blair had said about the settlement negotiations, perhaps the marquess was beginning to lose his temper.

Blair, seated at her side, met her gaze, his expression unhappy. The idea of the evening had been for the family to spend convivial time together, for her to meet his brothers. Perhaps the two families could not get along.

But if not, could a settlement be reached, or would Forebridge decide on another husband for her? Father had tales of the difficulties thrown in the path of the marriages of him and his siblings, how one of his sisters had two engagements fall through because of settlement issues. He never said so, but Augusta wondered if that was the reason her normally calm, somewhat cautious father had chosen to elope.

Would Blair be willing to do such a thing, or would he let her go if Forebridge and Rutherglen couldn't reach an agreement?

"I understand the Regent's plan for a grand fete in the summer are moving forward," Lady Eastleigh said, her voice louder that would usually be considered proper at the table, cutting off Forebridge's response. "I know you are often in attendance upon His Highness, Lord Blair. Any details you can share?"

The question was ridiculous and innocuous following the matters of law Forebridge and Rutherglen had been discussing. With her words, though, came a slight lifting of tension at the diversion. "I'm not privy to the latest details," Blair said, picking up the cue. "The Regent has been generous in allowing me to be absent from his presence due to the family issues you are aware of. However, I can tell you that he is determined the event should be a wonder, showing support for the Duc de Bourbon and other members of the French nobility driven into exile." A pause. "He's also celebrating the King's birthday."

A mixture of snickers and clucking of tongues around the table. The common wisdom was the birthday was the Regent's excuse to throw himself a grand party. "I know he has an elaborate scheme planned for chalking the floor for dancing. Which shall, of course, be quickly spoiled, but those who are present early will be able to view it before the dance begins."

Blair shrugged. "I imagine there will be other extravagances by the time we are done. He was speaking of allowing the public to visit that area of Carlton House afterwards."

The conversation fell to generalities, though much of the talk remained centered around the Regent's fete. Leaning toward Augusta, Blair said quietly, "Is your grandfather deliberately trying to upset my father?"

"To be honest, I don't understand what goes on in his mind sometimes," Augusta admitted. "I just hope your father won't be riled."

In some ways, it was a relief to rise from the table. The food had been excellent, the company pleasant, but throughout, underlying currents of tension which threatened to spill the banks of courtesy. Those among her own family were familiar companions, but the tensions between Forebridge and Rutherglen worried her. She sensed they worried Blair as well, but there was more than what met the eye.

Blair offered her his arm as the company began moving from the dining room to the salon where the music was to be presented. The gesture brought smiles from the others, including one gentleman who clapped Rutherglen familiarly on the shoulder. "Lovely girl. She'll make the lad a fine bride. Good to know one of them is marrying at last."

The last was said with a glance at Lord Strathern, Blair's oldest brother, who offered a weak smile in return. Another current, one Blair had warned her about.

"He's not married yet," Rutherglen said, leveling a meaningful glance at Forebridge. "There are still a few details to work out."

Forebridge responded with a grunt as the party entered the salon. Three of the chairs and small chaises set out were already occupied, Finola and Caitlin rising at the guests' entrance. The gentleman they had been seated with did not, his leg carefully propped on a footstool. That and the uniform he wore marked him out as Lord Hamish MacDonald. No, he did not look well.

Blair led her directly to Hamish and the girls. "You remember my sisters, of course. And this is my brother, Hamish. Hamish, Miss Augusta Eastleigh, and her parents, the Baron and Baroness Eastleigh."

He looked about as if to include Forebridge, but her grandfather had been swept into another conversation. "I am acquainted with Lord and Lady Eastleigh. You must forgive me for not rising to greet you. I'm afraid my condition does not allow me to at the moment."

"No worries, sir," Eastleigh said easily. "Glad you are well enough to be out of bed."

Hamish chuckled. "I would not put it that way, but the change in view is pleasant." He turned his head toward Augusta. "I find my sisters did not exaggerate. You are quite the beauty."

Augusta's cheeks warmed. "I will accept the compliment, Lord Hamish, but I'm afraid your sisters exaggerate somewhat."

"My sisters were charmed by you, even with some unrest at the opera, from what I understand. I'll take their opinion over Blair's any day. Let me add you should keep leading him a merry chase. It's no less than he deserves."

"How terrible, Hamish!" Fiona sounded indignant and smacked

him lightly on the arm. "You shouldn't talk to Miss Eastleigh that way."

He chuckled, casting a fond glance at his sister. "You're right. I shouldn't. Pray forgive me, Miss Eastleigh. A pleasure to meet you at last, and a pleasure to welcome your family in our home on what I hope will not be the last occasion."

It was easy to see why Blair was worried about his brother. There was a warmth and easiness about him which told Augusta she would be welcome here as more than the conduit for the next generation. Her mother had relaxed, and any distaste she might have for Blair did not seem to carry to his brother. "I hope you can sit in the gardens," Lady Eastleigh said. "With the weather as fine as it is, I'm certain the view would prove a tonic."

"Or at least another change of scene." He glanced over his shoulder toward where a woman quietly stood against the wall. "I have not had the chance since I returned, sad to say. A visitor would not be amiss. We must arrange a visit for Miss Eastleigh during the day when Blair can show her the garden."

"Is the pear tree still flourishing?" Lady Eastleigh asked. "You would love it, Augusta. There is the most beautiful pear tree, with wonderful blossoms."

"I do remember you were particularly fond of it." Hamish looked up toward Blair. "Do you think we can arrange a cutting for Lady Eastleigh to plant in her garden at home?"

"I'm certain we could," Blair replied. "Though perhaps closer to the end of the season for easier transportation."

"We'll consult with the gardener. A symbol of the bond between our families." His smile became somewhat wistful. "I just ask that when you look at it, you remember me."

"Don't talk so," Caitlin said. "You sound as if you're going away."

"Not on purpose," he said, patting his sister's hand. "I hopefully won't. But it is good to be remembered."

With a sign, he shifted and winced. "Too somber a topic for this evening. We're supposed to be happy and gay, and give Miss Eastleigh here every good reason to marry Blair."

"It would mean she would be with us much more," Finola said. "She could teach us all the latest dances."

"We have a dancing master," Caitlin said.

"You have a dancing master," Finola retorted. "I only get to watch and he's far too self-important. I wager Miss Eastleigh would be much more fun."

"I would do my best," Augusta replied. "I would be happy to show you, if things are settled."

The words felt strange, along with the realization she was looking forward to things being settled. Not because she wanted to be on the other side of this entire painful season, but because the idea of a life with Blair held more and more appeal.

A slight squeeze of her hand, and she turned her head to find Blair smiling from where he stood beside her. She hesitated for a moment, then gently returned the squeeze. This new understanding between them was at once powerful and fragile, and she wished for an opportunity to explore it somewhere other than in the middle of a crowd. "We should take our seats," Blair said. "Catlin, Finola, you're keeping Hamish company?"

The girls nodded, and Blair led Augusta to another small chaise, this one big enough for two. Her parents found another nearby, but far enough away she and Blair would be able to speak with relative privacy. Not that they would be chattering while the musicians performed. The chance to sit together without being watched was one she would not ignore.

Rutherglen said a few words of introduction, then took his own seat. The musicians struck up their first piece, a lively work which showed the small quartet to advantage. Would this be a common thing, she wondered, the family gathered with guests to listen to musicians. Would there be other evening where they would gather after supper to amuse themselves with their own playing and singing. Perhaps she needed to more practice on the piano.

Those thoughts drifted away as she let herself relax into the music. This quartet offered fewer breaks than at Lady Gresham's, music flowing from one piece to another with only the smallest pause for the musicians to re-arrange their sheet music. Somewhere during this, Blair's hand slid around hers once more.

Even with the glove she wore, Augusta felt the warmth of his palm against hers. She'd held hands with many a gentleman in London, dancing, being escorted into supper, but this was much more intimate. This was not something called for in etiquette, but a liberty allowed if she let her hand remain in his. Yet, it seemed natural and right to be sitting next to him, fingers entwined as they listened to the notes rippled up and down the scale.

Suddenly conscious of being observed, she shifted her gaze from the quartet at the front. Blair was watching her, his expression somewhere between fondness and curiosity. She tried smiling at him, earning a smile in return, along with a gentle squeeze of her hand. His thumb began to stroke along the outside of hers. Augusta couldn't help feeling a bit of a thrill at the pressure. They were racing toward some type of conclusion, one where no glove separated her skin from his. When liberties other than discreetly holding hands in a situation where they would not be noticed would not only be allowed, but sanctioned.

Another thrill went through her, this time provoking a shiver.

The piece ended, and the guests applauded. This time, there was a slight break, many of the guests rising to stretch their legs and mingle. "Are you chilled?" Blair asked. "I could have a shawl fetched."

"I'm fine," she said. "I was thinking soon you might hold my hand without worrying about being seen by others."

A puzzled expression on his face, he looked down and found their fingers still intertwined. He began to pull back, but Augusta did not let him go. "You are right. It would not be accepted for us to be seen so. Yet."

With that, he did pull his hand from hers, but let his fingers trail over her palm. "I'll speak with Father," he said. "See if we can hurry things along."

She began to tell him the move would please her, but one of the other guests approached and they were drawn into conversation. There was no further chance to speak before the music began again, and his hand sought hers once more.

CHAPTER 18

At last, the music came to an end, the musicians applauded before a servant discretely led them from the room. With the guests now rising to mingle, Augusta did not object this time when Blair's hand slid from hers. There'd be other evenings, other moments. Not now, though, when her parents were approaching. "This was a wonderful idea," Eastleigh said as both she and Blair rose from where they had been sitting. "A chance for Augusta to meet your brothers, and for us to enjoy beautiful music."

"Music is important to my family," Blair said. "We enjoy being able to share it with our friends."

"I doubt you'll hear much objection from Goose if you want to host parties such as this in the future."

Blair turned back to her, one eyebrow raised. "Goose?"

Augusta felt her cheeks grow warm. "I couldn't say my name properly when I was little, so I said A-goose-sta. Papa picked it up as a nickname."

"How charming. I used to be called—"

Blair broke off abruptly, frowning as he looked toward where the woman who hovered in the back of the room had come to help Hamish to his feet. Or rather, attempt to. Even with a footman's help,

Hamish appeared more than a little pale and drawn, as if the effort had been too much for him. "Pray excuse me," Blair said tersely, then moved to offer what assistance he could.

"He is not doing well," Lady Eastleigh said in a quiet voice as they watched Hamish be helped from the room. "Perhaps this proved too much for him."

"Perhaps," Eastleigh said. "But if he has been cooped up in his room, most likely he found the change of scene welcome. It also makes me understand why Rutherglen is anxious for Lord Blair to marry. Did you notice Strathern disappeared after we all assembled here?"

"I did. There are rumors—" Abruptly, Lady Eastleigh's tone and manner changed. "Lady Finola, Lady Caitlin, we must thank you for your hospitality."

The two girls dipped a curtsey. "Hamish wished us to send his regrets he was not able to speak with you again," Caitlin said, "and to say he greatly enjoyed meeting Miss Eastleigh and hopes to see more of her."

"Though he can't understand why she likes such a booby as Blair," Finola added.

"He told us not to say that part."

Finola rolled her eyes. "He was teasing. I think he believes she'll make Blair a fine wife."

"You must thank Lord Hamish for me," Augusta replied, doing her best not to laugh. "I was most pleased to meet him, and hope to see him again soon. Just as I hope to visit you both."

The girls dipped curtsies again and made their way from the room. "I think Lord Rutherglen will have his hands full when they make their curtsey," Eastleigh said.

Lady Eastleigh nodded. "They'll likely have a flock of suitors around them from the moment they step into a ballroom. I think he faces other worries at the moment."

Glancing toward where Rutherglen stood, Augusta saw Forebridge with him. The two men were speaking in low tones, but the conversation didn't seem to be going well. Forebridge ended things by nodding curtly and made his way toward them. "Are we done?" he asked, his voice tight.

"We've yet to thank Lord Rutherglen for his hospitality," Eastleigh said, his voice soothing. "Plus, I imagine Augusta will wish to say goodnight to Lord Blair who should be down soon."

Forebridge harumphed. "Let's not linger too long. The evening's been long enough already. Everyone else is leaving."

The guests were beginning to filter out, though not in any great rush. Forebridge was itching to go, however, and experience had taught them not to upset him in such a mood. So they made their way to Rutherglen. The marquess was charming, but a tightness to his jaw that signaled unhappiness with something. Worry about Hamish undoubtedly formed the bulk, but there was also his conversation with Forebridge and the tension between the two men earlier in the evening.

He managed a smile for Augusta. "Did you enjoy yourself, Miss Eastleigh? You and Blair appeared focused on the performance."

"I found it very entertaining. Love of music is something Lord Blair and I have in common."

"'Tis best to have a shared interest. Finola and Caitlin play, and sing. Blair possesses a passable voice, but I'm afraid the rest of us are only fit to serve as audience."

"Augusta plays quite competently," Lady Eastleigh says. "She has a charming voice, though I may be prejudiced in that matter."

"Then we must arrange another evening, just the family. A small supper and we shall entertain one another afterwards." He paused. "When Hamish is more up to it."

Lady Eastleigh reached out to lay her hand comfortingly on Rutherglen's forearm. He patted it, then let his grip close over hers for just a moment. "I know Blair would like to say his farewells."

"We should not linger," Forebridge said from behind them. "I'm certain you're glad for the evening to be over."

"I suppose we are." The words came out somewhat grudgingly, as if he didn't agree, but also understood Forebridge did not care to linger. "I'm certain Blair will understand."

With that, there was little else any of them could do to delay. They dawdled getting Eastleigh's hats and the ladies' wraps, but when Fore-bridge snapped his impatience, they started for the door.

Augusta was almost across the threshold when she heard feet on the stairs. "Miss Eastleigh! A moment!"

Turning, she found Blair hurrying across the open space of the entrance hall. "My apologies. I had to ensure Hamish was settled."

"I hope you did not rush on my account."

Blair answered with a bit of a wry chuckle. "He chased me out. Told me not to waste my time with him with a pretty girl downstairs waiting for me."

How many times had her cheeks grown warm that evening? "Of course you were worried about him. He's your brother."

"I'm glad you understand." His voice was warm as he reached out to take her hand. "He sends his regard and hopes very much that you and Lady Eastleigh will favor him with a visit. He asked I let you know when he can receive visitors."

"I'm certain Mother would be happy to visit." A slight pause. "So would I."

It felt right to stand with him here, halfway between inside and out. They were on the threshold in more ways than one, though she wasn't certain what the next step should be.

"Will you hurry up, girl! I don't want to stand here all night."

Blair glared in Forebridge's direction, but brought himself under control. "Let me escort you," he said.

He offered his arm and she laid her hand upon it, allowing him to lead her down the steps and across the sidewalk to the carriage. Fore-bridge glared at him as they approached, but Blair met him with a steady gaze. "Lord Forebridge."

With that, Forebridge was forced to at least acknowledge him with a nod before climbing in the carriage. A few final words of goodbye, and Blair helped Augusta in after her parents. Forebridge called to their driver and they were away almost before the door closed.

"That was certainly an interesting evening," Lady Eastleigh said, breaking the silence. "Lovely music."

"I like the idea of having a small, intimate party, rather than something large," Eastleigh said. "I noticed everyone who attended was most appreciative." He paused. "Almost everyone."

Forebridge did not respond, though he clearly understood who Eastleigh meant. He did not speak during the brief ride home, but Augusta was keenly aware he watched her. It didn't make her comfortable. Being under his scrutiny never did. Nor did it ever portend good things.

Blair was just climbing the stairs when Mrs. Petherbridge appeared. "Could you spare Lord Hamish a moment, sir? I would be grateful."

"I thought you had him settled."

"I did." Her voice was tart. "He is in bed, but says he won't sleep until he speaks with you. Given how much the evening took out of him, please come and see what he wishes."

Not for the first time, Blair sensed a bit of frustration in the nurse and he couldn't blame her. He knew firsthand what a difficult patient Hamish could be. "I'll come."

She breathed what could only be described as a sigh of relief as they turned their steps to Hamish's room. His brother was sitting up in bed, looking more awake than he should be after such a long evening, eyes almost fever bright. "Did you speak with Miss Eastleigh?" he asked.

"Briefly. Lord Forebridge found himself eager to be away."

Hamish's face scrunched in distaste. "Why Father gets along with that man, I cannot fathom. Hardly the most pleasant of souls. His son and daughter-in-law are thankfully a different story. I like her. If I were more mobile, I'd give you a run for your money because she is most assuredly a charmer. She genuinely likes music?"

"She does." Blair debated about taking the chair near the bed. It would be more comfortable for both of them, but he didn't want to encourage the conversation to go on for any length. "I'm not certain how it happened, but I'm looking forward to spending the rest of my life with her. Just one problem."

"Forebridge?" Hamish waved a hand at the chair. "Sit down, man. I'm getting a crick in my neck."

"You missed the bit at supper where he and Father clashed," Blair said as he took the seat. "Worse, Father snapped at him."

He did not miss Hamish's wince as he continued. "Forebridge seems to be acting as if he's doing us a favor by offering an alliance with his family. It's beginning to annoy Father."

"I thought he wanted the girl married off as quickly as possible because of all the rumors."

"He does, but he doesn't want to pay for the privilege. He's trying to take advantage of Father's worry. Augusta fears he'll pull out if he doesn't get everything he wants."

Hamish scowled. "Not what you want, if you've grown fond of the girl." He paused. "You called her Augusta, not Miss Eastleigh."

Blair started. "I...I didn't realize I had."

But he had called her such and the name had come easily to his lips. Was fondness becoming something else without his realizing?

He looked back to Hamish, who smiled. "Best talk to Father, encourage him to give a bit more. Remind him if you marry now, he could welcome a grandchild come spring." Hamish sighed. "With that, I should say goodnight. I'll wager Mrs. Petherbridge will be in any moment and let me know I am exerting too much energy."

"She takes fine care of you."

"Aye, that she does." Hamish shifted, grimacing at the effort. "Obviously of good breeding. Wonder where the doctor found her."

"Perhaps you should ask the next time he's here." Blair rose. "Lady Eastleigh and Augusta do hope to come visit if you can sit in the garden and your dragon allows it."

The sound of chuckling, even weak, sounded good in Blair's ears as he left. Hamish had given him much to chew on and given him a question which needed answering. What lengths was he willing to go to secure Augusta as his bride?

CHAPTER 19

Unlike last time, the note asking Blair to visit Simon was a plea, not a demand. *I need to speak with you as soon as possible. I need your advice.*

He and Simon had been on better terms of late, the rift in their relationship nearly repaired, but this was somewhat unexpected, delivered before Blair finished dressing for the morning. "The servant who delivered it stressed the urgency of the request," the butler said, as Blair scanned the lines again. "He is to return with word as to whether you will come."

The clock had not yet struck ten and most of the house would not be up yet. He wanted to speak with his father early, but something warned his attention was needed elsewhere. "Tell him I'll visit Lord Chalton as soon as I am presentable."

The butler bowed and departed. "So, it is to be a plain neckcloth, my lord?" Blair's man asked.

"Plain neckcloth and plain jacket. Simon isn't one to panic, so whatever he needs must be urgent. Tell my father I wish to speak to him when I return.

He was out of the door not fifteen minutes later, a tribute to his valet's efficiency when necessary. A brisk and brief walk to the Chalton townhouse, his mood much different from his last trip visit.

Whatever Simon wanted, it wasn't to read Blair the riot act this time. Upon his arrival, he was sent upstairs immediately, straight to Simon's chambers. Now he was beginning to worry. He expected the conversation to take place in the drawing room or where Simon did his business. Even among close friends, being sent to directly to the earl's chamber was not the norm.

"I'll need the black jacket," Simon was saying as Blair entered. "Not the evening one, but the one for church."

Simon's valet, looking more than a little harried, nodded, putting one jacket down and holding another up for his master's approval. Once Simon gave him the nod, he carried it to where a pair of saddlebags waiting and began carefully rolling it. Simon turned toward the collection of neck clothes he was considering, stopping as he realized Blair had arrive. "You're here. How is Hamish doing after your party last night?"

Not the expected greeting. "Tired, last I saw him. I think it may have almost been too much. He was in better spirits and glad of the chance to meet Augusta. Yes, I realize I'm using her name," Blair said at Simon's grin.

"Which is a good thing to hear. Hold on to that. No, I don't think I'll need that. Remember, I'm trying to pack light."

This last was addressed to his valet. "What is going on?" Blair asked. "Your note—"

"Said absolutely nothing. I received an express late last night. Mark Weir died. Fairly suddenly, from what I understand. Grandmother didn't specify. If I leave today and ride hard, I can make the funeral."

Hence the packing and the saddlebags. Eleanor Shelby a widow. A possibility Blair hadn't imagined. "You're not going to do some damn fool thing such as throw yourself at her feet in the middle of the church and declare your eternal devotion, are you?"

Simon managed a rueful smile. "Not such a damn fool as that. I should be with her at this time, to offer comfort at the very least."

You want to see if she shows any affection towards you. Blair knew how his friend's mind worked and he knew no other way to prevent Simon from making a damn fool of himself except by getting on a horse and going with him. There was no question of him doing that, not at this moment. "You know Lady Eastleigh will be upset when she learns. I think she's still hoping."

"Lady Eastleigh must learn to live with disappointment." Simon handed his valet the pile of neckcloths. "Yes, I understand they'll wrinkle in the bag. I'll be in the country, not holding up London standards. I am worried about Miss Eastleigh. Forebridge will be gleeful, I'm afraid. Which is likely to provoke Lady Eastleigh into some new scheme. The two of you appear to be getting along better. Are you willing to marry Miss Eastleigh quickly?"

"I am, but I'm not always certain Forebridge is. Father feels he's being unreasonable, unwilling to make a respectable settlement. I'm going to try to grease the wheels somehow. You're right. This needs to be settled. Any word you would like me to take to them?"

"I wrote notes They should be delivered soon. No, this won't bring Lady Eastleigh joy, but it should clear the way for you." He reached out to clap Blair on the shoulder. "Give her my regrets, and thank Augusta for me. She's made the last few weeks much more pleasant."

"They'll ask when you're returning."

"No idea. You can tell them that. It all depends on what happens. I promise I'll be here to dance at your wedding." Simon took a deep breath. "I should finish this. It's going to be a long, hard ride."

Blair was about to bid him farewell, but stopped on the threshold when Simon asked, "You will take care of her, will you not?"

"I promise. Go. Learn if your lady love still cares."

With that, he departed, leaving Simon to finish his packing. This changed the game. With Simon gone from the board, there were no other candidates of rank, only outside chances and Mr. Wilverton. As long as Augusta was as willing as he, nothing should stand in their way.

Maybe this was going to be a good day after all.

"Damn and blast! Did you know anything about this?"

Augusta glanced up from her book, to find Lady Eastleigh

frowning at the note in her hand. "Lord Chalton is called away from London unexpectedly."

"Does he say why?" Augusta was a bit surprised at the pang she felt at the idea Simon wouldn't be present to dance and laugh with her, even as a friend, not suitor.

"No." Lady Eastleigh glanced at the paper in her hand. "He's not explicit about the reason, but he makes it clear that he expects to be gone for some time. He sent a note to you as well. I suppose that settles things, then. No hope he'll change his mind."

Putting her book aside, Augusta took the note her mother offered. "I told you; I don't want him to change his mind."

"I told you why I believe it a foolish thing to risk. What does he say?"

"Same as what he wrote to you, that he's been called away," Augusta said. "He might be back, before the end of the season, but he's not certain. The business is personal."

"Is that what he says or what you're willing to tell me?" As Augusta opened her mouth, Lady Eastleigh held up her hand. "Don't answer that. I suppose it doesn't matter. He's gone, and no proposal. What we need to now is find someone else who might be interested."

"There is someone who's interested," Augusta countered. "Lord Blair—"

"Is subject to whether or not his father can come to terms with the old goat. I'm not holding my breath. Since we shouldn't expect Lord Chalton back too soon—"

"Shouldn't expect who back too soon?"

Lady Eastleigh and Augusta stood as Forebridge spoke from the threshold of the room. "I heard your outburst, madam," he said, addressing Lady Eastleigh. "What social disaster have you brought down upon our heads with your cunning plans?"

"Lord Chalton wrote to inform us he is called away from London." Each word sounded as if it was pulled from her. "He doesn't say when he expects to return."

Forebridge appeared more amused by the news than annoyed. "That puts paid to your plans, doesn't it? Can't offer for Augusta if he's not actually here."

"He believed it important enough he write to tell us he would be gone," Lady Eastleigh countered. "Likely we know before the rest of London. He also wrote Augusta a note."

"He did, did he?" Forebridge's gaze turned toward Augusta. "What does he write, girl? Are there protestations of love, enough to justify your mother's hopes?"

"I—" Augusta found herself unsure how to describe the words Chalton had written. "He says he wanted me to learn of his absence from him, not from gossip."

Forebridge harumphed. "Does show some consideration. No hint that he expects to ask a certain question upon his return?"

She looked down at the sheet of paper once more, wondering how to convey what had been written. "He says he hopes to visit me soon," she took a breath, "And has asked Lord Blair to keep me company while he is gone."

The smirk on Forebridge's face did not bode well. "Doesn't sound as if Chalton's in any hurry to make a declaration. Perhaps your girl isn't as alluring as you thought. Though I heard rumor there is another gentleman sniffing about."

"No one you would deem suitable," Lady Eastleigh responded.

"You don't know who I might find suitable if Rutherglen won't budge," he snapped. "Perhaps you should take a lesson from your mother's book, girl, be friendly enough with Lord Blair that Rutherglen will find himself obliged to agree if he wants to avoid a scandal. It's how she caught my son."

Her father had once compared the young girls seeking husbands during the season to a horse auction. The analogy was very apt at the moment. "I will do what I can, sir."

The words were uttered in a flat tone. The idea he expected her to act the tart with Blair niggled at her, as if there was some hidden worm within the happiness she felt. It was an ugly sensation and she tried to push it away.

To her relief, Forebridge accepted her words and departed. "He's determined none of us should be happy," Lady Eastleigh hissed, when he was gone. "Do you understand now why I think we should try to find you another suitor, just in case? He'll sell you off to someone else if he doesn't get his way. You need another plan."

"Don't you worry you'll look desperate because of how much stock you were putting in a proposal from Lord Chalton? Won't that make Grandfather happy?"

"Who let me believe a proposal was coming?" Lady Eastleigh snapped in reply. The two stared at one another, resentment hanging between them. Then Lady Eastleigh offered up a resigned sigh. "You're right. But if I can find another suitor, you are to give him due consideration. Just in case."

"What if I am willing to do as you did and elope with Blair if he'll have me?"

"Are you sure he would be willing to do that, bring shame upon his family in such a way?" When Augusta didn't answer right away, Lady Eastleigh continued. "There would be scandal. You would be cut off from scandal, never mind Forebridge attempting to drag you back by the hair for daring to besmirch the family name. Your Aunt Susan, married to a clergyman? She still maintains only the most formal of contacts even after twenty years. Your father and I would be forced to disown you or be cut off. Think of your brother and sisters."

She paced away. "How Lord Rutherglen would react? He's willing to settle things on Blair now, but will he feel the same way after an elopement? Or would he want to keep Blair on a closer leash, even with the possibility any son you bear might be a future heir to the title? Yes, you prefer Lord Blair above all else, but you need to be practical. Or else you might discover yourself at the altar with someone such as Mr. Wilverton. He'll likely be willing to take you with a much smaller settlement that what Rutherglen's being offered. Don't you think your grandfather would jump for that?"

Closing the distance between them, Lady Eastleigh grasped Augusta's hands. "I'm just asking you to be practical and not put all your future hopes in his hands, because he does not have your best interests at heart."

There was nothing Augusta could say in response, except, "I will consider it."

Lady Eastleigh smiled. "That is all I ask at the moment." Dropping Augusta's hand, her manner became brisk. "Now, we must make ourselves ready for our calls. It is possible some will know of Lord Chalton's departure and we must be ready. Remember, he did write you, which shows concern. That is all anyone need know."

A gentle pat to Augusta's cheek and then she was shooed upstairs. Not for the first time, Augusta wished they were done with this.

CHAPTER 20

They were almost through afternoon calls when the hostess at their latest stop said, "I'm certain Lady Eastleigh knows the news. Can you offer us any details as to why Lord Chalton left London suddenly? From the gossip, he was seen riding fast and unaccompanied."

The drawing room fell silent as all eyes turned toward Augusta and her mother. Lady Eastleigh let her face adopt a mournful, expression. "He received word of a death close to his family. Not a relation, but a long-time friend. He left London to see what assistance he can offer." She looked at Augusta. "He did say he was attempting to be at the funeral did he not?"

Lady Eastleigh had managed to worm that information out of Augusta in the carriage, insisting she needed what details she could gather to battle the gossip that would surely arise. "He did," Augusta replied, unwilling to offer more. If her mother wished to embellish, let it be on her head.

Embellish she did. "Hence the need for speed. Nor does he know how long he'll be gone from London, though he did take time to write both Augusta and I notes to let us know of his absence and that he hoped to see us again on his return. I imagine he'll be back in London for the Regent's Fete in six weeks."

Sympathetic noises were offered all around as the conversation turned to other topics. Lady Eastleigh looked a bit smug, especially when one of the gentleman present found an excuse to come sit next to them. In one stroke, she reaffirmed Chalton's interest in Augusta by the sending of personal notes but left the field open because of his absence. Save for the fact Augusta now found herself obliged to be polite to a gentleman she had no interest in, she would applaud her mother's skill.

Their time was thankfully up soon, allowing them to escape the gentleman and further talk. "On to the Careys and then Lady Watling. I think that should be enough for today," Lady Eastleigh said once they were in the carriage. "Do try to rest when we return home. You need to appear fresh this evening."

"I know you think this is helping," Augusta began, only to stop as her mother turned steely eyes on her.

"I'm trying to protect your future. I believe when your grandfather entered into negotiations with Lord Rutherglen, he did not under-stand how ill Lord Hamish was. He would like you married off in a way that did not embarrass the family, but do not think for a moment he wishes to see you in an elevated position."

She leaned back against the cushions. "Do you really want to be an object of derision and pity because the man you hoped would propose left town suddenly? He sent you a note, which speaks of consideration, even if he doesn't plan to make you his wife. I think you do not understand how much appearance counts for within the Ton, how much currency it holds. I learned those lessons the hard way, and it is my fault for not passing them on as I should."

She paused. "Does Lord Blair know Lord Chalton does not intend to propose?"

"Yes," Augusta said, remembering those somewhat painful conver-sations.

"Does Lord Rutherglen?"

Augusta shook her head. "I believe Blair told him he's willing to go through with the match."

"That much was obvious from the party. That was his father intro-ducing you to his circle. Did you just not use his title?" Lady Eastleigh sighed. "Be careful not to do that around others. It speaks of an intimacy that we don't necessarily want made public. It will cause gossip, and that will just make a certain person angry. He hates gossip about the family, though he's more than happy to share in it about others."

As they arrived at their next stop, Augusta wondered when she dropped the honorific Blair bore as the son of a marquess. Chalton, for all their easy friendship, had never been more than Lord Chalton.

This had become such a mess. She could only hope Blair had good news for her when they saw one another next.

The news of Chalton's departure had spread, given the number of gentlemen approaching that evening whom Augusta had not seen for several weeks. Tonight, she found herself at no loss for partners. Worse, the sitting at the House of Commons was running late, which meant Blair was not present at first. So she smiled and danced, and watched the door, hoping each new arrival might be him.

When Wilverton appeared before him, the only comfort she took was the possibility his presence might signal Blair was on the way. What was unpleasant was when he managed to catch her at a moment between the dances when Lady Eastleigh's attention was elsewhere. "We've not had a chance to speak to speak for some while, Miss Eastleigh."

"Yes. The House is done sitting? Was Lord Blair there?"

Wilverton's face darkened. "He was, looking most somber. I hear rumors of some difficulty between his father and Lord Forebridge in the matter of settlements."

He stepped closer. "I understand you must bow to the requirements of your elders, but please be comforted if Lord Forebridge cannot reach an accommodation, I am still interested in an alliance."

Had he not listened the last time they spoke? Had he not noticed he was told they were not at home each time he called, even as others were admitted? Or was it that, having fixed his sights on her, her wishes did not matter? In that instant, he reminded her of Forebridge, and she had no desire to be matched with her grandfather. "I am sorry for you, sir, for I have no interest at all. Excuse me."

Without waiting for a response, she turned and walked away, heading for the only place a young lady could safely escape a suitor: the retiring room. Once inside the precincts, she asked the waiting maid for a cool cloth, a request likely all too frequent that evening. With cloth in hand, she applied it to the back of her neck, hoping to slow her breathing.

She shouldn't be surprised. Not after months of increasingly terse hints that had been ignored. Somehow, Charles Wilverton had fixated on her as low-hanging fruit which could serve him well. Not until a match was safely made would he search elsewhere, though she doubted any young lady of good family would be eager to be treated in such a way. She hoped Blair had had a chance to speak with his father, so this matter might be settled.

"There you are, you little baggage."

Mrs. Hibbert's voice was unmistakable, causing Augusta to sigh as she turned. Mrs. Hibbert in here and Wilverton possibly waiting outside. *This is not my evening.* "How may I help you, madam?" she said, offering a respectable curtsey.

Always florid, Mrs. Hibbert's complexion held a darker hue that hinted at either rage or apoplexy. "Don't play coy with me. I want answers. What did you do to drive Lord Chalton from London?"

"I did not drive him from London. He departed on family business.

Mrs. Hibbert snorted. "So convenient the only two who tell such a story are yourself and your mother."

"Mama," the younger Miss Hibbert reached out a hand as if to calm her mother somehow. The elder daughter was not in evidence, either dancing or not yet recovered socially from her attempt to trap Chalton.

"Lord Chalton was kind enough to write me a note. Please excuse me."

She stepped forward, only to find herself pushed back with enough force she stumbled and found herself sitting ungracefully on the couch. "You're not going anywhere, you strumpet. Not until I make certain you understand you are going to stay away from Lord

Chalton in the future. He is marked for my eldest and neither you nor your harlot mother are going to stand in my way!"

"If you're going to call me a harlot, please have the courtesy to do it to my face."

Mrs. Hibbert spun at the sound of Lady Eastleigh's voice. "I have no difficulty with that, madam."

At this moment, Lady Eastleigh's walk was not the elegant glide she usually used in the ballroom, but firmer and somewhat menacing as she advanced on Mrs. Hibbert. "I was the one who encouraged Lord Chalton in his attentions, so your quarrel is with me. The choice is ultimately his. That he chooses not to associate with you only shows his taste."

"Best you ensure your spawn stays out of my way. Which I suspect she won't. After all, I imagine you tutored her in all your ways."

"Shouldn't we be getting back to the dance?" Augusta asked, hoping to avoid the confrontation she knew was coming.

At the same moment, the younger Miss Hibbert plucked at her mother's arm once more. "Mama, please. Let us go."

Neither woman acknowledged their daughters' pleas. Worse, Lady Eastleigh's eyes had narrowed, never a good sign. "Say what you will about me. I've heard it all through the years. Your dull tongue is not quick enough to strike a wounding blow. Say anything against my daughter, touch her again as you did just a moment ago, and I will show you what I am made of. Do I make myself clear?"

She fixed Mrs. Hibbert with a deadly glare, not moving until the woman flinched beneath it. Then she turned to Augusta, her tone now solicitous. "Yes, we should return. Gentlemen are waiting to speak with you, unlike some ladies I could name."

The implication was clear, and Mrs. Hibbert drew herself up. For a moment, Augusta feared there would be another attack, but she turned on her heel and stomped away. Miss Hibbert did not follow immediately but dropped a curtsey. "I am sorry, Lady Eastleigh. My mother didn't mean it. Well, she did mean it, but she didn't mean to—"

"Annis! Come here!"

At her mother's voice, Miss Hibbert dropped another curtsey and hurried away. Lady Eastleigh shook her head. "Poor girl. Bad enough to have Mrs. Hibbert as a mother, but Annis? What a name to be saddled with."

She turned back to Augusta. "She didn't hurt you, did she?"

Augusta shook her head. "I was more surprised than anything. Mother. Are you certain she won't make more trouble?"

"As her eldest daughter finds a number of doors closed because of her behavior, I imagine she'll try to avoid any public displays." She held out a hand to help Augusta up. "Only one thing could make me feel worse about Lord Chalton deciding not to propose. That would be if he were fool enough to decide he was going to marry one of that silly woman's daughters. Now, Lord Blair has arrived, best return to the dance. There are other gentlemen who are disappointed with your absence. It is proof you are esteemed by them, and we can use that in your favor with your grandfather."

Can anything be used in my favor with him? Augusta didn't voice the thought, but it rang loud inside her head as they made their way back to the main salon. Blair was waiting, looking nowhere near as solemn as Wilverton had implied. Not that she expected him to. Nor did she argue when her mother ensured he would enjoy her next dance. "Would you rather talk or dance?" she asked as they moved away from her mother.

"Talk," Blair confessed. "We haven't had as much of a chance as I would have liked the last time we saw one another."

"It was a musical evening. We were supposed to listen, not speak."

He chuckled. "You always manage to puncture my expectations." He glanced about. "This way."

Swiftly, he moved her out of the room into the hallway. There were alcoves here, one tucked under the staircase as it curved upward, complete with a small couch. A screen half-shielded it from general view, but not completely. "We are not so secluded we can risk improper behavior," Blair said, "but we can talk without too much interruption."

As they settled on the cushions, the instruction from Forebridge to do what was necessary to ensure Blair was compelled to marry her flashed through Augusta's brain. "We shouldn't," she said abruptly, standing once more.

Before she could move away, Blair caught her hand. "What's wrong?

She looked down at him and wondered how much she should say. She could claim she did not wish to be the object of even more gossip, but that wasn't the truth. At least, not the whole truth. "Grandfather suggested I try to put you in a position where you were obliged to marry me. He," she swallowed and tried again, "he said I should understand because I'm my mother's daughter."

Her reward was a dark frown. "Your grandfather's an ass. Sit down." When she didn't, he said, "I'm not angry with you, Augusta. If you planned on doing such a thing, you wouldn't give me warning."

Another gentle tug on her hand. "Sit down. Please."

As she did, Blair said, "It shows me he isn't willing to move in what he's willing to give, and he'll resort to underhanded trickery to get his way. Nor does he care what it might mean to you."

"I don't want you to be angry," Augusta said. I don't want you wasting your time thinking about him. One thing, though."

"What is that?"

She let her hand slide forward to rest on his arm. "Living down to his expectations almost gives me permission to do what I want to do."

"What do you want to do," he asked, his voice softer now.

"This."

With that, she leaned forward to kiss him.

Kissing Blair was easier than Augusta expected. In fact, it felt rather natural, like falling into a soft feather bed. She didn't expect a feather bed to make her tingly, or anxious for more. Blair's arms wrapped around her, pulling her close, meeting her lips with more force than she had expected.

He was warm and strong, and she was comforted within the circle of his arms. This was more than she meant to do, but it was as if a natural fit existed between the two of them. "Augusta," he murmured, the words vibrating against her lips before kissing her again.

Oh, yes. In this instant, she understood why her parents were frequently caught kissing one another if it was as wonderful as this.

They also couldn't go on forever and when he pulled back, she knew a combination of loss and a need to pull more air into her lungs. "You're not marrying anyone but me," Blair said, his voice hoarse.

"I don't plan to."

With that, she kissed him again, in this moment not caring if anyone caught them. If they were, so be it. A quick marriage and they'd be together and—

She pulled back as another stray thought crossed her mind. "We shouldn't. I mean, we shouldn't be seen."

"Because it's what your grandfather wanted you to do?"

"Because he would be glad I settled the issue and despise me at the same time, think me unworthy."

The implications sank in and Blair nodded. "We don't need any more trouble with him."

He helped her to her feet, then pulled her close once more. "There will be a day soon when I will kiss you for all the world to see and I won't care what anyone thinks."

The words brought a smile to Augusta's lips. "I look forward to that day. And your father?"

"Don't worry. My father and I are going to have a long talk about this. I planned to today, but with Simon leaving—"

"He's going after the woman he couldn't marry?" she asked as they made their way back into the salon.

"I'm not certain it's the right thing to do, but, yes. Hopefully, he'll only offer his sympathy and renew the connection. I'm worried he'll do something foolish."

"That was why he said he couldn't ask Father for my hand," Augusta said. "He said he still loved her. I'm starting to understand."

He stopped for a moment, they were in a crowd now, but his voice was low, his eyes focused on her. "We are not like Simon and Eleanor. There is no relative who is determined to keep us from marrying at any cost. Simon's father was so determined his would marry a woman 'worthy of his station,' he didn't care what it did to his son. I strongly suspect it was the late Earl of Chalton who engineered Eleanor Shelby's marriage to Mark Weir. It happened quickly and was clearly designed to remove her from Simon's path."

Augusta couldn't help the shudder which rippled through her body. "I think I might feel more kinship with her than you would imagine."

"It. Won't. Happen. To. Us." His tone was firm. "I'll speak with Father, make certain he understands how much I want this."

He looked out across the room. "We should return to your mother. She's watching us."

The trip back was short, shorter than she would like, given the look she received from her mother. Blair bowed over Lady Eastleigh's hand, asked for her indulgence in a second dance that evening, and the pleasure of sitting with them at supper. Lady Eastleigh agreed to all these things, but the moment he excused himself to speak with another gentleman, she said in a quiet voice. "I'm not going to ask any questions because what I don't know, I can't accidentally tell. But be careful, Goose. Don't let yourself get in too deep. Not until things are settled."

"I understand, Mother. I won't." Even as she said the words, Augusta couldn't help wondering what she would have done if given half a chance.

CHAPTER 21

Blair was in a fine mood as he climbed the stairs to the Forebridge Townhouse. The ladies of the family were officially At Home this afternoon, and he planned to take the opportunity to let Augusta know his father had promised to do his best to get the agreement pushed through.

He wouldn't mention Rutherglen warned he would make no promises, preoccupied with Hamish and the fever he developed during the night. It was mild, but a warning the infection was getting worse. The doctor had assured the rest of the family his remedies would help Hamish make it through, but seeing the concern on Mrs. Petherbridge's face, he wasn't so certain. Another reason for this all to be done.

The butler took his hat and cane and indicated the way to the drawing room. This time, he saw no sign of Forebridge lurking. Blair was of two minds about that. He didn't particularly care for the idea of the man looming over the proceedings like a black crow, but he wondered if the chance for conversation might be of some use.

Stepping into the drawing room, he discovered a number of women present. They all looked at him. "Lord Blair," Lady Eastleigh said, all cordiality. "So kind of you to visit. Augusta, will you greet Lord Blair?"

Augusta rose and made her curtsey, then indicated he should take the chair next to her. Blair did so gladly, saying, "I didn't expect you would enjoy so many visitors this afternoon."

"They want to know more about Lord Chalton. A few formal notes were delivered to hostesses saying he was called away on business, but only Mother and I received ones of any substance it seems."

"I think you were the one he worried about. He said he hoped his absence wouldn't cause you difficulty. He also—"

"Lord Blair, can you give us any details about Lord Chalton's departure?" The speaker was an aged dowager sitting not far from them. "I know what Lady Eastleigh and Miss Eastleigh tell us, but as you and he are friends, surely you can offer us more."

He didn't think the word he muttered under his breath reached anyone, but there was mischievous amusement in Augusta's eyes as he turned to address the dowager. "Only that his business was personal, came up most unexpectedly, and he is unsure if he will be away from London for a week or maybe two. It depends on what is required."

The words seemed to satisfy the woman and she returned to her previous conversation, old heads bending close to one another. "If Simon doesn't step carefully," Blair said, turning back to Augusta, "he'll be back in London with his tail between his legs."

He looked her in the eye. "I worry that if he thinks his hopes are lost, he may regret his choice to not speak with your father. I spoke with mine, and he says he will do his best to—"

Blair stopped as the butler announced, "Mr. Charles Wilverton."

The unhappiness was clear on Augusta's face, just as she threw a glance to her mother. Lady Eastleigh did not look happy, and it was likely someone would be spoken to in most severe tones once the guests departed. At the moment, though, she could do nothing without causing talk. A fixed social smile graced her face, polite, but not welcoming as Wilverton approached and offered her a slight bow. "A pleasure to see you again, Lady Eastleigh," he said. "Good to greet this charming company as well."

A few appreciative murmurs from a few of the older ladies, other smiles were not so kind and snickers partially hidden by hands. One corner of Lady Eastleigh's mouth twitched. "It would not be an afternoon to receive visitors if you did not present yourself, Mr. Wilverton. Won't you have a seat?"

She indicated the seat next to her, an honor for a visitor of relatively modest rank. Which also had the advantage of being a distance from Augusta. He ignored the gesture and took the chair on Augusta's other side instead. "I will forgive you for your words the other evening, Miss Eastleigh."

"I do not recall asking for forgiveness, Mr. Wilverton. I wanted to make my position clear due to the misunderstanding on your part. Again."

The rude snort escaped Blair despite his best effort. She did sound a bit like her mother. Cool, collected, and determined not to be cowed by a gentleman who tried the last edge of her patience.

Wilverton's eyes narrowed as he was forced to acknowledge Blair's presence. "Lord Blair."

"Wilverton."

Augusta rolled her eyes, but said, "Lord Blair and I were discussing the opera. Apparently, the company will be doing a production of Der Zauberflöte soon, which sounds most exciting. Do you enjoy opera, Mr. Wilverton?"

That he didn't was obvious from the sour expression on his face before he spoke. "Gentlemen usually attend the opera for the dancers on display in the ballets. Not exactly the place I would think respectable women would want to be seen."

"There are any number of respectable women who attend the opera," Blair said, rising to the implied criticism. "In the boxes, of course. The demi-monde hold sway in the orchestra. The two do not mix."

A sniff from Wilverton. "I do not believe I would allow a wife of mine, nor any well-brought up young lady, to expose herself in such a manner. I'm certain your grandfather would not approve, Miss Eastleigh."

"Lord Forebridge enjoyed himself when Lord Rutherglen invited us to join him in his box. He didn't behave as if he found anything inappropriate about the evening at all."

Wilverton's smile became fixed. "He didn't?"

"No." She turned and smiled at Blair. "I'm certain he will appreciate the invitation to join your family when *Der Zauberflöte* begins. Can we hope your brother, Lord Hamish, will be well enough to join us?"

"Unfortunately, I think Mozart would be a bit taxing for him. It is somewhat long."

"A pity. I was hoping you would have good news. Perhaps your sisters will be present."

Somehow, Augusta had managed to turn her back almost completely on Wilverton, effectively cutting him, her distaste clear to any who watched. Unfortunately, etiquette would demand Blair's departure before him, though he wondered how long Lady Eastleigh would allow him to extend. She did seem more friendly these days, though he did not put too much faith in such appearances.

"Lord Cardenly," The butler announced signaling another arrival.

That Lady Eastleigh greeted the gentlemen with a warm smile was not lost on anyone. "Lord Cardenly, you naughty, naughty man. It has been far too long since you crossed our threshold."

"Not my intention, Lady Eastleigh, but things kept me occupied. Horseflesh is damn unpredictable. I beg your pardon," he amended with a smile that said his intent had been to shock as the ladies present tittered slightly. "Having dealt with it, I'm able to once again pay the calls I would like to pay."

He turned around and smiled at Augusta. "Here is your charming daughter. I hope I can claim a dance when next we meet on an evening."

"It would be my pleasure." What else could she say to such a public request. Now the gossips would set to buzzing with the news of a competitor for Lord Chalton and Lord Blair's place in her affections. Just perfect.

Having made his address, he took a place near Lady Eastleigh, listening attentively to her conversation. Augusta turned toward Blair, intent on picking up the threads of her conversation again, but she'd barely begun when Lady Eastleigh called, "Augusta, please come join us. I think Lord Cardenly would enjoy hearing your description of the music we heard the other evening."

Augusta hesitated, but Blair knew she couldn't refuse her mother's request. Still, she didn't move.

"Augusta." Her name was said sweetly, but firmly. There was no doubting the note of steel underneath. Not request, but a command.

She took the seat beside Lord Cardenly. "I look forward to hearing you description," he said, smiling at her.

Blair couldn't believe it. Even as he pushed his father to give in to Forebridge's demands, Lady Eastleigh was still chasing a rich man in possession of his fortune, no third son. Was she pursuing Cardenly or was he a distraction of some kind? Only time would tell.

According to the clock on the mantel, his time was almost up.

CHAPTER 22

"I see you find no more favor with our hostess than I do," Wilverton said, leaning in.

"It's not a matter I wish to discuss," Blair replied stiffly.

That should put the matter to rest, but Wilverton, as usual, didn't take the hint. "There's much you won't be able to discuss. Lady Eastleigh's against you marrying her daughter. That means she'll make certain Lord Eastleigh is never available for you to speak with."

"I've had a number of discussions with Lord Eastleigh." Blair's tone was cold. Perhaps he should bid his hostess farewell now. It would get him away from Wilverton.

"I have as well," Wilverton countered. "Quite amiably when we meet at some social gathering. The moment I wish a more private interview, however, he's suddenly unavailable."

When Blair didn't respond immediately, Wilverton leaned forward. "If she has her way, you'll never get your interview, because the surest way to ensure Eastleigh isn't obliged to consider your offer is to ensure you never make your offer."

It really wouldn't do to bloody the man's nose in the middle of the drawing room. Still his hands curled into fists as Wilverton leaned back with a bit of a smug smile. "A cunning man might bypass the father and go to the purse strings. After all, Forebridge is the one who—"

The words shut off abruptly. For a moment, the man sat, lips pursed, then, he rose to his feet. "I'm afraid my time is up, Lady Eastleigh, and I must depart. I hope that I will see you soon, and, of course, Miss Eastleigh."

With that, he bowed and departed. Lady Eastleigh had smiled appropriately while he spoke, but the moment his back was turned, she looked more unsettled, as if something in his manner signaled some type of change. After a moment, though, the hostess returned, leaning in to acknowledge a remark Cardenly addressed in her direction.

With a sigh, Blair rose to make his own farewell, knowing little could be accomplished here, even if Augusta looked in need of rescue. There was no rescue he might affect, though, and he soon found himself on the sidewalk once more.

He should ignore Wilverton's words, but they pricked at him. Unsurprising Eastleigh had avoided an interview with the man. Augusta had made her disinterest clear, yet he continued in pursuit for some reason. It couldn't be in hope of a rich settlement, given how little Forebridge wished to settle on her in his talks with Rutherglen.

As much as he wanted to discount it, he didn't trust Wilverton not to go to Forebridge and make his case. If an agreement had not been reached by the time he did, Blair didn't trust Forebridge to make the leap in an effort to rid himself of Augusta.

He needed those negotiations settled, then they could relax. At least, Blair tried to tell himself that as he strolled away.

Standing in yet another assembly room, feeling more than a little warm, Augusta did her best to smile at Lord Cardenly. He flirted, but with more than a hint of naughtiness underneath, the type of naughtiness Viscount Tilney had tried on her earlier in the season.

He might be saying all the right things to her mother, but Augusta doubted his interest in anything beyond amusement. The "accidental" touches to her arm told her that. Once the music began and they were out on the dance floor, she wagered the "accidents" would increase. Too much, she might be forced to trod on his toes. Then speak bluntly with her mother, let her know Cardenly should not be considered a viable option.

"I will claim at least one dance," Cardenly said. "Though perhaps not the first one. Later in the evening, there will be more chance to linger and speak with you."

Again, Augusta did her best to smile, though it seemed stretched and false. He sounded confident, as if he didn't expect opposition from her or competition from anyone else. Certainly not Wilverton, who approached to bow first to Lady Eastleigh. "It wouldn't be an evening's amusement if you did not appear, I suppose," she said dryly. "You are as dependable as ants at a picnic."

He ignored the thinly veiled insult, looking a bit smug. "What type of suitor would I be if I didn't come to claim a dance from my lady fair?"

Turning, he bowed to Augusta. A pause and then he bowed again. "Lord Cardenly."

Cardenly barely acknowledged him before turning back to Augusta. "The supper dance, perhaps? With a promenade after? It will give us so much time to speak together."

The last thing she wanted. "I must seek Mother's permission, of course," she replied demurely. "I am not certain she will agree to a promenade."

She said the words loud enough her mother was certain to hear. Given the way her head tilted, Lady Eastleigh listened to every word.

"I had intended to claim the supper dance," Wilverton said, a petulant note creeping in.

"Afraid you're too late, old man." Cardenly flicked a piece of lint from his jacket. "I asked first."

The smugness faded from Wilverton's face, replaced by an unpleasant annoyance. "Tonight, perhaps. I anticipate a meeting with the Earl of Forebridge which will change many things."

He what? Augusta's attention now focused on Wilverton as Cardenly shrugged and said, "Of no matter to me. I'm more occupied with securing the lady's company this evening. Tomorrow can handle itself."

Further proof Cardenly's attentions were not sincere, but not why she wanted to drag her mother away for a private conversation. Only, where? It was early enough in the evening the retiring room would be filled with young women making last-minute adjustments to their toilettes, which would not allow for conversation one didn't want overheard. Nor could she leave at the moment, not with Blair coming across the floor toward her.

He acted as if Cardenly and Wilverton were invisible as he made his bow. "Good evening, Lady Eastleigh. Miss Eastleigh. "Do I dare hope at least some of your dances are still free?"

"Augusta saved the supper dance for you," Lady Eastleigh said. "She has been too polite to tell these gentlemen outright without your presence, but I know she anticipated your arrival."

They were almost the same words used the night Augusta and Blair had met. Funny to remember how her mother had done her best to ignore him in favor of Chalton. Funny to find herself smiling warmly at him and saying, "My mother is not exaggerating. I hoped you would ask for the supper dance."

A noise of exasperation from Wilverton as Blair said, "As I hoped you would agree. I am told a German Waltz is intended for later in the evening. Might I partner you for that?"

Given the intimacy of the dance, which was the talk of society, Augusta eagerly agreed. She didn't worry making her preferences known now with Blair present. The idea of being in his arms in the middle of the dance floor was irresistible. Even if she felt unsure of the steps.

"Having settled that," Lady Eastleigh said, "I think it best if Augusta and I retire briefly before the dancing starts. I promise we shall return shortly."

Her mother's grip on her arm was firm, steering her firmly away before she could protest. "I thought you agreed you would offer Lord Cardenly at least some encouragement."

"He's not genuine in his attentions. At least, not any honorable attentions. He's been touching my arm frequently."

"Forward but does show a certain amount of interest." For all her mother's casual tone, a certain concern appeared in her eyes.

"And manages to 'accidentally' brush his hand against my breast when he does so."

"Damn. I hoped. You'll tolerate him this evening, but best we limit him to a country dance. Most definitely no promenade. One thing when Blair MacDonald attempts to drag you into a quiet corner. We know his intentions to be honorable."

Lady Eastleigh sighed. "You're risking everything on this match coming off."

"Did you not risk everything when you eloped with Father? What if Grandfather had caught you and dragged him back?"

A shudder. "I don't want to think about it. My reputation would be ruined, and that man would do everything he could to blacken it further out of spite. This is why I worry. Your future is in his hands, in the settlement he's willing to make out of the estate. I heard Mr. Wilverton say he's applied for an interview with your grandfather. Another thing to worry about."

Lady Eastleigh pulled her to one side in the hall, away from the other guests who were arriving and circulating. "Do you think Grandfather would stop the negotiations with Lord Rutherglen in favor of him?"

"If he were angry enough, perhaps." Lady Eastleigh shook her head. "We must rely upon the fact Forebridge is an incurable snob. Mr. Wilverton is a minor member of Commons, with no land or fortune of his own. While it would be a great step up for him, it would be most assuredly a step down for you and some would say it'd reflect badly upon the family. Your grandfather might not receive him, anyway. At least, I hope not."

"Mother—"

"All we can do at this moment is hope, Augusta. This is the curse of being a woman. Try as we might to shape our future, they lie in the hands of the men around us and all we can do is influence, convince, and hope." She smiled. "Perhaps it is best if you suggest to Lord Blair he seek an interview with Lord Forebridge himself. Show him the seriousness of his intent. That might do much to help things along."

It was unlike her mother to admit to any type of helplessness. All she could do was agree and follow when Lady Eastleigh suggested they return to the ballroom.

It only took a moment following Augusta and Lady Eastleigh's departure for Wilverton to draw himself up self-importantly in Cardenly's direction. "I'll have you know, sir, an understanding exists between myself and the young lady."

Cardenly deigned to lift an eyebrow. "Strange. I had heard negotiations were ongoing between Lord Forebridge and Lord Rutherglen, though no settlement reached yet." He turned to Blair. "Is that true, sir?"

"We are hoping to conclude them within the week," Blair said. *He* hoped they would, but no need address the details. "Once that is done, the banns should be cried directly."

"The family knows I wish to ask Lord Eastleigh for permission to make my addresses directly to Miss Eastleigh." Wilverton almost sputtered the words. "I just need to obtain an interview."

Blair knew he shouldn't, but he couldn't resist saying, "Which you are unable to do. You said yourself he's been actively avoiding you. I take that as a sign the man isn't interested in giving you his daughter's hand."

Cardenly snickered, not bothering to hide his amusement. Wilverton shot him a dirty look, but his worst was reserved for Blair. "You don't seem to be faring much better, sir. I saw how eagerly Lady Eastleigh pulled Miss Eastleigh away from you when she thought a bigger prize dangled."

"You know damn little about me, sir. Or my relationship with the Eastleighs. I'll thank you not to be so free in discussing the lady. Or implying you enjoy some claim on her."

"One might say the same of you. Everyone knew it was Lord Chalton who was the prize. Now that he's gone, she's searching in greener fields."

Another glare at Cardenly, who did not wither beneath it. Frustrated, Wilverton turned back to Blair. "Expect an announcement in the next few days. After that, I will have a say in whom Miss Eastleigh consorts with, and I can assure you neither of you gentlemen will be included in that circle."

"I imagine Lady Eastleigh will have something to say about that."

"Not if I have my way. She's not the best of influences, is she? She'll lead her daughter into scandal without a restraining hand."

Blair stepped forward at that, closer than socially polite. "Again, I warn you as to how you speak about a lady. One could take offense."

"As amusing as that might be to watch," Cardenly said, stepping forward and inserting his arm between the two men, forcing both of them to step back, "I doubt our hostess would appreciate a brawl breaking out as an adjunct to the evening's entertainment."

He nodded toward the door which led out to the retiring room. "Not to mention, Lady Eastleigh and Miss Eastleigh are returning and I doubt it would help your cause."

Realizing Cardenly was correct in his assumption, Blair stepped back without a word. Wilverton looked as if he had something he wanted to say, but he bit off the words in favor of plastering a smile on his face as Augusta and her mother approached. They were smiling, but something was not right about it all. What had their conversation been?

Probably maneuvering Augusta into agreeing to pursue Cardenly.

The words slid into his brain like a black fog. One thing he did agree with Wilverton on: Augusta would do much better when she had space away from her family. Lady Eastleigh had her daughter's best interest at heart, but did she understand what her daughter wanted?

"I believe we were discussing the supper dance," Wilverton said once the ladies were close enough for conversation.

"Which Augusta promised to Lord Blair," Lady Eastleigh said briskly. "You were there for that portion of the conversation. Nor do I believe any appointments you may or may not expect give you any prior claim over the gentleman."

Wilverton opened his mouth to argue, but Lady Eastleigh continued. "What's more, I'm afraid my daughter will be unable to dance with you at all this evening. Her time is promised elsewhere. Perhaps your time would best be used finding another lady to partner."

There was the formal refusal, the bald statement she would not accept the man as a suitor for Augusta's hand. Bald enough that even Wilverton seemed to recognize it. Cardenly's snicker likely helped drive the point home. Face flushing, he straightened himself. "I see. I will go, but I'm certain we will be dancing to a different tune soon."

With that, he offered a curt bow and marched away. Looking amused, Cardenly offered his own bow. "Until later?" he said and wandered away.

"Mr. Wilverton's a demented fool if he thinks anyone in my family is going to be anything more than civil to him," Lady Eastleigh muttered darkly. Then, she centered herself and asked, "How is Lord Hamish? Better than when last we spoke, I hope?"

Blair chose not to comment on the change in affect. "There are some concerns, but he was greatly cheered by the evening. Father suggested perhaps something more intimate, your family and ours. A small dinner and then a show of our musical talents. I'm told I'm an expert at turning pages."

He said the words to Lady Eastleigh, but was relieved when Augusta's face lightened at the joke. "I think that would be a wonderful idea," Lady Eastleigh said. "Now, since it is such a warm evening, would you do me the favor of escorting Augusta in search of a breeze. There are some people I should speak to."

Time alone with Augusta? Blair did not object and offered her his arm. As she took it and they moved away, he asked in a low voice, "How serious is your mother about Cardenly?"

CHAPTER 23

Cardenly? Wilverton had been insisting he was going to upset everyone's plans once he spoke with Forebridge and Blair was upset about Cardenly? "My mother is worried about the negotiations. Grandfather said something which hinted he might search elsewhere if he didn't get what he wanted. She thought I needed an alternative just in case."

"But Cardenly? I doubt the man is interested in finding a wife. She might make demands on him for small things, such as food and clothing. Make him choose between his horses and a wife, and he'll choose his horses any day."

"I didn't say it was a wise alternative. My mother is trying to find me a husband possessed of a good name and fortune." The words came out tighter than she liked. "I don't agree with her methods, but she is doing it out of affection for me."

"But Cardenly."

"You keep repeating that. Would it help if I told you Lord Cardenly does not have any interest in me? Certainly not any interest with an honorable intent."

She did not mean the words to be snappish, but she found his behavior irksome. "To tell the truth," she said, trying to make her tone softer, "I never thought he was interested and when he disappeared from London, I did not miss him. Do you know why he disappeared in the first place?"

"It had to do with horses and an unpaid debt. Things must be settled for him to show his face again." He considered her as they walked. "Your mother didn't know? I thought she vetted your suitors carefully. She must be worried."

"She is. She and I disagree over whom she thinks I should choose as a husband."

"Who would you choose?"

Now she could smile. "I believe there is a certain younger son who's caught my fancy. I'm not certain how he feels about me, though. There are hints, but he does not speak his mind."

The corner of his mouth was twitching. "Perhaps he should, then."

"Perhaps."

They strolled on in comfortable silence. Funny how easy they felt with one another now. Easy enough that she felt comfortable saying, "Mother thinks it would not go amiss for you to pay a call on Grandfather, speak about our future together. No matter what problems he's having with your father, the assurance might do well to smooth things over."

The music began, and he asked, "Do you wish to dance?"

Augusta shook her head and drew herself a little closer to him as they continued to walk. "Your mother is right. Speaking with Lord Forebridge would not be a bad thing. It might make him more assured things are moving forward."

He took a deep breath. "You might prefer a moon-swept terrace, but I'm afraid tonight all I can offer is a too crowded room, weak lemonade, and somewhat dubious company."

"I had noticed both Mrs. Hibbert and Mr. Wilverton were admitted."

Blair patted her hand. "They were both instrumental in bringing us together. Simon first asked you to dance to avoid Mrs. Hibbert, while you accepted my invitation because Mr. Wilverton annoyed you."

The sharpness of her words that night was etched across Augusta's memories. "I'm afraid it was almost our last."

"I believe I've apologized several times for being an ass. I can also admit I was wrong. Perhaps this is not as passionate as your parents—"

"No one, can be as passionate as my parents."

"But I have come to care for you deeply."

He stopped, pulling her close to the open windows, away from the other couples who strolled seeking a hint of a breeze. "That care has a name. My love, will you do me the honor of becoming my wife? Of living with me all our days, no matter what may come?"

There was no hesitation in heart or mind as she met his gaze. "I will, my love, and I will do so happily."

A look of pure joy crossed his face and he leaned, only to catch himself at the last moment. "I don't think your mother would appreciate it if I caused a scandal by kissing you in rented assembly rooms."

Augusta stepped closer, her hand rising to rest lightly on his chest. "I think it's the rented assembly rooms which would upset her the most. She believes such things should happen in wildly romantic places." Sobering, she added, "Grandfather would use it as a reason to force your father to make concessions."

"Then let's not give him the satisfaction." He lifted her hands to his lips and planted a gentle kiss upon her gloved fingers. "As much as I would like to linger, because there is a breeze here, we should continue our promenade and return to Lady Eastleigh. I imagine your mother is trying to keep an eye upon us."

As they began to walk again, Augusta realized her mother was not the only one who might be watching them. She caught sight of Wilverton, eyes fixed her on her with an unhappy, angry expression. No. Not at this moment. Not when all the world seemed right. They would stroll back to her mother, tell her they had settled it between them, Blair would go to see Forebridge, and perhaps everything would be well.

Unfortunately, the moment they drew near to Lady Eastleigh, it was clear everything was not well.

. . .

It took Blair a moment to come to terms with the idea his valet was standing beside Lady Eastleigh. "What are you doing here, Baxter?"

"Your father sent me, sir," the man said. "I did not see you at first, but Lady Eastleigh told me you were with her daughter and she expected your return soon. I need you to come home. Lord Hamish is worse."

The world which was so secure and steady a moment ago dropped out from under Blair's feet. No need to ask how much worse if Baxter had been sent to fetch him. "I must go," he said, turning to Augusta.

"Of course you do." She reached to grasp his hand. "I'll keep him in my prayers."

"We both will," Lady Eastleigh said. "When you can, send us word."

"I…" There were things he wanted to say, but the words seemed lost or inadequate. "Do not stand on ceremony," Lady Eastleigh said, as if she understood his distress. "Your brother needs you and that is most important in this moment. Go."

They were not words to rid her of him, but the impetus to get him moving. Nodding to them both, he gave Augusta's hand a squeeze and turned toward the door, Baxter falling in step beside him. "Sorry to interrupt your evening, my lord."

"They would not send you if the matter were not urgent. You called for the carriage?"

"Yes, but we also need to find Lord Strathern. He is not at home, and Lord Rutherglen hoped you might know his whereabouts. We would ask his man, but he was given the evening off, and left the house."

Which meant James had gone somewhere their father wouldn't approve. If his valet wasn't present, he couldn't answer uncomfortable questions. James had played this trick before, and he had an unerring sense of timing to do so right before something went wrong. "I can guess. Be warned; none of them are going to be particularly savory."

As he retrieved his hat, Blair hoped the short list he remembered would serve them well and James could be found in one of those haunts. The reckoning of what that list meant would come later.

Even at the door, he wanted to turn back, realizing he and

Augusta had not had a chance to tell Lady Eastleigh their news. Nor would he be able to call on Forebridge. Lady Eastleigh was correct. Hamish needed to be his focus. A note. He'd do his best to send Forebridge a note and with luck that would serve.

Settling his hat firmly on his head, he followed Baxter out into the night.

"I don't think I want to dance anymore this evening," Augusta told Lady Eastleigh as she watched Blair slip out of the room.

"I understand, but you departed early several times this season, leaving gentlemen to whom you promised dances hanging."

Augusta didn't even try to keep the anger from her voice. "If you mean Cardenly—"

Lady Eastleigh scowled. "Lord Cardenly said he would ask later in the evening but made no specific request. No, I'm talking about Mr. Fischer and Mr. Erickson. Both asked for a dance and you will honor those. I understand you might find this difficult, but you must keep up appearances."

"Why is it so damn important?"

"Because it affects how others see you. Don't discount such things, Augusta. Never discount it. Social standing is a currency. It allows you to ensure you can get to the people you need when something is important. Do not spend it foolishly. As an unmarried girl, you possess little."

"I won't be unmarried forever." The words came out as a grumble.

"You won't. Lord Blair is not what I wanted, but he seems to be making you happy and despite your start, you appear well matched. I just wish…" She shook her head. "I suppose I was still hoping Lord Chalton would arrive to save the day."

Augusta couldn't help laughing. "The business out of town? Eleanor Shelby's husband died unexpectedly."

"Oh." A pause. "*Oh.* That puts a different light on things. You had a lucky escape. Things would be bad if he asked and your betrothal was announced. He would likely stay the course because he is a man of honor. I fear, however, under those circumstances, he might come to hate you. I know if I'd been forced to marry someone else and your father found himself single, I would grow to despise my husband."

Another long pause. "How bad is Lord Hamish, do you think?"

"He's been ill for a while now. Fetching Lord Blair home is not a good sign." She turned toward her mother. "I should have told you."

Lady Eastleigh shook her head. "Best you didn't. All too easy to throw it in your grandfather's face during an argument. He doesn't want you to succeed. Anything goes awry with Rutherglen, he'll marry you off to anyone he chooses.'

"Does he have the power to do that?" Augusta asked. "I know he could impact some of Father's income."

The long hesitation which followed hinted at something left unsaid. "You have no partner for this dance. Perhaps we should step out of the room. It is far too close."

The air was close, but Augusta doubted was why her mother led her away. Once more, they did not venture into the retiring room itself, but found somewhere out of the way. "Your father and I made a devil's bargain," Lady Eastleigh said. "Your grandfather would pay for your season, as well as the seasons of your sisters in two years, on the condition you found a husband before the end of June. If not, he would choose the man you married."

There was no pride here, no sense she managed to gain the upper hand in any way. Instead, Augusta saw bitterness and regret. "I didn't like it, but I was certain there'd be at least one gentleman who would suit. More should be dancing attendance. You are lovely and charming, and the gentlemen do find you attractive. But they don't take the next step."

She wrapped her arms around herself, almost as if she was in pain. "Some of this may be my fault. I should have realized your appearance would bring up all the old gossip surrounding the elopement. People counting stupidly on their fingers backwards from your birth didn't help."

"There is a man who wants to marry me," Augusta said. "Blair proposed tonight and said he would speak with Grandfather."

For a moment, Lady Eastleigh's face lit up. "That's wonderful. It's a clear statement of intent, exactly what he's looking for."

Then reality sank in. "His brother—My dear, his brother must come first right now. No telling when he'll be able talk to Forebridge."

She stretched out her hand to touch Augusta's cheek. "That you and Blair reached this point is wonderful. I hope the news of it will be enough."

CHAPTER 24

The night was far closer to dawn than Blair liked by the time he and Baxter found James and they could make their way back to the Rutherglen home. Sullen and resentful when he learned his younger brother had been hunting for him through the less savory parts of London, James had changed his tune once he learned the reason why

"You'll say nothing of this to Father?" he asked as they climbed the steps to the front door.

"That we found you in a gambling den which also serves as a Molly House?" Blair shook his head. "Nay. He doesn't need that worry."

He paused for a moment, hand on the knocker. "The tale of you and the pox. It was a story to get him to stop asking about marriage."

James scowled and he opened his mouth, but anything he might say was forestalled by the door opening. "Thank heaven you're home," the butler said. "I prayed it was you when the carriage arrived. The marquess is in Lord Hamish's room and you're to go up immediately."

No bow and none of the usual courtesies as they passed over their hats to waiting hands. Instead, the butler urged them upstairs. "You didn't say it was this bad," James muttered as they went.

"I didn't know."

Servants aplenty gathered in the corridor, more than would normally be awake at this hour, an absence of jackets and wigs among the footmen who seemed to be awaiting instructions. All stood aside to let Blair and James pass. As they entered the room, Rutherglen looked away from his conversation with the doctor, scowl turning to relief. "Thank god Baxter found you, both of you."

A few quick steps and both of them were wrapped in a tight, desperate embrace. Blair held on, feeling his father take in deep, shuddering breaths, as if holding back some great emotion. At last, Rutherglen straightened, calmer than before. "I want you to hear what the doctor says."

The doctor appeared grim, Mrs. Petherbridge just behind him. "I was telling Lord Rutherglen that the infection is spreading and I fear the wound has turned septic. The time has come to take his leg. I know Lord Hamish does not wish—"

"No!" The cry from the bed caused them to turn. Hamish propped himself up on his elbow, the pain from the effort writ across her face. "Don't let them do it, Father. They take my leg, that will be the end of me. I won't be able to go back to the army. It's what I trained for. I've earned that place. Don't take it away from me."

He was sweating, his eyes unnaturally bright. Blair found himself avoiding looking to where the covers had been turned back to expose the ugly wound. He wasn't ready to face the truth of it, knew he couldn't show Mrs. Petherbridge's calm as she moved to Hamish's side. "We'll need to do what's best for you, so you can live."

Hamish grasped at her hand. "But if I lose my leg, I might as well die because my life will be finished. You understand, don't you?"

She picked up a cloth from the bed table, dipping it in a basin before pressing it to his forehead. "I do. I also know you're not doing yourself any good by getting upset. Lie back, conserve your strength. Lord Rutherglen hasn't agreed to anything yet, and you need to let him speak to the doctor."

She coaxed Hamish to lie back down, his hand still wrapped around hers. Once he was settled, she slowly withdrew his hand and adjusted the cloth—only for him to snatch her hand back again. "You won't let them take it?"

"I will ensure he understands your wishes," she said.

For some reason, her words satisfied him, and he let her hand go. She stayed for a moment before rejoining the others. "I may be presumptuous, Doctor, but I think it best this conversation continues in the corridor."

The doctor nodded. "I think that is wise, Mrs. Petherbridge. Please join us."

They stepped out into the hall as the waiting footmen straightened, suddenly at attention. Grimly, Blair realized why they waited. If the leg was taken, the doctor would need strong men to hold Hamish down during the awful act of cutting. "Father—"

"Aye, I know. Any way we can save his leg?"

The doctor frowned. "We need to bring the fever down, help his body fight the infection. If we can't do that…"

Rutherglen nodded. "He will die. I understand. You think the battle's already lost."

"It is generally held that in cases such as these, an amputation, while unfortunate, is the best method of ensuring the patient survives."

It hurt to watch his father grow older before his eyes, but Blair hated to think of the weight pressing down on Rutherglen at this moment. "There is no other way?"

Before the doctor could say anything, Mrs. Petherbridge spoke up. "There are possibilities, but no guarantee. Doctor, might you cut away the dead flesh so it is no longer a cause of infection? Cleanse the wound constantly and treat him with some of the older herbal remedies, might we not stand a chance?"

For a long moment, the doctor was silent, pursing his lips as he considered. "You're schooled in these?"

Mrs. Petherbridge nodded. "From both my mother and grandmother. I have their recipes close to hand."

Another pause, longer still. "A chance," he said at last, each word slow and drawn out. "Mrs. Petherbridge and I must consult, of course, agree on the treatment, but we might be able to save his leg."

As Rutherglen sagged with relief, the doctor spoke again. "Even if this succeeds, you must understand it is unlikely he will ever regain full use of the limb. He may never be able to sit a horse and the Army might still declare him not fit for the battlefield. We must also face the possibility things may get worse. Then there will be no time to waste. The leg will have to come off."

"If we wait, are we any worse off than now?" Blair asked.

"Only that your brother is at greater risk for death than if we took the leg immediately." The doctor turned to Rutherglen. "The decision is yours, my lord."

"How long?" The words can out in a croak. Rutherglen cleared his throat and spoke again. "How long should we wait?"

"We'll try to wait a day," the doctor said after a moment's thought. "We'll see where we are. If we see improvement or he's grown no worse, we wait another day after that. We must to take this one step at a time. I would advise the family stay close, because things may change with little warning."

"We'll need help," Mrs. Petherbridge said. "Lord Blair, would you be willing to help with the cleaning and change of bandages. You have some experience with this."

"What can I do to help?" James asked. "The three of you can't work without respite."

The doctor cleared his throat. "I was told of your condition, Lord Strathern. I appreciate the offer, but there is always the possibility of passing the infection along and I doubt you want to do that."

James looked crushed. Then, he drew himself up straighter. "I'm sorry, Father, but I lied because it's a long story, but I didn't want you asking anymore, so I blurted that out as it cut off all chance."

The expression on Rutherglen's face was a mixture of shock, relief and fury. Blair wanted to strangle his brother. "You lied?"

"You can hate me later, but I can help care for Hamish. I *want* to care for Hamish."

"I suggest you rest for the moment," Mrs. Petherbridge said. "I can smell the whiskey, and your brother will need us to be at our best."

"Best tell Lord Hamish something," the doctor said. "I doubt he fully understands the situation, but if we tell him we will not amputate immediately, it might calm him. Calm will help at this point."

With that, he strode back toward Hamish's room and gestured for Blair and Mrs. Petherbridge to follow. Casting a glance over his shoulder, Blair saw Rutherglen take James by the arm and drag him along the corridor. There was a conversation he was glad he wouldn't be a part of. Stripping off his jacket, he waited as the doctor told Hamish what was happening, his thoughts fluttering briefly toward Augusta.

If he wished for anything at the moment beside his brother's life and leg being spared, it would be that Augusta was in the house so in whatever brief moments he had of rest, he might lay his weary head on her shoulder.

He knew, though, that even if she was with him, those moments would be few and far between. All he could do now was get through this.

Augusta heard nothing the next day, not that she expected to. Little chance Blair would come calling if the situation was as bad as she feared. She pleaded a headache for both the afternoon calls and the supper they were to attend that evening. Lady Eastleigh started to object but stopped. "I think you're right," she said, considering Augusta. "You look worried, enough so that it will raise questions. An evening in would likely do us good."

She was grateful she could retire to her bedroom and not speak to anyone. Augusta knew the peace couldn't last forever. She should tell Forebridge about Blair's proposal, but he had no time for her yesterday before her claim of a headache, snapping when she had attempted to speak with him. Staying in her room had been safest, keeping her out of his sight for the moment.

Augusta stared at the toast on her breakfast plate, her appetite all but non-existent. Today. She would tell Forebridge today. Hopefully, he would be in a better temper and glad of the news.

Luck was not with her.

They were just preparing to rise from the table when they heard the noise. "I wonder if he's learned about Lord Hamish," Eastleigh said.

"Something's set him off," Lady Eastleigh replied, dropping her napkin to the table. "Augusta——"

"If it concerns me, I should be there," she said. "Otherwise, I'll leave."

Together, they moved into the hall, and were met by Forebridge, emerging from his study as his solicitor made a hasty retreat for the door. "Seems Lord Rutherglen declared himself 'too busy' to continue talks about a marriage settlement."

"That's not exactly what the marquess said," the man of business began as he was handed his hat, but fell silent at Forebridge's glare and made his exit.

"Lord Hamish is gravely ill," Lady Eastleigh said. "So ill, Lord Blair was summoned from the assembly."

"You did not see fit to tell me?" Forebridge rounded on her. "Was it illness or did Lord Rutherglen decide against the match and wanted his son as far from your clutches as possible? He's been less and less enthusiastic about the negotiations of late."

"Yet he arranged an evening in his home specifically so Augusta could meet his other sons," Lady Eastleigh countered. "You saw Lord Hamish's condition. Are you surprised at news he's not doing well?"

Forebridge didn't answer but turned on Augusta. "I told you to make certain Blair MacDonald was tied to you. For all the tricks your mother taught you, you couldn't manage it?"

"He said he wanted to marry me," Augusta blurted out, any speech she planned vanished. "Just before the message arrived, he asked me to be his wife and said he planned to come speak with you. He was going to tell his father as well, hoping that would spur an agreement. If you could just wait——"

"For weeks I was told to wait, that something was about to happen. Your mother swore Chalton would propose, and he didn't. Left town chasing after the woman his father wouldn't let him marry. Oh, yes, that tale's come out. Rutherglen was certain we'd reach a settlement 'any day', but now I get this," he brandished the note in his hand, "so I'm left to wait and foot the bill. If Rutherglen wanted this marriage, so eager to ensure an heir, he would show more concern about making concessions for the settlement. Lord Blair may fancy himself in love with you, but I'll wager there's a hook in the water elsewhere."

He turned to Eastleigh. "We made a bargain and your time is up. I warned you to keep a close rein on your wife, but you chose not to listen. The girl will marry whom I choose, and you'll raise no objections. You understand the consequences. We'll have a special license, too, so she will be gone from my house as soon as possible, you can take your baggage home, and I'll stop having to pay for gowns and frippery."

"Won't you show some consideration for your granddaughter, Father?" Eastleigh's clenched fists warned he was far less calm than his tone.

"What proof she is my granddaughter?" Forebridge countered. "I know the tale your wife sold you, but what proof do you have?"

"Because Augusta was born precisely nine months and two weeks after Richard and I wed," Lady Eastleigh said. "If I was with child when we eloped, I would have been at least four weeks along. Which meant she was born ten and a half months after conception. I am certain you can count on your fingers, even if the gossips can't."

She moved and took a step toward him, danger in every line. "You don't care, do you? You're ready to believe the worst of her for no other reason than she's my daughter and you hate her because of that. Don't think I haven't noticed how you treat Caroline and Charlotte, or your comments about 'worthless girls.' You accept Robin because he's the heir and your future, but if you had your way, you'd see all my daughters left with nothing for their portion, wouldn't you?"

The only reason she did not advance again was Eastleigh caught her by the arm. Forebridge stepped back a pace, putting more distance between them. "Truer words were never spoken. There will be a match, and she will cheerfully accept, or face the consequences. I'd better not find you're bemoaning her fate, either."

With that, he turned on his heel and strode back to his study, slamming the door behind him. "Richard—"

"We made a bargain," Eastleigh said. "I asked if you understood what could happen. You said you did. Now Augusta must live with the consequences."

He wrapped his arms around Augusta, trying to give her comfort. Augusta burrowed as close as she could, but panic burned within her breast.

CHAPTER 25

The summons came much sooner than Augusta expected.

She spent the rest of the day waiting in hope of a message from Blair, only to be disappointed. She wrote him a note but who knew when he would have a chance to read or respond.

They had not kept their plans for the evening activity, either. Not because of Augusta's plea she did not feel like smiling or sparkling at other gentlemen while Blair's brother was so ill, but because Forebridge gave instructions the carriage was not to be made available to Lady Eastleigh. "I suppose he believes it saves him money," she said bitterly when she brought Augusta the news.

Augusta had another suspicion, that such a move kept more control over both of them. Had her plea to Blair been intercepted as well, or was she letting herself give in to dark fantasies?

When the summons came in the early afternoon of the next day, it was almost a relief. As unpleasant as whatever he had to tell her might be, at least she would no longer be waiting. Perhaps she could make one last plea with him, to forego a marriage, return home, and settle into spinsterhood. He might like the idea of her 'shame' not being passed along to anyone else. Once home, she could more easily get word to Blair. Perhaps he still wanted her, and they could arrange a way around her grandfather.

Never before had she understood why her parents eloped to Scotland or why they believed they had no other choice.

To Augusta's relief, her parents were not present in the hall. If he summoned only her and not them, perhaps he would listen to her offer, beg his forgiveness for any disrespect she might have shown. The idea of swallowing her pride hurt, but it was the last card she had to play.

Taking a deep breath, she opened the drawing room door and stepped inside...

Only to discover Charles Wilverton waiting for her. Alone. "Good afternoon, Miss Eastleigh," he said formally.

"I..." The words died on her lips. She swallowed and tried again. "I did not realize you were here, Mr. Wilverton. Allow me to summon my mother."

"It was you I came to see, not Lady Eastleigh."

Augusta began backing toward the door. He wore a smug smile, as if possessed of knowledge she was not privy to.

"That is flattering, but we should not be alone. It is not proper. I'm not certain what the servants were thinking. If you'll excuse me."

"Lord Forebridge knows I am here, so it is perfectly proper," he said, just as she reached for the door. "In fact, he granted me the interview I had tried to obtain with your father."

A chill passed through Augusta. "He did."

"He states your parents have not taken proper responsibility for you and your future. I wrote him Lord Eastleigh had actively been avoiding me, and he wished to rectify the discourtesy."

I'll be he did. She turned back and found Wilverton had moved closer. "If he chooses to tell me the result of that interview, I will be more than happy to listen. Now, though, I must ask you to leave."

"I have no intention of leaving." He moved and Augusta countered, doing her best to keep a distance between them, even if it meant moving away from the door. "We had a productive conversation. He gave me permission to seek your hand."

"I'm happy for you." Taking a few quick steps, Augusta managed to place one of the couches as a barrier between them. "I wonder, though, given I did my best to discourage you, sometimes rather rudely, at every step, why you insist on continuing your pursuit. Surely there are other ladies who would be more amenable."

Wilverton moved, and she moved again. She had almost circled the room and the door would soon be in her grasp once more. "Others, but none who are the granddaughter of an earl, will someday be the daughter, then sister to an earl. Marriage to you will help my standing in both the county and in Parliament. For the connection, I'm willing to overlook any irregularities of your birth."

A vase was close to hand. She considered throwing it but decided to hold that in reserve. "You're very charitable. I'm afraid I must refuse your offer."

"I haven't made it yet."

"I don't care. My answer is no."

His face took on the same piggish, angry look he wore each time she refused to comply at an assembly or other gathering. "You don't understand. The matter is settled. Lord Forebridge and I agreed upon a settlement and shaken hands as gentlemen. Your assent is merely a formality." He smiled, a sight which sent shivers down her spine. "The wedding is set, my dear."

Augusta made a dash for the door, throwing aside any concerns about the proper behavior of young ladies in her rush to escape. Not bothering to see if he followed, she headed straight for the room where Forebridge often spent his days. Bursting in, she announced, "You must be mad if you think I'll accept Charles Wilverton's offer."

Forebridge put down the papers he was reading. "This is no joke. I footed the bill and have seen little return for the cuckoo in the nest. Mr. Wilverton is positively grateful to be allied with a superior house, no matter how dubious the connection." He leaned back. "I'm getting off cheaper than with Rutherglen."

"But Blair—"

"Blair MacDonald proposed. So what? Rutherglen couldn't come to terms and brushed me off like I was a tradesman. I'll not stand for that."

"I'll forgo marriage, not come to London again. No need to worry about the old stories because I'll sink into obscurity."

His fist came slamming down on the desk, rattling the small items scattered across the surface. "Enough! I want you gone. Not back to the country where you can be a curiosity for everyone but gone from my house and my family. The last farthing I'll spend on you is for a special license and a wedding breakfast. Your mother can find you something to wear, given everything she bought. Don't think about refusing at the altar, either. I'll disown you. Rather, I'll give your father the choice of disowning you, or I'll rewrite the entail so everything is settled on your brother and your father is forbidden to touch any part of it. Should have done that years ago when my son married the harpy who bore you."

He'd won. Here and now, she had no choice but to agree. Still, some little part she inherited from her mother couldn't resist saying, "I thought you tried to break the entail before and found you couldn't."

"Don't think you can get around this. Marry Wilverton, or you'll not only be disowned, I'll ensure there is no money for your sisters. Not for a season and not for a marriage"

Coming out from behind his desk, he stalked toward her, his face dark. "Now go and give him your answer. And smile. Men like it when the ladies smile."

Realizing retreat was her best option, Augusta returned to the hall. For a moment, she considered fleeing upstairs to her mother, but she doubted the usefulness in such a gesture.

Her swift departure must have convinced Wilverton she was not happy for his attentions, for he stood with hat and stick with in hand, as if about to depart. Seeing her, he handed them back to the servant. "Well?"

"I spoke with my grandfather. I understand this is what he wants."

She did not smile, but he did, and gestured for her to lead the way back into the drawing room. "I'm glad you came to your senses, my dear Augusta—for I may now properly call you my Augusta. I fear your grandfather may be behaving a bit harshly, but he has his concerns and I'm happy they mesh with my wishes."

He closed the doors and turned back to her. She was going to come to hate that smirk, she realized, hate it with a passion. Still, she did her best not to shrink back as he stepped toward her. "I'll do my best to make certain you don't regret your choice."

With that, he took her in his arms and kissed her. Augusta did her best to respond, but she felt nothing. No spark of passion, no surge of desire. She was reminded of lukewarm tea.

Wilverton seemed pleased, though, when he pulled back, and she did her best to return the smile. She was regretting this already.

Wilverton didn't stay long, but it was an eternity to Augusta. When he left at last, cheerful and triumphant, she sank to a chair, numb.

"My darling, I just heard. Don't worry, we'll think of something."

Looking up, she found Lady Eastleigh kneeling in front of her, face filled with concern. "We'll find a way," she insisted. "You won't have to go through with this ridiculous match that old fool is insisting on."

As her mother continued to pour forth invective regarding Forebridge and his ideas, Augusta slowly started to come back to herself. The words were familiar, the complaints and promises heard since before their arrival in London. "Stop it, Mother."

Surprised, Lady Eastleigh stopped, sitting back on her heals. Taking a deep breath, Augusta shuddered. "Yes, Grandfather acted badly, and he doesn't care about my feelings. But you are not helping by arguing with him all the time."

"I just want you to be happy." There was puzzlement in Lady Eastleigh's voice.

"I was happy. I love Blair, he loves me, and he wants to marry me. When I first told you I was willing to consider this match, you didn't like the idea, kept hoping someone 'more suitable' would make an offer. All the while, you fought with Grandfather at every opportunity."

"Might I remind you that you are the one who didn't tell me Lord Chalton decided against proposing?"

Augusta groaned. "Did you ever stop to think if he had asked me to marry him, Grandfather might refuse to agree to the match out of sheer spite?" She rose and began to pace. "I didn't tell you because I knew you would frantically look for another suitor. Blair and I were just starting to communicate. You might not want to admit it, but if he was the match Grandfather favored, what were the odds I'd end up married to him? I wanted to be able to get to know him without you complicating matters by trying to find me another suitor. When you found out, you didn't want to tell him because you worried Grandfather would push for the settlement to be finished quickly and you didn't want me to marry Blair for the simple reason he was Grandfather's choice."

"He didn't think of your feelings when he planned this match in the first place. I'm sorry you thought I would react badly at Chalton's decision." Hurt colored Lady Eastleigh's words. "I'm sorry I didn't recognize you had come to care for Blair MacDonald earlier than I did."

Augusta knew she was supposed to assure her mother everything was fine. She was in no mood to play the game. "He threatened to make Father disown me if I didn't go through with the marriage. Threatened to ensure there'd be no money for Caroline and Charlotte."

"Did he threaten to change the entail?" Lady Eastleigh asked as she rose. "That's an old favorite."

"Don't dismiss his words, Mother. He's determined the wedding happens as soon as possible. Unless Blair can make a case to him and change his mind, there is no easy way out for me."

"Blair would need to come armed with agreement to all the demands. Even then, it might not be enough."

Lady Eastleigh reached out to grasp Augusta's hand. Let's speak with your father and see if he has any ideas, though I'm not hopeful. Somehow we need disrupt this match, even if that means smuggling you out of the house and off to one of my sisters."

It was, as Augusta expected, a drastic suggestion. They were reaching the point where drastic might be her only hope.

CHAPTER 26

Hamish showed only the slightest improvement during the first twenty-four hours, but enough to buy him another day. Whatever Mrs. Petherbridge administered allowed him to sleep, even if the fever didn't break. Hamish looked calmer, as if the pain no longer preyed on his mind. Remembering the long trip back from the Peninsula, Blair knew his brother slept better than on their journey. For himself, he caught a few winks at odd moments, not ready to relinquish the work to James.

The second day saw the fever diminish slightly and some of the farthest areas around the wound look less angry. He didn't understand all that portended, but the fact Mrs. Petherbridge and the doctor both seemed pleased was enough for him.

They did need the footmen on the third day, when the doctor decided some of the dead flesh needed to be cut away. Seeing the panic reflected on Rutherglen's face, panic likely reflected on Blair's, the doctor assured him this was a positive sign. This was a more difficult treatment, but he hoped this would prevent further infection. "The flesh would be removed if we had taken the leg. Here, we are removing it because we hope to keep the leg."

Blair was sent to rest during the surgery as the doctor preferred the family not be present. He also suggested Caitlin and Finola's governess take the girls on an expedition so they wouldn't hear any noise. Blair was glad of it; he feared nightmares from hearing Hamish's cries before his brother passed out.

After that, the days began to blur together, marked only by assisting in changing the dressings, holding a basin while the wound was cleaned, catching sleep when he could. Between treatments, he watched and waited, all other thoughts driven from his mind.

At last, the doctor sent for Rutherglen and James. Asking Blair to join them in the hall, he said, "There is still cause for concern, my lord, but as of now, I am cautiously optimistic we saved not only Lord Hamish's life, but his leg."

Rutherglen muttered a prayer of thanks as the doctor continued. "I cut away more flesh that I had hoped I must. I'm afraid he won't be able to do all that he could before, but he will keep his leg. He might be of some use yet to the army."

Hamish resuming his army career was likely the furthest thing from anyone's mind, but the optimism was welcome after what they'd been through. Even the warnings the recovery would be long and difficult were dismissed in the general rejoicing. "I would suggest— please, a moment, my lord—I would suggest that once he is well enough to travel, he be removed to the country where the air is more healthful."

"I know just the place," Rutherglen said. "Blair, you and I will speak, for this may impact your plans. Now, though, you should get a proper rest." He sighed. "I'll get some, too, once I've thanked Mrs. Petherbridge."

Blair didn't need any further encouragement, half-walking, half-stumbling down the corridor to his own room. He wanted to sleep, he wanted a bath, but he most definitely wanted sleep. Shedding clothes worn too long, he lay down atop the covers, too tired to pull them back. Body sinking into the mattress, he let his eyes drift closed...

...And opened them only moments later, exhausted, but stubbornly awake. With a groan, he sat up, and rang to order a bath. Perhaps that would help. Even if it didn't help him sleep, he would be in better shape when he went to speak to his father.

The experience of the past days warned him not to let things slip through his fingers without a fight, and there was one person who was very important to him. He wanted Augusta as his wife. Not because his father wanted him to secure the dynasty, but because he wanted Augusta by his side for the rest of his days.

He didn't want to be like his brothers, shutting themselves off from love. He was willing to accept Forebridge's terms because it was the only way the man would agree. Rutherglen might mutter about pride, but Augusta was worth far more.

Waiting for the tub and water to be delivered, Blair began to shuffle through the letters on his desk. He found one in Simon's hand, and couldn't resist tearing into it. *You were right to remind me not to declare my love for E. when I saw her in the church. It was my instinctive reaction, but even I, love-sick fool that I am, realize swearing undying love while she buried her husband would be, if nothing else, extreme poor taste.*

I received mixed signals, though. She appeared happy to see me, with as lovely a smile as any that graced the dance floor during her season. We did get a chance to speak, but not until after the internment, as those attending were offered refreshments in her father-in-law's home. She said she was pleased I made the effort to attend and found it a comfort to her to see my face. Yet, at the same time, she appeared guarded, checking the location of her husband's parents every few moments. I'm not certain what to make of that.

I know nothing can be said properly for six months, but she did allow she would not be averse to correspondence. By these means, I shall remain in her thoughts until her formal mourning period is done.

Blair shook his head. If Simon wasn't careful, he would prove a fool for love once more. Hoping this time would turn out better than before, he continued sorting through the letters. Invitations, a tradesman bill he needed to deal with, and another letter, this in an unfamiliar and feminine hand. Augusta?

Eagerly, he broke the seal, but the greeting told him it was not from Augusta. Rather, the page bore Lady Eastleigh's signature.

Lord Blair,

I am hoping this will reach you. I know Augusta wrote you at least one note, but I suspect our mail is not allowed to leave the house. I came to this conclusion when I learned several notes I sent did not reach their recipient. Nothing has been said, and I do not feel it is wise to ask. Therefore, I have bribed one of the kitchen boys to carry this note directly to your home.

Under normal circumstances, I would ask how Lord Hamish is doing, and I assure you Augusta and I keep him our prayers. I hope things are improving and your silence is not a sign things have taken a turn for the worse. I hope that silence is because your focus is on him and not because you decided you do not wish to continue your courtship of Augusta.

Those words had Blair sitting upright. Where would she get such an idea?

It is possible you wrote and the missives were intercepted. I fear this is likely because Forebridge took offense in the last communications he had from your father. Augusta and I tried to convey the seriousness of the situation, that you were summoned home urgently, but he was unwilling to listen. Instead, he decreed the negotiations a failure and sought a match for Augusta elsewhere. He found an eager candidate in Charles Wilverton and the wedding is set for Wednesday next.

What was the day? Everything had blurred together in the sick-room and this letter had been written several days before. "Wednesday next" now loomed close to hand.

I regret whatever part I played in bringing things to this pass, but I hope you will not dwell on that. Instead, if you care for Augusta, do whatever you can to put a stop to this madness. Augusta will be pleased by your arrival, and I pray Fore-bridge will show some care for once and agree to award her hand to you instead of Mr. Wilverton. If he does not, I will do everything in my power to help facilitate your elopement to Gretna Green if you are so willing.

There was more to the letter, but Blair didn't bother to read the rest, instead on his feet, out the door and down the corridor to see his father as the servants carried the bathing tub into his room.

With barely a knock, he entered Rutherglen's private chamber, finding his father sitting in a chair by the window, head back and eyes closed. For a moment, he hesitated, struck by how Rutherglen had aged in these past days. Some of it was weariness, but also a new feeling of years which hung about him.

A step forward and the floorboard creaked beneath his foot, enough to cause Rutherglen's eyes to open. "Blair? What is it? Has something changed with Hamish?"

"No, but something upset Lord Forebridge. He decided you broke off negotiations and found someone else for Augusta to marry."

"What?" Rutherglen held out his hand for the letter Blair still held. Scanning the lines, he swore and passed the pages back. "Damn the man! He sent a request asking my agreement to one of his conditions shortly after Hamish grew worse and I'm afraid my response was somewhat curt. So while my son possibly lies dying, he chooses to take that as a sign we weren't interested. Probably found someone who would take a smaller settlement. Since you did not give a statement of intent—"

"I proposed to Augusta the night you called me home," Blair said. "I love her. Not because of James or Hamish or the future of the line, but because I want Augusta Eastleigh as my wife."

For a moment, Rutherglen's face brightened, only to darken again. "*Damn* the man." Still grumbling, he rose and made his way over to his desk, pulling out a clean sheet of paper. "I'm writing to our solicitors, telling them to draw up final papers. I'll also write one, which I want you to deliver yourself. Tell him we'll accept his last offer, no quibbling, which means his granddaughter gets a handsome marriage for little cost."

Blair knew it meant Augusta would bring precious little to the marriage except herself, but he didn't care. He should, but having her with him was more important than a settlement which favored the estate. "Thank you, Father."

"Thank me by ensuring I get some grandchildren out of this." He paused for a moment, then looked up at Blair with a sly grin. "If you truly love the girl, I imagine that will not be a hardship."

With a chuckle, the marquess turned his attention back to his letter. Blair sighed in relief, but then a worry stopped him. "What if Forebridge doesn't accept your offer, says he's sticking with Wilverton?"

Rutherglen put his pen down, lips pursed. Then, he asked, "Do you love her enough to face a scandal over an elopement?"

Blair couldn't believe what he heard. "Would you accept that?"

"Accept? I'll make certain the carriage is ready for you." He leaned back in the chair. "No, I don't want an elopement. I'll wager

Miss Eastleigh, who appears to be a very sensible young lady, doesn't want an elopement either. She's had to live with the shadow and gossip of one all her life. Does she love you as you love her?"

"Yes." The word came without hesitation.

"You're certain she doesn't want to marry this gentleman Forebridge contracted her to?"

That required no hesitation as well. "I can assure you she despises the gentleman, and with good reason."

"Then better a scandal. The girl you love marries another, I doubt you'll find another girl you wish to marry for some while. I want the nursery filled. Given all we've been through this past week, you can now understand why. Bathe and change. We can spare you long enough for you to pay a visit this afternoon. The letter will be done by the time you're ready."

Blair stepped forward to lay his hand on his father's shoulder. "Thank you," he said.

Rutherglen covered Blair's hand with his own. He said nothing but squeezed. That gesture of support was enough, and Blair went to ready himself. He needed to look his best, and he needed to be prepared to grovel a bit, most likely. If it meant Augusta could be his, it would be worth it.

CHAPTER 27

Bathed and freshly dressed, Blair did his best to appear calm as the butler answered the door of the Forebridge townhouse. "I'm here to see Miss Augusta," he said. "Also Lord Forebridge, if he is at home."

The butler looked none too certain, as if admitting Blair would run counter to instructions. Even so, he bowed and ushered Blair into the front hall, asking him to wait while his card was presented. *They didn't slam the door in my face. I'll take that as a good sign.*

He doubted he'd be allowed to see Augusta. If what Lady East-leigh said was true and not just malice attributed to her father-in-law, she was being kept close. Forebridge likely guessed she was not going to this match willingly, and it seemed in his nature to take no chances if he put his mind to something. Asking for her, however, set a certain tone and increased the odds she would hear of his visit.

Forebridge appeared, looking none too happy. "I brought a letter from my father, sir," Blair said, "and I hope we may discuss it privately."

He placed the papers in Forebridge's hand, dismayed when he opened it immediately. "So, he's finally come around. Shouldn't have waited so long."

"My father regrets any curtness in his words. The only explanation is that my brother was very ill, and my father focused almost entirely on whether Hamish would live or die. I hope you can understand why any communication might not have been couched in the politest terms at that moment."

Anyone who had sympathy or empathy would be able to, even if the words had vexed them. Blair was beginning to suspect Forebridge possessed neither. Nor did it appear would there be any private discussion. "You had an agreement in principal," he continued, "and it was only the details which need finalizing. As to that, my father has instructed his solicitors to finalize the papers for the marriage settlement, accepting everything you offer."

"He says that now, but given how he dragged his feet, and how unenthusiastic you were for this project, what was I to think? Don't deny you didn't want the match. I remember hearing you and the girl at the opera, arguing before you came into the box."

It struck Blair that Forebridge never referred to Augusta by name, as if she was unworthy of the attention. "I admit I was not eager initially. The suggestion of the match was unexpected and I, too, held my brother higher in my thoughts than marriage to a girl I didn't know. As time passed, I came to value and esteem Miss Eastleigh. I, in fact, asked her to be my bride. Unfortunately, there was a crisis."

Forebridge waved his hand, dismissing the words. "Yes, I heard. Summoned home from some damn party because your brother was at death's door. Is he better now? You're not wearing black, so I suspect he's still with us. Pity you came to your realization so late. I did a deal with Charles Wilverton. The man's determined to climb the social ladder, and for some reason he thinks he'll get value out of Augusta. No idea why, but she'll be off my hands."

He tore the letter in half, letting the pieces flutter to the floor. "The settlement's been signed as well. He was more than happy to accept what I offer, no quibbling."

"I want to see Augusta." If Forebridge could behave insultingly, so could he.

"You may wish all you like, but you won't. I don't want someone filling her head with the idea she can defy me in this. I get enough of that from her mother. You had your chance; you weren't quick enough. Now, I'll ask you to leave my house."

By all rights of courtesy, he should go. He should accept Forebridge's decree and be done with it. "Augusta!" he shouted. "I'm here!"

His cry shocked Forebridge, and that was enough to give Blair the chance to make for the stairs. "Augusta!"

"Get him out of here!" Forebridge shouted to the servants. The sound of footsteps warned Blair they were hurrying to obey their master's command, but he did his best not to be distracted. Instead, he kept climbing the stairs, hoping to make it to the upper floor. "Augusta!"

Burly footmen grabbed him before he reached the landing, physically dragging him backwards. Blair struggled, but the odds of three against one were not in his favor. Then, as his feet hit the hall's tiled floor, he saw her, Augusta at the upper railing, Lady Eastleigh just behind her. "I'm here! I have not forgotten you! I'll find a way!"

He wanted to say more, but the footmen did their work, expelling him from the house, down the steps and to the sidewalk. The butler followed, offering Blair his hat and came with marked courtesy. "I suggest you do not call again, my lord. It would not be taken well."

Blair settled his hat on his head and took the cane, then bowed politely to the gawping passersby as the butler retreated inside. No, he wouldn't visit again. This was not the end, though. He had plans to make.

"What are you doing?" Lady Eastleigh demanded, hurrying down the stairs as Blair was evicted from the house. Augusta followed quickly, overtaking her mother and making straight for the door. Until Forebridge caught her roughly by the arm. "No, you don't, miss. I'll not have you upsetting my plans."

Keeping his hold on Augusta's arm, he turned back to Lady Eastleigh. "This is your fault. If you hadn't been so scheming and conniving, we wouldn't be in this position. The girl would already be married or at least betrothed to someone respectable."

"You're so worried about respectable, yet—"

"*Quiet!*"

He shoved Augusta back toward Lady Eastleigh. She stumbled, not falling only because her mother caught her. "The wedding is in two days. You are both confined to the house, and any visitors who call will be told you're preparing for the wedding, so are not available. I'll be checking your letters as well."

"I suspect you are doing that already," Lady Eastleigh said.

"So, you figured that out?" He smirked. "Given what you wrote to Lady Gresham, good thing I was. I won't stand for you trying to concoct some obstacle at the last minute or arrange an elopement. Once was enough to stain this family. Your daughter will marry Wilverton on Wednesday."

"What if I refuse?' Augusta said. "What if I stand at the altar and say I am being coerced into the match. What will you do then?"

"Exactly what I said. You'll be disowned, and no money for your sisters." He stepped closer, his expression grim and menacing. "What's more, if you cause a ruckus, you won't be allowed back in this house. Find refuge on the street for all I care. Don't be too certain Rutherglen will let his boy take you in your shift, either. Blair MacDonald may think one thing, but his father controls the purse strings."

Having delivered his dictum, he stepped back. "Go, both of you. I don't want to look at you for the rest of the day. Oh, and don't think of trying to bribe the servants again to take a letter out. That's what you did, didn't you? Your maids won't be going anywhere as well, and a close watch will be kept on who they speak to within the house and what it's regarding. Try to use them as a conduit, and they'll be on the streets without a reference."

With that, Forebridge turned on his heel and walked away. Lady Eastleigh urged Augusta upstairs, not that it took much effort. "Any suggestions, Mother?" she asked as they climbed the stairs.

"I don't know," Lady Eastleigh replied, a shocking admission from her. "I fear we may have run out of choices, and I am sorry for that. If you do refuse—"

She closed her mouth, nodding to the housemaid that passed, then ushered Augusta into her rooms. "If you refuse at the altar," she said once the door was closed, "do not doubt he'll make good on this threat. He will, at the least, refuse you admittance to this house."

Augusta paced the carpet, her fingers lacing and unlacing. "If I could get word to Blair, knew he would still want me."

"If we were certain, I would tell you to refuse loud and clear. Forebridge may be right that Blair says one thing and his father says another. Families are usually not in favor of an elopement."

"He came for me. He was trying."

"Will he keep trying? Would Lord Rutherglen be willing to take you in if you showed up on his doorstep?" She stepped forward to grasp Augusta's hands and stop the pacing. "I'm not so sure. Men make grand, sweeping promises until the moment comes. Then they retreat into respectability. Taking you after you refuse a man at the altar might be too much." A deep sigh. "You are the one who must make the choice to risk it."

As Augusta chewed on the words, Lady Eastleigh said, "I will tell you one thing. If you do decide to refuse, stay silent. Tell no one of your decision. Not me, not your father, nor your maid. Your grandfather gets the slightest hint you might do something, he'll try to outmaneuver you somehow. Like it or not, the law is on his side in this matter. He is the head of the family, and he has great powers over us who hold our living from him, women especially. Which is why you need surprise on your side. I'll lay my hand on what cash I can, make certain you have it on you on the day. You decide to refuse, you'll need something because he will make certain there will be no help from us, no matter what your father and I want to do. He'll likely cut off our funds, send us packing back to home."

She'd felt so brave saying the words to Forebridge, so certain of her path, but Augusta could feel herself begin to waver, wondering how badly such a choice would harm those she cared about. It must have shown in her face, for Lady Eastleigh squeezed her hands again and said, "He won't let his heir starve. He'll make it difficult for us, if for no other reason than to ensure we have no funds to give you."

"And the entail?"

The question evoked a small, sly smile. "He's been saying that for years, ever since your father and I married. So far, he's found no way to break it, though he's tried more than once. I think the failure eats at him." She sobered. "It will be hard, but you need to make this decision for yourself. Do you take the risk or condemn yourself to a life with a man you despise? All I ask is you be certain of the choice, because once made, there is no going back."

They were uncomfortable words, but Augusta knew them to be true. She had two days in which to make that choice.

CHAPTER 28

On a warm Wednesday morning, Augusta moved down the aisle of the church on her father's arm, each step mechanical. The man waiting for her at the altar was not the one she wanted. But she was not given a choice. Her grandfather controlled the purse strings, and she must follow his wishes.

She would be married, Wilverton would gain a connection to a titled family, and she would be out of her grandfather's sight. Did Forebridge plan to make good on his promise to help Wilverton, she wondered, or offer the bare minimum and pretend the connection didn't exist? How would that shape Wilverton's view of her.

No, she couldn't see a happy union.

They reached the altar and her father led her into place beside Wilverton. Kissing her on the cheek, he stepped backward into the pew next to Lady Eastleigh. As the minister cleared his throat, Augusta couldn't resist stealing a glance at the man next to her. Wilverton focused ahead, a smug smile on his face.

"Dearly beloved," the minister began, "we are gathered together here in the sight of God, and in the face of this congregation, to join this man and this woman in holy Matrimony; which is an honorable estate.

She should be paying attention, but Augusta's mind at this moment flew rapidly from subject to subject, a bird caught within an orangery, frantically beating its wings against the panes of glass in an effort to escape.

"It was ordained for the mutual society, help, and comfort," the minister continued, "that the one ought to have of the other, both in prosperity and adversity. Into which holy estate these two persons present come now to be joined. Therefore, if any man can show any just cause, why they may not lawfully be joined together, let him now speak, or else hereafter forever hold his peace."

The church fell silent as the minister paused, in case there might be an objection. This was all form, because dramatic objections only happened in the climax of Mrs. Porter's romantic novels, when the heroine would be rescued from the clutches of the villain at the last second.

Augusta tensed, knowing her own moment was about to come. She would be asked if she took this man, then run in the disarray her refusal would surely cause. She had no plan after that, except to somehow find her way by foot or hackney carriage to Blair's home. The coins in the pocket of her petticoat were more than enough to pay the fare.

"I object!"

Blair's words were followed by a gasp and the rustle of fabric as the congregation turned. Augusta kept her eyes fixed ahead on the minster and the altar beyond. She didn't want to look, didn't want to hope that it was Blair come to rescue her. "You had something to do with this," she heard Forebridge demand, followed by her mother's insistence she was as surprised by this as he.

"Please, please," the minister called. "If there is an objection, we must hear it, or the ceremony cannot proceed. Who are you, sir, and what objections do you bring?"

"Lord Blair MacDonald, son of the Marquess of Rutherglen, and this lady cannot marry this gentleman as she is contracted to marry me."

The minister frowned and looked down at Augusta. "Is this true, my child? Are you already contracted to this man?"

Now she had no choice but turn. Blair stood in the middle of the aisle with an expression which said he'd brook no resistance, the one which always made her push back. "You came," she said.

"I told you I'd find a way. That is, if you are still willing."

He gave her the choice, she realized, something others denied her. Turning back to the minister, she took a deep breath and said, "Yes, we pledged ourselves to one another."

Wilverton's brows drew together. "But that ended. Lord Forebridge assured me there were no impediments."

"There are no impediments," Forebridge shouted, louder and angrier than one should sound in church. "The contract was never signed."

"The lady says there was an agreement." The priest looked at Augusta again. "An agreement between the families, or did you promise to be his wife?"

This time, the answer came easier. "I promised to be his wife. Before Lord Forebridge spoke to Mr. Wilverton, while our families worked to reach an arrangement."

"You promised to be my wife as well," Wilverton said. His tone was angry as well. Augusta took a step back and he reached out to hold her in place. "If you gave him your promise, why give me the same?"

"Because I was forced to," Augusta answered, her own voice becoming heated. "I am not at this altar willingly."

Murmurs began in the church, the small group of guests gathered buzzing among themselves. The vicar moved to insert himself between Augusta and Wilverton. Wilverton released her, but only reluctantly. "That is a most serious statement, miss. I am certain your family has a tender care for you. Perhaps there is some reason to object to the young man."

Behind her, Blair said, "I have here several letters showing Lord Forebridge is the one who suggested the match. He only withdrew from discussions of the settlement when my father said he could not continue at the moment because my brother was deathly ill."

The murmurs increased as Augusta snuck a glance at Forebridge. His complexion, often somewhat florid, had grown even darker. "I ended the negotiations and awarded her to someone else, as is my rights under law. Now get on with it."

The last, dismissive words uttered as one might to a recalcitrant servant, were perhaps a miscalculation. The vicar drew himself up straighter. "You have a legal right, but marriage is a sacrament, and the Church looks most unkindly on coercion. I think it best if we retire to the sacristy and try to—"

"There's nothing to discuss! I don't want her to marry him" he jabbed a finger in Blair's direction "I want her to marry him. Will you let me pass, woman?"

Lady Eastleigh looked more pleased with the chaos than she should. She didn't move. "He was willing to grant Augusta two thousand a year," Blair said to Wilverton. "How much did he offer you?"

"Must you make me sound like a horse you're trading?" Augusta asked.

"I think you'll like the answer, my love. Well?"

"Those are private arrangements!" Forebridge protested. "They're not to be—"

"Seven hundred and fifty pounds."

The church went quiet. "He said that given the circumstances of her birth, he did not feel he could offer more as it would take away from the other, more legitimate children, but he would offer his friendship and assistance." Wilverton turned toward Forebridge. "Did you intend to honor your word at all, sir? Or would you conveniently find a way to wriggle out of your promises once you achieved your desired results?"

Forebridge sputtered more. Wilverton nodded, and said, "I will take that as an answer, sir. I wish you good day."

He stepped away from the altar, and said to Blair, "I wish you luck of her, sir. You'll need it." With a bow to Augusta, he added, "I am sorry to have importuned you, Miss Eastleigh."

Augusta wanted to laugh in his face. Importune her? Is that what he called it? Forebridge shouted as Wilverton headed down the aisle and out of her life, "We had an agreement. I'll sue!"

Turning on Lady Eastleigh, he said, "This is your fault. You put the girl up to this to embarrassment. You think this is your revenge on me? You'll see what revenge is."

"Be quiet, old man," Lady Eastleigh shot back. "You lost. Can't you do it gracefully for once in your life?"

As the two began to argue, Eastleigh turned to Augusta. "Go now. Before anyone can stop you."

It was what she'd planned, though not in the way she planned, but she found herself hesitating for a moment. Eastleigh turned to Blair. "Take her, man. You go with my blessing."

"I'll thank you for that, sir." Blair tugged on Augusta's hand. "Let's go, love."

This time, she didn't hesitate, the two of them running toward the church door. Outside, a phaeton waited. "This will not get us to Scotland," Augusta said. "Or did you make other plans?"

"Other plans." He helped her up, then climbed in beside her. "This will get us back to the house where a carriage is waiting. That will get us to Scotland."

"Grandfather will try to prevent us from reaching Gretna." As they started to move, she reached up and tugged at the ridiculous piece of veiling which adorned the back of her bonnet.

"They'll assume we'll be making for Gretna. We own a small estate just over the border, and that's where we'll be married. What are you doing?"

"Getting rid of this veil. Your father won't object to an elopement?"

"Father absolutely objects. But he was insulted by Forebridge's behavior, so he's decided he'll live with the scandal and has every intention of letting it be known he aided us in this. Given his performance in church, I think most of the gossip will center on your grandfather. The tongues were already wagging before we left the church."

With the veil removed, she bundled the lace in her hands. She had dropped her bouquet somewhere, not that it mattered. No wedding for her, at least, not today. Augusta felt relief, but other emotions crowded in as well. Chief among them were anger and annoyance at the idea Forebridge had not just sold her to Wilverton, he sold her on the cheap.

"You're being quiet," Blair said after they'd driven several minutes in silence. Rutherglen's house was not far, but the streets were thick, slowing their progress.

"I was thinking," she began, before deciding she did not want to dwell on her feelings toward her grandfather. Not when she was away from him. "You, Wilverton, or poverty on the streets. I believe I'll take you."

He laughed as they cleared the congestion and he could bring his horse to a trot. "It won't be poverty for us, love. Father is arranging a settlement that won't hinge on Forebridge agreeing to anything. Though I'll wager he'll do something to save face, since all of London will know how parsimonious he tried to be. I don't care. I'll take you with the clothes on your back."

"I'm bringing more than that," Augusta said. "Mother managed to give me five pounds in notes this morning. Just in case."

"Just in case? Why would you need five pounds?"

"I was going to object and run, try to find you. I hoped you would take me in, though Mother warned your father might not permit it." She took a deep breath, shuddering as she recalled her nightmare of a closed door and being forced to turn away. "Even not knowing the outcome, the chance was better than the certainty."

"I'm glad you were willing to give me the chance."

He spoke of more than today, she knew. If she had refused to give him a chance, he could have easily been the one she dreaded facing the altar with. "We would take you in. Five pounds is a magnificent dowry."

"Five pounds and twenty-three shillings, if I'm being honest. Are you sure about Gretna? Your brother—"

"Hamish is out of danger, or at least much improved to the point where I think I can safely be away for a week or so, though I wish to come back straightway, once we're married."

"We could apply for a special license, stay close to your family."

"The longer we stay in London, the more chance for Forebridge to bring the law to bear." Blair shook his head. "Scotland's the best answer, even if it is a scandal."

The Rutherglen house was in view, a carriage waiting in front.

Blair maneuvered in behind it, and helped Augusta to descend . He began to lead her toward the house, but stopped when she said, "I've lived with scandal all my life because of my parents. What's a little more, if it's with you?"

Blair's face lit up as he gathered her into his arms and kissed her on the street. Yes, this was scandal she could live with.

CHAPTER 29

Five months later…

At her writing desk in the parlor which overlooked the garden, Augusta paused in the letter she was writing to glance out the window of Whiterose's parlor. The sight of gold and red leaves on the trees filled her with warmth as she picked up her pen to continue the letter to her mother.

I am not surprised to learn Grandfather made such an effort to break the entail. I fear the wedding was the last straw for him after years of harboring resentment against you and I. Worse, he appeared a parsimonious fool before Society, which greatly touched his pride.

Looking back, I think we all knew he would never be happy with my season in London, that he would always find fault. Given his behavior with Lord Rutherglen regarding the settlement negotiations—negotiations which he initiated—I doubt he would have been willing to reach an agreement with any gentleman save one who would take me cheaply. Whom he would despise for agreeing.

I do not fault you for trying as it led to my current happiness. Blair's father has been more than generous, and we are happy in our establishment. Hertfordshire is lovely now that autumn is here. Whiterose reminds me much of home, with old casements, whitewashed walls and floors which creak as they've undoubtedly done since Queen Bess' time.

We are, however, going to replace the windows in the bedroom as the sills have shrunk enough the wind whistles in as it will. I know you sympathize when I tell you the price of new glazing is dear.

I am glad to hear Caroline and Charlotte are well, and I believe being banished from Grandfather's presence for some time will suit them nicely. Blair suggests when spring comes, you and Father should bring the family to visit. Lord Rutherglen will be here as well, along with his daughters.

As Caitlin is the same age as my sisters, we thought it right they should become better acquainted with one another, so there will be an established friendship when the three of them face their season. Yes, I know Grandfather swears he will offer no help, but we will find a way.

Hamish will be likely be here as well. He is with us now, him and Mrs. Petherbridge, his nurse. Not what I envisioned for my first few months of marriage, but the air does seem to be helping with his recovery, though his return to the army is still in doubt.

A kiss on the back of her neck caused Augusta to lay her pen down. Laughing, she shifted in her chair to find Blair hovering above her. "You laugh more than you did in London," he said.

"I often didn't find a great deal to laugh about," she replied. "I find life rather different here."

He pulled her to her feet. "I'm glad of that." He kissed her. "My wife."

"Husband."

Blair kissed her again, deeper this time. Augusta did not protest, willingly letting him pull her toward the window seat. The freedom to touch one another as they wished still seemed new and exciting, and she didn't mind such interruptions. Most of the time.

Now, with no pressing business needing her attention, and she was glad as he drew her to his lap, hands sliding her skirt up to expose her legs. A sudden breeze and she shivered. "Something wrong, Augusta?"

She shook her head. "Nothing, save that I fear we may need the glazier to look at these windows as well before winter comes."

"As my lady commands. As long as my lady focuses on me and not on household details."

"Kiss me again and I might not have to."

He did as she asked, and all thoughts of windows vanished from her mind. Instead, she focused on his lips upon her skin, trailing down from her mouth along her throat to bury his face in the valley between her breasts. Augusta wiggled on his lap, rewarded with a growing firmness beneath her. Desire pooled within her, anticipating his touch. Before long, his hand was sliding up her leg, lingering on the ribbon garter which supported her stocking. "Don't," she breathed.

"Don't what?" He'd managed to free one breast from the confines of her stays and sucked her nipple into his mouth. Augusta sucked in her breath with a gasp, back arching. "Don't...untie...the ribbon," she managed.

Blair chuckled against her skin, and Augusta closed her eyes, reveling in the sensation. Her breathing came quicker, compounded by the moment his fingers traced over the top of her stockings and continued up her thigh. Closer, closer, there.

His mouth swallowed her cries as he stroked her, a finger slipping inside for a moment, then returning to stroke her bud once more. She could feel herself tensing, beginning the climb, but she wanted more.

Shifting wasn't easy, as she caught him by surprise. When her hand reached for the buttons on his trousers, though, he eagerly accommodated her, hands clasped around her waist as she moved her legs to straddle him. All the while, they kissed, devouring one another as if their life depending on it.

The buttons undone, Augusta reached for her prize, glad to find it hard. She had been more nervous on their wedding night than she wanted to admit, but any nervousness had long since vanished. Now, she slid her hand down his shaft, then up again to brush her thumb over the head, smiling as it was his turn to gasp.

There was more she could do, but her pulse was pounding with need, and it was such a simple thing to lift herself up and slide down, steadying herself with her hands on his shoulder.

With him seated inside her, she paused, letting the tension inside her build further. Not too long, but enough for her to look into his eyes and see the desire. She began to move, setting a steady rhythm, their eyes never leaving one another. That was, until he leaned forward and caught her breast in his mouth once more. Augusta threw her head back as her movements became quicker, more erratic. Everything was tightening, she was climbing, then she felt him pulse within her and tumbled over the edge, crying out as she did.

She collapsed against him, head coming to rest on his shoulder. They both breathed hard and heavy, not moving, but she was keenly aware of him next to her. A pain in her knee and she moved, separating to sit next to him on the long seat. "I keep reminding myself we need cushions here."

Blair chuckled. "Not the most romantic thing you've said to me after we've joined, but I understand your point. You're right about the windows. We need to have them checked."

They cuddled for a few minutes before beginning to straighten themselves. "What did I interrupt when I came in?" he asked.

"Answering mother's letter. She says Grandfather gave up the fight to break the entail, but he's strangled their income as best he can. Things are a bit tight for them at the moment, but they'll manage. I know," she said as he rolled his eyes. "I don't want to get drawn into their fight, either."

"Are you telling her the news? That should provide a distraction."

Augusta smiled. "Not yet, but I will."

He took her hand. "I'm glad you didn't conceive immediately after the wedding. Our child won't endure the same whispers you had to."

A shrug as she stepped closer. "Some will count on their fingers anyway, and I don't care. There's a difference between what I knew and our child. Your family is happy, wants us to be happy, and will welcome this baby. That happiness lets me leave the rest of it behind."

Blair slipped his arms around her and drew Augusta into a gentle embrace. She let her head drop to his shoulder, enjoying the closeness. Her past was behind her. Her future lay here, in his arms.

AUTHOR'S NOTE

First, and always, thank you for taking time to read *To Lure a Lord*. Our lives are busy ones, and I hope this tale offered at least a small respite. If you enjoyed the book, please leave a review.

Hamish MacDonald's tale isn't over yet, though his story is in the future. Next we'll follow Simon Mercer's efforts to win Eleanor Weir née Shelby, the woman his late father prevented him from marrying. But Eleanor, now a widow with a small daughter, is not the same woman Simon knew in London, and is struggling to find her way froward when Simon tries to take up residence in her life once more. *Easy for the Earl* will arrive in Spring of 2021.

If you'd like to know when my next book will be released, enjoy the odd history tidbit or adventures in knitting, along with cute cats, please subscribe to my newsletter. You'll also receive a free short story exclusive to my subscribers.

Until next time, stay safe, stay healthy.

ACKNOWLEDGMENTS

Writing one book is hard enough. Writing a second and getting it to market can sometimes feel even harder. I'd envisioned this book releasing much earlier, but a pandemic, the implosion of a writers' organization and the struggle to rebuild, along with family issues made for a bumpy road. That's in addition to the usual writer neuroses.

But life has not been all grim this year, and I'd like to thank Ophelia Bell, Claire DeWolfe, and Alexis Morgan-Roarke for being friends, cheering me on and sometimes just letting me vent. Debbie Decker deserves thanks for stupid, funny memes on Facebook when I needed a laugh. Thanks also to Lynda Ryba, with whom I shared many a Starbucks session until March and lockdown. Via her company, FWS Media, she also provided copy editing, though final responsibility for any final errors rest with me.

Stock image for the cover was provided by Period Images.

Love and appreciation to my husband, Fred. He did his best to give me space to work in a house which found itself unexpectedly crowded, fetched lunch, made certain I ate, and sometimes insisted I get away from the computer when I showed signs of getting too stressed out. My books wouldn't get finished without his support.

ALSO BY CARO KINKEAD

Just a Touch of Scandal (Historical Romance)

The Accidental Viscountess

Non-Fiction

Surviving 30 Days of Literary Madness

Contemporary Romance

Will You? (Kindle Unlimited)

ABOUT THE AUTHOR

As a child, Caro Kinkead was told Dr. Seuss' job was "writing books," and decided that was her goal when she grew up - along with being a ballerina and an archeologist and about a dozen other things. A fear of snakes signaled the end of her ambition to find the next Tutanka-mun's tomb, the dancing (and acting) didn't quite pan out, but the love of writing remained, allowing her to enjoy those varied careers and more in her imagination.

Born and raised in Houston, TX, Caro grew up in a family of readers, where she developed a love of science fiction and fantasy thanks to her father, and old movies and the art of costuming from her mother. These days, she and her husband share a home in the Los Angeles area with their cats, a sizable book collection, and more yarn than she'd care to admit to.

Want to know when Caro's next book is coming out? Subscribe to her newsletter or visit her website at CaroKinkead.com